the Color of Love

SHARON SALA

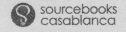

sourcebooks
casablanca

Published by Sourcebooks Casablanca, an imprint of Sourcebooks, Inc.
P.O. Box 4410, Naperville, Illinois 60567-4410
(630) 961-3900
Fax: (630) 961-2168
sourcebooks.com

Printed and bound in the United States of America.
OPM 10 9 8 7 6 5 4 3 2 1

This book is dedicated to those in search of a place to call home, and to the people they find along the way who become the family they never had.

Chapter 1

RUBY DYE WAS GETTING READY FOR CHURCH, BUT HER thoughts were anything but angelic. Peanut Butterman, the local lawyer, was taking her to Granny's Country Kitchen after the services. She'd spent the entire time she was putting on her makeup thinking about him and wondering, even hoping, that he was her secret admirer. For the past few months, someone had been showering her with flowers and gifts, and the idea that a man even found her desirable anymore had resurrected every dream she'd had about heroes—and Peanut was at the top of her list.

There were plenty of single men in Blessings, and most of them came through the Curl Up and Dye at least once a month to get a haircut. Each time one of them had shown up, she'd done her best to see if they were acting any differently toward her, or if their conversation was in any way alluding to more than chitchat.

However, the acquaintance she'd had with Peanut had grown from friendship to a crush to very shocking dreams of the two of them in bed. If he wasn't the man secretly courting her, her heart was going to break.

She sighed, then paused in front of the mirror, looking past the makeup to the older, wiser woman she'd become—a far cry from the young woman who showed up in Blessings nearly fifteen years ago as a frightened, newly divorced woman in her early twenties. Her dark, expressive eyes were set above high cheekbones in an oval face, and while she would have loved to be taller, she'd come to terms with her appearance.

After one last look, she walked back into her bedroom, eyeing the two outfits she'd laid out on her bed. She still couldn't decide what to wear—the pale-blue blouse that went with her navy-blue suit, or a long-sleeved wraparound dress in a dark mulberry color. Either one would look good with her strawberry blonde hair, and still suit the cool weather. She decided on the dress and was about to put it on when she heard a knock at the door.

"Who in the world?" she muttered.

Still barefoot and wearing only her slip and underwear, she grabbed a robe, tying the belt around her waist as she went to the door.

A knock sounded again.

"Coming!" she called, and hastened her steps. Someone was certainly in a hurry.

She was smiling as she opened the door, then a moment of pure horror washed through her. For a split second, she was standing outside herself watching this happen, and by the time she came to her senses and tried to slam the door shut in her caller's face, it was too late.

Jarrod Dye shoved his boot into the space and pushed his way inside, shutting the door behind him.

She hadn't seen her ex in fifteen years, but the sight of his face was still enough to cause panic.

"What are you doing here?" Ruby cried.

Jarrod grinned. "Why, darlin', I came to see you."

"Get out!" Ruby cried, and hated that her voice was shaking.

He lunged forward before she could escape and locked his fingers around her wrist.

"No way, baby. I just got here."

—∿∿—

Ruby Dye didn't show up for church.

Her friends were concerned when she didn't answer their texts. By the time church was over and she had not answered their calls either, they gathered in the parking lot, deciding who would go do a welfare check.

Vera and Vesta Conklin worked with Ruby and knew where she kept the spare key to her house. "We can go," Vera said. "If she's sick, we'll go in and check on her."

"Let us know," Lovey said. She owned Granny's and needed to get to work.

"We will," Vera replied.

Everyone walked off except Peanut. "I'm going with you. I was taking her to Granny's after church. I want to make sure she's okay," he said.

"Of course," Vesta said. "Follow us."

Peanut was a tall, slim man with clear, blue eyes and a ready smile, but his expression could sharpen quickly when he was challenged. He didn't like to think of Ruby being sick. She was the brightest light in Blessings.

The Conklin twins drove at a fast clip through the streets, cutting through neighborhoods to take the short route to Ruby's house. As they pulled into the driveway, Peanut drove in behind them. The twins waited for him to get out, and then they went up the steps together.

Vesta knocked, then waited.

Then Vera knocked, and they waited again.

"Well, her car's still here, so she has to be too,"

Peanut said. He stepped in front of the women and knocked even louder, then, out of frustration, jiggled the doorknob.

To his surprise, the door swung inward.

"Well then," Vera said, and giggled.

But Peanut wasn't laughing. Something wasn't right. He walked into the house.

"Ruby! Ruby! It's me, Peanut! Are you okay?"

It was the silence that raised the hair on the back of Peanut's neck.

"Ruby! Damn it, girl! Answer me!"

He started through the house with a long, anxious stride that ended as he reached the kitchen. He saw the overturned chairs, the knife block on the floor, and Ruby's knives scattered around it. He was trying not to panic when he saw the blood.

Vesta and Vera were right behind him. They screamed at the sight and grabbed each other for comfort, but Peanut was already following the blood trail as he ran down the hall toward Ruby's bedroom.

The bed had been made, but it appeared there had been a terrible tussle atop it. Ruby's purse had been dumped on the bed. Her wallet was empty, and her cell phone was three feet away beneath the windows. Clothes were on the floor, and one bloody pillow had been slashed. The stuffing was scattered all over the sheets, and the bedspread was missing. Peanut groaned, picturing her lifeless body rolled up inside it and being carried away.

His heart was pounding as he raced into the bathroom and saw bandages and alcohol scattered all over the counter. Then he saw something had been written in blood beneath a roll of bloody gauze. The hair stood up on the back of his neck as he carefully moved the gauze aside.

HELP ME

"Don't touch anything," he yelled, then pulled out his phone and called 911.

———

Jarrod Dye was cursing a blue streak as he raced out of Blessings with Ruby bound, gagged, and rolled up in her own bedspread in the back seat of his car. He hadn't planned an abduction or expected her to fight back, and he sure hadn't expected her to pull that knife. If he hadn't blocked her with his forearm, she would have stabbed him straight in the chest.

Rage had made him hit her with his fist, but instead of being cowed by it as she had been when they were married, she came back at him again, clawing and scratching. That's when he had pulled his gun and forced her to bandage his arm.

It wasn't until he'd tied her up and threw her on the bedspread that he saw fear in her eyes.

"You better be scared, bitch! After what you did to me! I didn't come to start trouble. All I needed was a little money to tide me over."

Then he'd rolled her up in her bedspread, carried her over his shoulder to his car, and dumped her in the back seat. He hadn't decided yet what to do with her, but if he let her go, she'd file charges and put him in jail, so he just kept driving.

———

Ruby was scared. As afraid of Jarrod Dye as she'd ever been. She had no idea how he'd found her, but she knew after the fight they'd had that her chances of coming out of this alive were slim to none. What broke her heart was the thought that the secret admirer could have been Jarrod trying to weasel his way back into her good graces. She'd built up such hope, dreaming of a man she could spend the rest of her life with, not the man she'd been hiding from.

She thought of her friends back in Blessings, especially Peanut. They would certainly find out she'd been abducted, but she doubted there'd been a witness. Everyone on her block attended church somewhere and was likely already gone when all of this occurred. The only option she had was to save herself.

In his haste, Jarrod had tied her hands in front of her rather than behind her back, using one of her own leather belts as a tie. The belt was thin and narrow, and he had wrapped it multiple times around her wrists before tying it into a hard, tight knot.

She struggled within the spread until she got her wrists up to her mouth and pulled down the gag. Her head was throbbing, and her lips were swollen and bleeding, but she couldn't think about the pain. In a desperate effort to free herself, she began biting and pulling on the knotted leather, trying to get it loose while the miles between her and Blessings grew, taking her farther and farther away from the people she loved.

―᠁―

Police Chief Lon Pittman was in charge of the abduction scene. He already had crime scene tape around the front of Ruby's house and had sent his deputy, Howard Ralph, to interview everyone on both sides of the block in hopes someone had seen a stranger around Ruby's house.

He'd already called the county sheriff for help. The sheriff sent his crime scene investigators, who promptly photographed the destruction and blood in the kitchen, then followed the blood trail to the bedroom and bathroom, taking pictures and collecting evidence as they went. They had moved into the bathroom and were now taking fingerprints and bagging up the bloody bandages to run blood types and DNA.

The people in the neighborhood were in shock, but none more so than Peanut and the Conklin twins.

Vera and Vesta had given their statements and, the moment they were released, began making calls. Vera called Mabel Jean, the other employee at the Curl Up and Dye, while Vesta called Lovey Cooper at Granny's. They went home in tears.

Peanut had also given his statement, but he wasn't budging. He sat in a chair in Ruby's living room—the same chair he always chose when he was here—and kept imagining she would come bursting into the house at any moment, eyes shining and a smile on that beautiful face, saying it was all a mistake. But there was no getting around those two words written in blood.

HELP ME

Dear God, sweet Ruby, if only I could.

And then Lon came striding through the house on his phone, talking as he went. "What did he say? Is he sure? Stay there. I'm on my way."

Peanut stood up. "What's happening?"

"A neighbor may have seen something," Lon said.

"I'm coming with you," Peanut said.

Lon frowned. "This isn't your business yet, Peanut. You need to—"

"Anything to do with Ruby is my business," Peanut said.

Lon saw the fear and the pain in the lawyer's eyes and understood. "Follow me, but I talk. You listen."

"Yes, yes, I won't say a word," Peanut said, and followed the police chief out of the house, across the street, and then two houses down.

"This is where Arnold Purejoy lives. He's my secretary's brother-in-law," Peanut said.

"Let's hope he saw something helpful," Lon said.

Deputy Ralph was waiting for them on the porch. "Mr. Purejoy has a broken leg, which is why he wasn't in church and why he was, as he said, 'sitting at the window watching the world go by.'"

"I want to talk to him," Lon said, and then followed his deputy back into the house with Peanut behind him.

"Good afternoon, Mr. Purejoy," Lon said, and then nodded politely at his wife, Arlene, who was sitting nearby in a recliner. "Mrs. Purejoy. Hope we didn't disturb your Sunday dinner."

"It will all heat up," she said. "We're happy to do anything that will get our Ruby back. I don't know what we'd do in this town without her."

Peanut was sick at his stomach from the thought.

Lon pointed at Purejoy's cast.

"What happened to your leg?"

"I stepped off the back porch wrong. Broke my leg just above my ankle."

"Sure sorry to hear that. So, about Ruby… My deputy tells me you saw someone at her house earlier."

Purejoy nodded.

"Arlene says I've turned into a nosy busybody, but I'm used to going to work every day. It's hard to just sit around."

"I'm going to videotape your statement," Lon said as he pulled out his phone, then handed it to his deputy to film. "Tell me what you saw at Ruby Dye's house that made you think something could be wrong."

"Well, I saw this guy drive up in her driveway in an SUV. It was a black Chevrolet TrailBlazer with a blue front fender on the driver's side. Looked like a 2001. I didn't recognize it or him, so I watched. He got out and knocked at her door, but she didn't show up, so he knocked again. I saw the door open, but I didn't see Ruby."

"What made you think something was wrong?"

"It seemed as if he pushed his way in, but then when he went on in and stayed, I thought I was just imagining things so I got up to check on the roast in the oven like Arlene told me to do before she left for church. I'm slow moving around, so I was gone a little while. When I came back to my chair, the guy was putting something in the back seat."

"Could you tell what it was?" Lon asked.

"Didn't get a clear look, but it looked like a rolled-up rug. I thought maybe she was sending one out to be cleaned or something. I sure wish I'd paid more attention."

Peanut's soft moan said everything. Lon looked over his shoulder. Peanut's elbows were on his knees, his hands covering his face.

There was nothing Lon could do or say that would

change what had happened, but he could do his job and hopefully be a part of Ruby's recovery, so he refocused on Purejoy.

"Describe the man for me," Lon said.

"Hard to see his face from this distance, but he was probably early forties with short brown hair. Skinny guy, and average height. Oh…one other thing. I'm not positive, but I think there was a Tennessee tag on the back of that car. My son lives in Tennessee, and the tags looked the same."

"Is there anything else you can remember?" Lon asked.

"No, sir," Purejoy said.

Lon signaled his deputy to stop filming.

"You've been a big help, Mr. Purejoy."

"I sure hope you get her back," he said.

"Yes, sir, so do we," Lon said. "Mrs. Purejoy, we'll be leaving now. Thank you for your hospitality."

Deputy Ralph gave the phone back to Lon and followed him out. Peanut's legs were shaking as he started down the steps.

"I'm going home now, Chief, but I would take it as a personal favor if you kept me updated."

"This info is going out as a BOLO, a be on the lookout, so if I get news, I'll let you know."

Peanut's steps were dragging as he went back across the street to his car and drove away. The knot in his belly was getting tighter, and the pain in his chest was spreading. He'd planned this dinner at Granny's for weeks, waiting for what he thought would be the perfect time to reveal his feelings.

Please God, don't let me have waited too long.

Jarrod was driving as fast as the law allowed on his way back to Tennessee, but fuel was low and getting to the critical point. He had taken the ready cash from Ruby's wallet, but he'd counted on more than the eighty-three dollars she'd had in it. Still, it was enough to get him home. He glanced over his shoulder into the back seat. As far as he could tell, she hadn't moved, wasn't crying, or trying to escape. It occurred to him that she might have suffocated, which gave him the creeps. He didn't want to be driving around with a dead body. As soon as he fueled up, he'd take off out into rural Georgia. First bridge he came to, he was tossing her into the water below.

About five miles further, he saw an exit road leading to a big truck stop. He took the exit and was thinking about getting something to eat when his phone began to ring.

Ruby had chewed and bitten on the knots until she finally had the last knot loose enough to get her hands free. She'd swallowed enough blood in the process that she'd made herself sick, but her ankles were still tied with the belt from her robe. She couldn't undo them without revealing the fact that she was conscious, but she *could* come out of the bedspread fast enough to get her leather belt over Jarrod's head and around his neck. She was willing to risk the wreck this might cause rather than be murdered later. Just as she was about to make her move, his phone rang. She paused, holding her breath as she listened to Jarrod's voice.

"Hello? Oh hey, baby. Yes, I finished my business, and I'm already on the way home but just now stopping to refuel. You made me some ribs? Oh man, I wish I had some now. I'm starvin'. I'm gonna get some snacks to eat on the way. Yes, I'll be careful, and it's likely to be midnight before I get home. Okay, yeah, love you too."

Ruby heard him disconnect, then drive forward at a much slower rate. That's when it hit her. *Oh my God, if he stops for gas, I have a chance to escape.*

She heard him get out. The click that followed had to be the door locks, then the gas cap being unscrewed. A few moments later, she smelled the fuel rushing into the gas tank beneath the car.

She didn't know if she had time to get out before he saw and stopped her, but she would have risked it, if not for the gun. She didn't want to be shot in the back trying to get away. As difficult as it was, she waited for the gas to shut off. If he didn't get back in the car right away, she'd know he'd gone into the store for something to eat.

When she heard him putting the gas cap back on and then his footsteps walking away, she tensed. *Thank you, God.* Now was her chance!

Her heart was pounding as she tore her way out of the bedspread, untied her feet, and reached for the door. To her horror, it wouldn't open.

But as quickly as she panicked, she realized what the problem was. Nothing but child locks. She leaned over the front seat and pressed the unlock button.

Moments later, she was out and running, unaware of the cold concrete beneath her bare feet or the chilly air on her face. She was twenty yards away and looking back over her shoulder when she ran straight into a trucker who'd been checking his tires.

He took one look at her bare feet and battered face—and the fact that she was wearing nothing but underwear beneath the open front of her bloody robe—and grabbed her.

"Lady! What the hell happened to you?"

Ruby was shaking so hard she could barely talk. "I was kidnapped. Help me. He'll be coming out of the station any minute."

"Which car? What's he look like?" the trucker asked.

"That black SUV with the blue fender, at the back pumps." And then her heart skipped a beat as she saw Jarrod exit. "That's him, coming out of the station now."

"The skinny guy with the red cap?"

"Yes, oh my God," Ruby moaned and tried to pull out of his arms.

"You're okay, lady. I got your back. Just stay here," he said, and hefted the tire iron he was carrying for a better grip.

"He has a gun!" Ruby said.

"I hear you, ma'am. Now, when I get his attention, you just run on inside and tell Melvin at the cash register that Joey B said to call 911."

Ruby slipped back behind the cab of his truck as the driver started toward the old SUV. Jarrod was eating and walking as if he didn't have a care in the world, and he didn't seem to be aware that the man at the pumps was waiting for him.

When Ruby saw the trucker step out from between the gas pumps swinging that tire iron, she knew Jarrod was startled. She couldn't hear what they were saying, but when she saw Jarrod drop his snacks and go for his gun, she took off toward the station with her bathrobe flapping and her bare feet flying.

She heard shouts, a *thunk*, then silence just as she reached the door. Without looking back, she pushed her way inside and ran straight to the man at the register.

"Melvin!"

He looked up, startled that a stranger knew his name.

"Joey B said for you to call 911. I think he just took out the man who kidnapped me."

That's when Melvin focused on her condition. He shoved the cash register shut and reached for the phone as the other men in the station began running outside. She could see Melvin talking, but his voice was fading. People were coming up around her now. A man had his hand on her shoulder, a woman's lips were moving, but Ruby couldn't hear what she was saying. The room was spinning. Her last thought was she needed to identify herself.

"My name is Ruby Dye. I live in Blessings, Georgia, and I think I'm going to faint now."

And down she went.

———— ∿∿ ————

It was almost four o'clock when Mercy Pittman stopped by the police station on her way home from work to bring her husband a piece of her coconut pie.

Mercy did all the baking at Granny's Country Kitchen, and pie had been on special today. She'd carried out the last piece of coconut for Lon, and now he was eating it while they talked about Ruby.

"It's all anyone talked about today," Mercy said.

"Poor Lovey keeps tearing up when she thinks no one is looking. I know they're old friends, and she's scared she won't see Ruby again."

"Nothing like this has ever happened here in my time," Lon said. "The BOLO has been out a few hours now. I keep hoping some highway patrolman will spot that funky TrailBlazer."

"With that off-color front fender, it would definitely stand out," Mercy said, and then her voice began to shake. "I keep imagining how I would feel. She has to be scared out of her mind...if she's still alive." And then Mercy clapped her hand over her mouth. "I can't believe I said that aloud."

"It's nothing I haven't thought too," Lon said, and then the phone on his desk rang. "Excuse me a minute, honey." He set the pie aside to answer. "Chief Pittman."

"Chief Pittman, this is Lieutenant Farley of the Georgia State Highway Patrol. We have your kidnap victim, Ruby Dye. The man who took her was Jarrod Dye, her ex-husband. He is in handcuffs and on his way to jail."

Lon stood up, almost afraid to ask for details. "What are her injuries? What hospital will she be sent to?"

"She'll be in the local hospital in Dublin, just off Interstate 16. Her injuries are minor."

"But there was so much blood at the scene," Lon said.

"Probably from your kidnapper. He's got a mean cut on his forearm and likely a concussion from the trucker who took him down. He'll be taken to the hospital for stitches before booking."

"Thank you. Please tell Ruby we're coming to get her."

"Yes, sir. My pleasure, Chief Pittman."

Lon hung up the phone, grinning.

Mercy ran to him. "They found Ruby, didn't they? Is she hurt bad?"

"Yes, they've got her. It appears most of that blood at the scene was from the guy who kidnapped her. And get this. It was her ex-husband. She got in her licks before he took her down. I've got to call Peanut. I'll be late coming home, honey. We're going to get her."

Mercy threw her arms around his neck, her dark eyes dancing. "What wonderful, wonderful news! Is it okay if I tell people?"

Lon grinned. "You can shout it from the rooftops for all I care. This is news I was too scared to hope for. For sure call the Conklin twins, and tell Lovey. They're best friends. I'm calling Peanut."

"Why would she need her lawyer?" Mercy asked.

"I think he's more than her lawyer. I think he's head over heels for the woman. Thanks for the pie. Love you to pieces, and I'll call you when we head home."

He gave her a quick kiss and a pat on the backside as she left the office. He had the lawyer's info on his cell phone, and Peanut answered on the first ring.

"Hello?"

"They found her. She's on her way to a hospital in Dublin, just off Interstate 16. I'm going to get her."

"Take me with you," Peanut said.

Lon heard the desperation. "Be there in five," he said, and disconnected.

Chapter 2

PEANUT RODE IN THE FRONT SEAT. AFTER ASKING FOR details, learning Ruby's abductor was her ex-husband, and finding out she hadn't been the one bleeding, he went silent for miles. He knew she'd been married before, but she'd never once mentioned her ex's name. Now he was a reality they both had to face.

Lon drove with his lights flashing all the way to the Interstate 16 connection, which took over an hour. When they reached the interstate, he took the northbound route, turned on the siren too, and accelerated.

Peanut sent a message to Laurel Lorde, the woman who cleaned his house, to please change the sheets in his guest room and make sure there were fresh towels in the adjoining bath. Ruby couldn't go back to her home the way it was, and while he hadn't invited her to be his guest just yet, he was hedging his bets in case she accepted. While he was waiting for Laurel to text him back, he was trying to gather his thoughts, but it was hard to focus. He kept thinking of how quickly their lives had been turned on end, and how close they'd all come to losing Ruby today.

A few minutes later, Laurel returned a text, letting him know she'd received the instructions. Now that that had been taken care of, he dropped the phone back in his jacket pocket and looked up. The scenery out the side window was a blur.

Despite the raucous sound of the siren's scream and the flashing lights, they quickly faded from consciousness and became nothing more than background music to the drama in which they'd been caught. The lights and siren sent cars veering off the highway onto the shoulder, giving the cop car all the leeway needed as Lon flew past.

Peanut didn't look at the people in the cars. He didn't want to see their curious glances or disgruntled faces from drivers who had been forced to stop. Everyone was always in such a hurry to get someplace. They needed to slow down, think about the people they loved, and let them know it before it was too late. Life was too short to waste. He was still thinking about Ruby when something else occurred to him.

"Hey, Lon, what do you think the odds are of this going to trial?" Peanut asked.

"I don't know," the chief answered. "A sane man would get a lawyer and plead out. He was caught with her, and might get a worse sentence once Ruby got on the stand to testify."

"That's what I was thinking," Peanut said.

"Why do you ask?" Lon said.

"I'd have to ask someone else to advise her because there's no way I could be rational about the kidnapper. It would take every ounce of control I had not to break his neck."

"Can I ask you something personal?" Lon asked.

Peanut sighed. "If you want to know if there's anything between Ruby and me, I'd say yes and she'd say no, because everything I feel for her has been left unsaid."

Lon frowned. "But why? I see you guys together a lot. I just thought—"

"That's because I volunteer for every damn committee she's on so we can meet for lunch and so I can take pizza over to her house at night while we're planning the next agenda."

Lon grinned. "What's the holdup?"

"Mostly me," Peanut said. "I love her so much that I was afraid if I told her and she didn't feel the same way, it would ruin the friendship. I've been sending her presents and flowers for a while now, but with no card."

"Oh, going the secret admirer route? So how's that working for you?"

Peanut shrugged. "It wasn't, and I knew it. I was supposed to take her to Granny's after church today and then planned to confess it when I took her home. Only all this happened." He wiped a shaky hand across his face. "I spent the whole afternoon thinking of the time I'd wasted and what she might be going through. I thought I'd lost her."

"I thought we had too," Lon said. "So you got yourself a second chance, my friend."

Peanut nodded. "I won't waste it, either. Do you know how much farther to Dublin?"

"Maybe another thirty-five minutes or so…maybe less," Lon said.

Peanut glanced at the time and then took a deep breath. He was fresh out of patience.

———

Ruby was in the emergency room at Fairview Park Hospital, trying not to panic. As fate would have it, the patient in the next bay over was Jarrod, with the cops who were guarding him. They'd had to bring him in for stitches and X-rays before they could transport him to jail to be booked.

Logically she knew she was safe, but being able to hear her ex's voice didn't make her feel that way. She was alone and stranded in a strange place. Then when they told her the police from Blessings were coming to get her, she almost cried. Seeing Chief Pittman or one of the deputies would be a godsend. They knew where she belonged. They would take her home.

She thought about Peanut, wondering what he'd thought when she missed church and then wasn't there for their Sunday dinner date at Granny's.

She closed her eyes, thinking of how the right corner of his mouth tilted up just a little higher than the other when he smiled, and how blue his eyes were. He was a fixture in her life. The hero in all her dreams, and she loved spending time with him. Yet the closest thing between them was when he held her hand to help her in and out of a car.

He was a lawyer. She cut and dyed people's hair. He would likely never think of her as anything but a friend…and the lady who was his barber.

She looked down at her hands—at the scratched and bloody knuckles, and fingers swollen from fighting for her life. She didn't even want to see her face. She'd lost count of how many times Jarrod had hit her, but the whole incident brought back everything she'd been running from when she first appeared in Blessings.

All she knew was that one eye was swollen because it hurt to blink, and if her mouth looked as bad as it felt, people would be horrified by her appearance. It would take a while before she'd be able to go back to work.

The girls would have to pick up her appointments, at least until her hands healed.

She heard a scream and then a long round of curses and guessed Jarrod was getting stitches. She hoped they hurt. She had three stitches of her own on her upper lip. They'd hurt when the doctor was sewing her up. He told her it would probably leave a little scar, but she didn't care. It would be a reminder that Jarrod Dye no longer held power over her.

A nurse popped into Ruby's room. "Can I get you anything, honey?"

"Water? Thirsty," Ruby mumbled.

"Be right back," she said, and hurried away.

A few minutes later, she returned with a pitcher of ice water, a cup, and a straw. She poured some for her, and then added the straw, making it easier for Ruby to drink.

"Here you go, honey," the nurse said.

"Thank you," Ruby replied, and then winced because talking hurt.

"You'll be drinking your meals for a bit, but you'll heal. Oh...I'm supposed to tell you that your ride will be here soon. They radioed to have all of your paperwork finished so they could sign you out directly after they arrive," the nurse said.

Ruby clasped her hands against her breasts, and her breath caught on a sob.

"Home. I'm going home."

The nurse patted her arm. "I can't begin to imagine how frightening your ordeal was, but I have to say you are a remarkable woman. Talk about wearing scars. You put some on your kidnapper."

"Shhh," Ruby whispered, pointing to the next bay.

The nurse waved away Ruby's concern. "Oh, he's gone. They just moved him out. You rest a bit. You're going to have a long ride back to Blessings. The doctor has some pain pills for you to take home and a prescription you'll get filled there, as well."

"Thank you," Ruby said, pointing at the water.

"Welcome," the nurse said, and left.

Ruby closed her eyes, intending just to rest, but she drifted off to sleep. She was still asleep when Lon and Peanut walked into the room.

Lon stopped in the doorway, stunned by Ruby's appearance.

Peanut nearly went to his knees and reached for the wall to steady himself.

"Son of a bitch," Lon whispered, then put a hand on Peanut's shoulder. "I'll go sign her out," he said, and closed the door behind him as he left.

Peanut moved toward Ruby in a daze. He'd never realized how small she was until now. She'd always been such a bright light that he'd seen her as a kind of Amazon, able to take on whatever she chose to do. What the hell did he say to someone who had endured this?

When he touched her arm, she woke.

He leaned over and kissed her forehead.

"I thought I'd lost you," he said.

Ruby's heart skipped a beat. Peanut was here, and he'd just kissed her!

The empathy was her downfall. Tears welled. "Thought I lost me too."

"Are you in much pain?" Peanut asked.

"Some."

That one word made his heart hurt.

"I need to tell you something. This isn't how I imagined I would say it, but I've spent the whole damn afternoon thinking I was never going to get to say it, and then God gave me a second chance. I have been sending you flowers and gifts for weeks and weeks and telling you in every way except face-to-face that I am head over heels in love with you."

Ruby gasped, and then reached for his hand. "Once I hoped and then thought it couldn't be... Not in your league."

He lowered the bedrail and then sat down on the bed beside her. He slipped his hand beneath her fingers, wanting to hold her, yet afraid even to touch her.

"If I spent the rest of my life in sackcloth and ashes, I would still not see myself worthy of you, but I am a selfish enough bastard to want you anyway. If you could see your way to letting me properly court you in the hopes that you might learn to love me, it would pretty much make my day."

Ruby choked on a sob as she clutched his hand.

"Today when I thought I would die, your face was the first thing I saw. All the years I've known you and asked favors of you, and you always came through for me. You have been a white knight for so many in Blessings. I never dreamed you would ever be mine. Yes, to everything you just said."

The knot in Peanut's throat began to ease. Not only was Ruby going to be okay, but she'd said yes to being his girl.

"I'm taking you home with me for the first few days until we can get your house cleaned up. Right now, it is a crime scene. Besides the blood everywhere, there is fingerprint powder, as well as the footsteps of a team of crime scene investigators who've tromped all over."

Ruby blushed at the thought of being a guest in his house, and he saw it.

"You'll have your own guest room and bath, and all of your friends can come at will to my house to check on you and visit with you any time. I'm just offering shelter, darlin'. I won't ask for more. Whatever you give me comes on your time, at your speed. Deal?"

"Yes…and a good deal."

Peanut had a big, silly grin on his face when the chief walked in, but he didn't give a damn.

Lon was relieved Ruby was awake and talking.

"Hello, Miss Ruby. You sure gave us all a scare. The whole town went into mourning when you disappeared, thinking they might never see you again, and now I'm sure they all know you've been found. God only knows what kind of a celebration they'll be planning for you once you're back on your feet."

"Really?" Ruby said.

"Why would you be surprised?" Peanut asked. "Honey, everybody in Blessings loves Ruby Dye, including me."

Lon eyed the hospital gown she was wearing. "Do you have clothes to wear home? It's cold outside."

"I was in my slip and underwear when Jarrod knocked. I put on my robe to go to the door." Her voice began to shake, and her hands started to tremble. "There's blood all over the clothes. He…" She took a deep breath and started over. "He hit—"

Peanut couldn't stand it. "Doesn't matter. You don't need to explain. We saw it. Give me a second," he said, and walked out of the room.

Lon patted her leg beneath the sheets. "He's had a hard day too," Lon said.

A few minutes later, Peanut came back with a pair of scrubs, some fuzzy hospital socks with no-skid soles, and a clean hospital gown to wear as a robe. There was a nurse right behind him.

"Ruby, honey, she's going to help you dress."

Ruby nodded.

"We'll be right outside the door with a wheelchair. When you're finished, we're out of here."

The nurse grinned as the men left the room, shutting the door behind them. "Someone sure thinks the world of you."

Ruby put a shaky hand to her face. "I see that. I wish I'd seen it sooner, but better late than never, right?"

The nurse chuckled. "Absolutely. Now let's see if we can get this top over your head without hurting you."

A few minutes later, she walked out to get the wheelchair.

"She's ready to go," she told Lon. "I have to take her out and see her to the car. Hospital rules."

"I'll go pull the car around to the ER entrance," Lon said, and hurried out the door.

Ruby was sitting on the side of the bed when Peanut just walked over, lifted her up into his arms and put her down in the wheelchair as if she weighed nothing, then tucked a blanket around her legs.

"It's getting colder outside," he said.

"Then we need to get you on the road to home. Maybe you won't get there too late," the nurse said.

"I don't care what time it is when we get there, as long as I'm back in Blessings before I close my eyes tonight," Ruby said.

"Amen to that," Peanut muttered, and walked beside her chair all the way to the exit.

"So cold," Ruby said, shivering as Peanut lifted her out of the wheelchair and into the back seat of the cruiser.

"I'm riding with her," he told Lon, and crawled in beside her.

Lon grinned at him. "Don't forget to buckle up," he said, and shut the door behind Peanut.

Lon got inside the cruiser, then glanced over his shoulder to make sure they were settling in okay.

"Miss Ruby, I have the pills the doctor sent and a prescription to be filled, along with your discharge papers. I'm going to make this as comfortable a trip home as I can for you."

"I'll be fine," Ruby said. Then out of nowhere, she started crying again. "I'm sorry. It's so surreal...all of this. I thought I was going to die today, and then it turned out to be one of the best days of my life. I'm just so grateful."

"Yes, ma'am," Lon said, and put the car in gear, then keyed up the radio. "Chief Pittman to dispatch."

Avery Ames, the day dispatcher, responded. "This is dispatch. Go ahead, Chief."

"Be informed we're leaving Dublin. I'm bringing Miss Ruby home."

Avery let out a little on-air whoop. "Ten-four, Chief. Over and out."

Peanut put his arm around Ruby's shoulders and pulled her close against him.

"Lean against me all you want. Sleep if you can. I'll try to cushion the bumps for you."

Tears were still rolling as Ruby leaned in. At first, it felt awkward. Her reference points with Peanut had been in friendship. She didn't know how to be with him as a man who loved her, but she would figure it out.

Within minutes, she was asleep.

Peanut held her in his arms all the way home.

———— ∿ ————

It was dark when the chief drove back into Blessings. He'd killed the siren over an hour ago but kept the lights flashing, and they were still spinning as he passed the city limits sign.

Ruby woke up when he began slowing down. She was so stiff and sore she could hardly move, and speaking was almost impossible.

"Where?" she asked.

"We're home, sweetheart," Peanut said.

Ruby nodded and patted her heart to indicate how much it meant to her.

"Would you look at that!" Lon said, as he turned up Main Street.

People were lining both sides of Main, holding lanterns and flashlights, and some were holding candles. The ones standing beneath the streetlights were holding up WELCOME HOME signs, and signs that read WE LOVE YOU, RUBY.

When they saw the chief's patrol car and the flashing lights, they began cheering and chanting "Ruby, Ruby, Ruby," over and over as Lon drove past.

Ruby pressed her hands against her heart as tears rolled down her cheeks.

Peanut was nearly speechless. "Wow," he said softly, and gently hugged her. "This is how much you are loved."

Lon drove all the way up Main, then turned right toward Peanut's residence. "Someone left the lights on for you," he said as he turned into the circle drive in front of Peanut's house.

"Probably Laurel. She was here cleaning today."

Lon put the car in park and killed the engine, but left the headlights on. "I'll help you get Ruby inside," he said.

Peanut handed him the house key. "You unlock the door. I've got her."

"Will do," Lon said as he grabbed all of her paperwork and meds, then headed to the front door.

"Don't move, honey," Peanut said. "I'll come around to the other side."

Ruby sighed. It was hard to relegate herself to needing help. She was usually the one organizing it for someone else.

Peanut opened her door and then leaned in and picked up her and the blanket. She gasped as he lifted her up.

"Did I hurt you? I'm sorry, honey."

She patted the side of his face and then leaned her cheek against his jacket as he carried her inside.

Lon had lights on in the front of the house.

"Down this hall," Peanut said. "First door on the left. Open it please, and turn those lights on too."

Lon moved ahead of them, turning on lights as he went, and then stepped aside as Peanut carried Ruby into his guest room and sat her down on the side of the bed.

"Welcome back, Miss Ruby," Lon said. "I'll leave you to settle in. Rest well."

"I'll see you out," Peanut said, and followed Lon out of the room.

Ruby felt her mouth and her swollen eye, and then got up and gingerly moved to the bathroom. She dreaded facing what she looked like, but she had to know the extent of the damage Jarrod had done to her this time.

When she saw herself in the mirror, she groaned. *Oh my God! Will I even look the same when all of this is healed?* And then she took a deep breath and reminded herself that she was alive, and for now, that was all that mattered.

Peanut came hurrying back into the room and saw Ruby standing in front of the mirror. "That will heal," he said.

Ruby didn't know he was there until he spoke, and then she nodded. "Hurts much," she managed to say.

"Pain pills. You have some pain pills," Peanut said, and ran back out to the table where Lon had left the meds and her discharge papers. He came back with the pills and a glass of water.

Ruby slipped the pills between her lips, then managed to get enough water in her mouth to swallow them. She set the glass on the bathroom counter and then walked back out into the bedroom where Peanut was busy turning down the bedclothes.

"I don't have a nightgown for you. Are you okay to sleep in the scrubs?" he asked.

She patted her scrubs. "Sleep in these," she said.

Peanut sighed. "I want so much to hold you, but there isn't a spot on your body that I'd dare to touch. I'm so glad you're safe and that you're here. Will you be able to manage on your own tonight? My room is just across the hall. I'm going to leave the door open, so if you need anything at all in the night, just call out. I'll hear you."

Ruby walked into his arms and laid her head on his chest. "My forever hero," she mumbled, as he pulled her close.

"If you need, I could call someone to come sit with you," he offered.

Ruby shook her head. "I can do it," she said, and then winced.

"Do you want anything? Food? Some milk? I have straws."

"Tomorrow," she said.

"Then I'm going to leave so you can have your privacy. The remote to the television is on the table beside the bed. There's a night-light in the bathroom." He brushed a kiss across her forehead. "Sleep well, sweet lady. Tomorrow is a new day."

He shut the door on his way out, and now she was alone.

She sat down on the side of the bed and removed all her clothes, then walked barefoot into the bathroom. She wouldn't be able to close her eyes until she'd washed Jarrod Dye off her skin.

The warm water burned the skinned knuckles and cuts on her hands, but she didn't care. She wanted to wash her hair as well, but the thought of getting shampoo in her badly bruised eyes or infecting the wound on her mouth was enough to stop her. Instead, she stood in front of the warm spray and kept soaping and scrubbing, and then doing it again. Finally, she turned off the water and dried, put the scrubs back on for pajamas, and crawled into bed.

The last thought on her mind was that Peanut loved her. Now all she had to do was give herself permission to love him back.

Chapter 3

JARROD DYE HAD A BROKEN NOSE, SEVEN STITCHES IN HIS head, twenty-two in his arm, and he'd never made it home for ribs. He'd used his free call from jail to ask his girlfriend to contact a lawyer, but when she found out what he'd done, she freaked out and hung up on him. He should have called his brother.

Still, in the long run, it didn't matter. He didn't have money to pay a lawyer and was going to have to rely on a court-appointed one, although he didn't have a chance in hell of escaping his fate.

He'd crossed state lines and assaulted, robbed, and kidnapped his ex-wife. Without a doubt, it was the dumbest thing he'd ever done. He hadn't counted on Ruby fighting him. She never had before. And he sure hadn't counted on her escaping. If there was any kind of positive to be had from where he was at, it was that her escape had kept his charges to robbery, assault, and kidnapping. If she hadn't escaped, he would have had a murder on his conscience too.

The upside of spending what was left of his tomcat years in jail was that the collection agencies weren't going to be hounding him anymore. He'd have a roof over his head and three meals a day, compliments of the State of Georgia.

As for his damn ex-wife, he never wanted to see her

face again. He liked her better the way she used to be, before she turned into the bitch from hell.

—∿∿—

The pain pills Peanut gave Ruby eased the pain, but they also put her to sleep, and then to dream, resurrecting memories of every abuse she'd suffered at her ex-husband's hands—things she never talked about, things she'd spent years trying to forget.

She woke up twice in the night, once bathed in sweat with tears on her face, and the second time in mute panic, thinking Jarrod was throwing her bound-and-gagged body over the side of a bridge.

She threw back the covers and hobbled into the bathroom. When she came out, she sat down on the side of the bed, eyeing the wounds on her hands. She wanted the blood washed out of her hair. She could go to her shop and have one of the twins do it for her, but that would mean revealing the extent of what had happened to her, and she wasn't sure she was ready to endure that kind of inspection.

Still, the more she thought about it, the more she realized that what she was dreading had nothing to do with the way she looked, and everything to do with having to talk about the abusive ex. No one knew why she'd divorced him and ran, and now everyone would know.

Her shoulders slumped. *Damn Jarrod Dye to hell and back*. She'd tried so hard to escape her past, and just when she thought she was home free, he'd dragged his sorry ass back into her life and broken the fragile wall behind which she'd been living.

Then she thought of Peanut asleep in the bed across

the hall. He was so dear to her, and the knowledge that he loved her was the best gift she'd ever received. Still, there was something she had to tell him, something she had to confess that might end her happily ever after.

Finally, she lay down and pulled the covers up over her shoulders. The sheets were smooth and soft and smelled of a rain-washed morning. She shifted slightly, trying to find a comfortable place to lay her head, and drifted off to sleep again, dreaming this time that she was standing in a doorway looking down the aisle of her church. The pews were full of people she knew, but she was looking for Peanut. She was supposed to have dinner with him at Granny's, and she was certain he hadn't forgotten.

The organist began to play, which was the signal for the services to begin. Now she didn't know where to sit because all the seats were taken and people were frowning at her. She wasn't in her proper place.

All of a sudden, Peanut was down at the end of the aisle, in front of the pulpit. He beckoned to her. She knew if she took that first step, she was accepting way more than a seat at church, but there was no hesitation when she started toward him.

She was halfway down the aisle when something woke her.

To her surprise, it was morning and someone was knocking on her door.

-~~-

Peanut hadn't slept worth a damn and was up before daylight. He'd sent a text to his secretary to reschedule all of his appointments for the next two days and told her not to call him unless it was a big-ass emergency. He knew she'd laugh at his phrasing, but he didn't care. He was a man in love, and soon everyone in Blessings would know it was Ruby he loved.

Then the sun came up and the morning was passing, and Ruby hadn't let out a peep. He ate a bowl of cereal, drank two cups of coffee, and couldn't stand it any longer. He had to know if she was okay, or if she needed any help. He poured her a cup of coffee, stirring in the two spoonfuls of sugar she liked, then took it to the guest room and knocked.

"Come in," she said.

Thank God, he thought, and entered. He tried not to react to the darkening bruises and smiled.

"The swelling has gone down in your eye. Does it feel better, baby?"

He called me baby. This is real. This is really real.

"Yes, better," she said.

"I brought coffee the way you like it, and I let it cool enough so that it won't melt the straw."

She held out her hands. He leaned over and kissed her cheek, then put the cup in both hands.

Ruby took a quick sip, grateful for the sweet, warm liquid running down her throat.

"Sit with me?" she asked.

He pulled up a chair near her bed and then leaned forward, his elbows on his knees, watching as she took a few more sips before setting the cup aside.

She glanced up at him again, and he thought he saw panic come and go in her expression. He was suddenly afraid she was going to tell him she couldn't possibly love him after all.

"Talk in shorthand," she said, pointing to her swollen lips.

He couldn't bear the distance between them and abandoned the chair for the side of her bed. When he held out his hand, she grasped it like a lifeline.

"Have secrets to tell," she said.

"You don't have to do this until you feel better," he said.

She shook her head. "If we work, no secrets."

His gut knotted, but he understood what she was trying to say. "Okay then. I'm listening."

She looked at him then, seeing him as a man to love instead of just a friend.

"Before Blessings…lived Sparta, Tennessee. Born there. Knew Jarrod since kids," she said, and then drew a deep, shaky breath. "Married him because pregnant."

"Happens to lots of people," Peanut said. "Doesn't change a thing about how much I love you."

She glanced at him again and then looked down. "He drank. Sometimes get mad and slap me."

Peanut stifled a curse.

"Then with his fist…a lot. Lost baby. I can't have more. So sorry."

Tears were running down her face now, and Peanut had heard enough. "Look at me, Ruby."

She wiped away tears and looked up.

"Those aren't secrets, they're tragedies, and I wish to God you'd never experienced them. But if you think any of that matters to me, or what I hope for our future, you are mistaken. I'm forty-five years old. I cannot imagine being a fifty-year-old man with a kid in first grade, okay?"

The heaviness within her lifted. "Really?"

"Hell yes, really," he said.

She'd heard that tone in his voice too often to doubt the authenticity.

"Is that it?" Peanut said.

She nodded.

"And it's still okay that I'm crazy in love with you?" he asked.

"Dumb question," she said, and cupped his cheek.

He sighed. "Probably won't be the last dumb thing you hear me say. However, I have another question. What can I make for you to eat? You can't just drink coffee. I have ice cream. I can make a vanilla shake."

"Yum," she said, and gave him a thumbs-up.

He grinned. "What else can I do for you?"

"Need clothes from home. Need to go to the shop."

He looked horrified. "You can't work."

She frowned. "Not work. Wash out blood. His blood," she said, pointing to her hair.

"Oh, hell yes, I'll take you," he muttered. "Can you get dressed in the scrubs on your own okay?"

"Yes."

"Then you dress. I'll make the shake. You can drink it on the way," he said, and stood up.

"Thank you," Ruby said.

He shook his head. "You saved your own life. The least I can do is help you put it all back together, especially since you're saving a place in it for me."

He winked at her as he left, closing the door behind him.

Ruby took a few more sips of coffee, then picked up the house phone and called Vera and Vesta.

Vera answered. "Hello."

"It's me," Ruby said.

Vera squealed, and then started to cry. "Lord, lord, Sister, it is a blessing just to hear your voice. Vesta and I prayed so hard for you to be okay. Finding out that you were safe and on the way home was the best news ever."

Ruby sighed. *This is how love feels.*

"Peanut bringing me to shop. Blood in my hair. Will you meet me there to wash?"

"Yes, absolutely."

"Can't talk much. Mouth stitches…swollen. Look awful. Be prepared."

"None of that matters. The only thing that matters to your friends is that you're back."

"Thank you. Be an hour or so. Need clothes. Going home to pack."

"Your spare house key is back under the mat."

"Okay. See you," Ruby said, and then hung up.

She shook the wrinkles out of the scrubs she'd worn home and carried them and her coffee into the bathroom. A few minutes later, she made her way to the kitchen with the empty cup, following the sounds.

"Hey, honey!" Peanut said, as he turned off the blender and poured the shake into a large red Solo cup. "My best to-go crystal," he said, as he popped a straw into the shake.

"Trade you," Ruby said, and gave him the empty coffee cup as he handed her the shake.

She took it with both hands and took her first sip. Besides water and coffee, it was the first thing she'd had in her stomach in over twenty-four hours.

"So good, Peanut!" she said.

"Just one of my more complicated gourmet meals."

She laughed and then moaned. "Ow…no laughing… no fair."

"Right. Turning on my lawyer face. No grinning. No jokes. Hard, steely gaze and stern jaw."

Ruby rolled her eyes. "Sexy lawyer. Not scary one."

A big grin spread across his face. "Really?"

"Your Eastwood look," Ruby said.

Peanut frowned. "My what?"

"Everyone says Clint Eastwood. Don't worry… younger version, not old, gray one. Ready to go. I have no shoes or coat."

Peanut lost his train of thought. *People think I look like Clint Eastwood? Really? Is that good, or is that bad?*

"Peanut!"

"Huh… What, honey? Sorry. What did you say?"

She pointed at her feet.

"Oh right! You have no shoes. I'll carry you to the car, and then you can get shoes at your house, okay? I'll get you something for a coat."

He strode out of the kitchen with haste and returned carrying both his coat and a lined flannel shirt that wound up hanging six inches past her knees.

"Feels good," Ruby said, as he buttoned her up in it.

He paused, then slowly cupped her face and brushed a kiss on her forehead, then on her cheeks. "Forgive me for repeating myself, but being able to say that I love you is quite a heady feeling. I just had to say it again."

Ruby shivered with sudden longing. "I dream of making love to you," she admitted, then blushed.

Peanut sighed. "So do I, sweetheart, so do I, but when you're well. Now, let's get you and your breakfast in the car."

He put on his coat, then she followed him through the house to the front door.

"Wait here a minute," Peanut said.

Ruby stood at the window, watching as he opened the passenger side door and headed back to the house.

"It's so cold," he said, as he came back inside. "One more thing," and he left the room on the run. He came back carrying a pair of white tube socks. "This is better than barefoot. Sit there."

She sat down and held out a foot. When he knelt at her feet and began pulling one sock up her foot and leg, her gaze fell on his hair—thick sandy-brown hair that she'd run her fingers through for years, washing and cutting it without any thought for him beyond being a customer. Never dreaming it could be more.

"One more sock," he said, and then looked up at her and grinned. "Are you my Cinderella? Is the glass slipper going to fit?" He pulled the last sock over her foot and up her leg, then looked up. "It fits! Where have you been all my life?"

"At the Curl Up and Dye, waiting for my prince," she said.

He laughed out loud.

"Forgive me, Cinderella. Your prince was sort of slow on the uptake. Now let's get going. Grab that milkshake, and hang on."

He carried her out of the house and into the car, buckled her up, then drove them back to the scene of the crime. As he pulled up in her yard, the sight of that yellow plastic tape flapping in the wind made the hair rise on Ruby's neck.

"Lord. Crime scene tape. Around my yard."

Peanut sighed. "It's worse inside."

Rage swept through Ruby so fast that she hit her hands on her knees in frustration before she thought, breaking open newly healing scabs.

"He intruded in my world. Didn't belong here. He was the past. Why didn't he stay in the past?"

Peanut grabbed her hands. "Look what you've done, love. You're bleeding again. Come on now... We'll get your clothes and be gone from here."

Ruby looked down at the knees of her scrubs, now splattered with tiny specks of blood. She shuddered.

"Yes. Out of here," she mumbled, and opened the door without waiting for him to help.

Peanut jumped out and caught up with her at the steps. He took her elbow to steady her.

"Key's under the mat," Ruby said.

He lifted the mat and picked up the key, then unlocked the door.

Ruby stepped in front of him, entering first with her head up. It seemed to Peanut that she entered with purpose, facing the waiting demons.

The disarray hit Ruby like a kick in the gut. The dark smears of fingerprint powder, the chairs pushed slightly out of place, a muddy footprint near the sideboard, the window shades hanging at awkward angles looked as bad as Jarrod made her feel.

She shook off the shock and started walking, unaware Peanut was watching her every move through the house, touching the back of a sofa, feeling the smooth surface of the dining room table, giving the ruby glass candy dish in the center of it a telling look—a kind of recognition that the giver was no longer a secret.

She moved to the kitchen without hesitation and then barely glanced at the blood and the knives as she turned and went down the hall to her bedroom. Her heart was pounding now, and she was sick to her stomach as she stepped inside her room.

The horror was still real, the pain too fresh to ignore. She touched her face, then her mouth, remembering the blows, the cursing, and the blood. It was all over him, and on her, and now her sanctuary had been tainted by his presence. Would it ever feel right again?

"I should have cut his throat instead of his arm," she said, and sank to her knees.

Peanut picked her up, then held her close, rocking her where she stood.

"I'm sorry. I'm so sorry. You're breaking my heart. Tell me where I can find a bag. You tell me what you want, and I'll do it for you. Anything…just let me make something better for you."

Ruby wrapped her arms around his waist to keep from running. She'd tried so hard to run away the first time and thought she'd been successful, but it had all been veneer. Distance hadn't made her safe. Jarrod had still found her.

"He'll be in jail for a long, long time," Peanut said.

"Maybe he'll die there. It's something to hope for," Ruby said.

Peanut frowned. He'd never heard Ruby talk like this. This was hard for her, and he couldn't blame her for feeling this way, but he felt her shutting down and didn't know how to fix this.

He gripped her by the arms. "Ruby…look at me."

She looked up and then blinked, as if she'd just realized he was still here.

"I need a bag. Where are they? The sooner we're out of here, the better."

"The closet," she said, and went into the walk-in closet. "Top shelf."

Peanut took the bag down and set it beside the bed, then removed all the items scattered on it, pulled off the stained sheets and threw them on the floor before opening the bag on the bed. But Ruby was swaying on her feet and getting paler by the minute.

She's crashing. Coming back here was a big mistake.

"You sit right here by the bag. I'll bring what you want and you can pack it in, okay?"

She nodded.

"What first?" he asked.

"Shoes. Ones I wear, and my house slippers. Floor of the closet. Underwear in top two drawers of the dresser. Nightgowns and socks in the third drawer," she said.

He ran from one spot to another, moving as fast as he could, then into the bathroom for toiletries until she had what she wanted. She'd chosen pull-up sweat pants and a pull-over sweatshirt for warmth. They'd traded his oversized tube socks for her own and chosen slip-on loafers for her to wear.

Peanut gathered up the loose items and put them back in her purse, dropped her cell phone inside, and unplugged the charger and dropped it in as well.

"He took my money," Ruby said. "He always took my money. I'm ready to leave now."

"I'll get you more money. Stand up, darlin'. You need to wear your coat."

She stood up, so ready to be out of this house, away from the turmoil in her home. Once her coat was on,

Peanut buttoned it for her, then gathered her things and led her through the house. He locked it back up and replaced the spare key back under the mat before he took her to the car. When he leaned in to buckle her up, she moved toward him just enough that their foreheads touched.

"Thank you," she whispered.

He brushed a kiss on the side of her cheek. "Stay with me, love. Don't shut down, okay? This is a hard day, but I promise it will get better."

She held onto the seat belt as he shut her in. A chilly blast of wind came into the car as he slid behind the wheel and then reached across the console and patted her knee.

"Off we go to the Curl Up and Dye, where the best haircuts, the latest news, and a whole lot of love are offered on a daily basis."

Ruby looked a little startled. "Is that what you think of my shop?"

"Not just me, love. Everyone in Blessings brings you bad hair and troubles, and you find a way to fix them all. We leave looking *and* feeling better than when we arrived."

"I like knowing that," she said softly.

He backed out of the drive and then drove away.

Ruby sank back into the seat every time he stopped at a stop sign or for a red light. She didn't want people seeing her like this.

Peanut knew she was uncomfortable with her appearance. He understood but had no way to reassure her. She would have to witness all that for herself. The people of Blessings might cry with her, but surely they would never judge her as anything but heroic for seriously wounding her kidnapper and then finding a way to escape.

When he finally pulled up in front of the shop, Ruby was trembling.

"I'll get the door," he said, so she waited for him to help her out, then ducked her head as they walked toward the shop.

The bell over the door jingled their arrival, and within seconds, Ruby was surrounded.

Mabel Jean was crying as she hugged and kissed her.

The twins hugged Ruby together, one on either side, both talking at once as they removed her coat, handed it to Peanut without a word, and led her back to the work area.

Peanut grinned as he hung up their coats. This was exactly what she needed. He followed the chatter back to the work area, then walked up to Ruby and gently touched her shoulder.

"Darlin', if you'll hand me your phone and charger, I'll plug it in for you while you're getting all prettied up."

Ruby dug them out of her purse, and Peanut took them to her empty station, plugged in the charger, and then sat in her styling chair and turned to face the room.

The twins were eyeing him and then Ruby, then him and then Ruby, until finally Vera spoke up.

"What's with you two?" she asked.

Ruby blushed. "I have been getting presents and flowers from a secret admirer for several months."

"Who turned out to be me," Peanut said. "Everyone in Blessings is going to know it, but I'm telling it here first. I love Ruby Dye...deeply...madly."

Ruby shivered with sudden longing as she turned to him. "It's mutual."

Peanut just sat there grinning.

The twins squealed. Mabel Jean cried some more.

It took several minutes before they all calmed down.

"My hair… Get that man's blood out of my hair," Ruby begged.

The twins gasped. "That's his?"

"She sliced him and diced him for what he did to her, and then escaped her own kidnapper. She is amazing," Peanut said.

Ruby rolled her eyes. "Just wash it out, please."

Peanut let their chatter and the joy that always abounded in this place wash over him. Ruby might have dreaded coming, but the love and acceptance here was turning out to be the medicine she needed most.

Chapter 4

VERA WAS GETTING READY TO DRY AND STYLE RUBY'S HAIR when they heard the bell jingle over the door. Then they heard running feet, and before anyone could move, Lovey Cooper was in the work area. She went straight to Ruby without saying a word, leaned over and hugged her, and wouldn't let go.

"I'm okay," Ruby said as she patted Lovey's shoulder.

Lovey turned Ruby loose, then stepped back and looked at her as if she'd never seen her before. "I can't believe this happened to you...in our town. Blessings isn't like this. I feel like we all let you down."

"Blessings had nothing to do with my past," Ruby said, and reached for her friend's hand, but when Lovey saw the wounds on Ruby's hands, she staggered backward.

Peanut leaped out of the chair and caught her just before she went down. "Sit here," he said.

Lovey just kept shaking her head. "I feel like I never knew you," she whispered. "I always knew you had a heart of gold, and you are one of the most giving people I've ever known, but I had no idea you had this kind of strength. My God, Ruby. My God."

Ruby sighed. "Wasn't a stranger. Might have been different if it had been. I'm okay. He's in jail." Then she glanced at Peanut. "But this has a silver lining. Found out who my secret admirer is."

Lovey gasped. "You have a secret admirer! You never told me!"

"Didn't tell anybody," Ruby said.

Peanut sighed. He was ready to be out of this den of females. Every time a new one showed up, the same story was likely to be told. And yet he held up his hand, proud to stake his claim.

"It's me, Lovey. I have loved her for so long that I thought it was already obvious to the world. I mean, I love this town as much as the rest of you, but when have I ever volunteered for stuff? And yet I have been on every committee in Blessings for the last year and a half just so I could hang out with Ruby."

All of the women turned and stared at him.

"Well, it's the truth," he muttered.

They laughed.

He shrugged.

Vera turned on the hair dryer and grabbed her round brush.

"Sister, before I start this, do you have any sore spots on your head?" Vera asked.

Ruby shook her head.

They sat then, watching Vera work her magic without talking while Ruby closed her eyes and gave herself up to the warm air on her head, and the massaging bristles of Vera's little round vent brush. Some days it was all about the small things, and today, having clean hair and a style was helping put the shattered pieces of Ruby together again.

Peanut got Ruby home within a couple of hours, then left her on her own as he went to run errands. His first stop was the bank to cash her check to replace the money Jarrod had stolen. Then he made a stop at the Piggly Wiggly for cans of soup and oyster crackers, and added a few other items with her in mind. All of the shoppers he ran into wanted to know about Ruby and sent their love.

When he stopped to get gas, he was once again fielding questions.

Arlene Purejoy came running out of the station carrying her can of soda and her purse. "Peanut! How's Ruby? Was she hurt very bad? Is there anything I can do?"

"She's hurt enough, but she'll heal up just fine. I'll tell her you asked, and if she needs anything, she can let you know."

"Well then," Arlene said. "I'd better be getting back to the mister. He's a bear right now because he's laid up, but then you already know that, don't you?" she said, and hustled away.

Peanut was waiting for his tank to fill when a car pulled up on the other side of the pumps and Niles Holland got out.

Niles Holland was the president of the Blessings Country Club and dressed accordingly by never being seen about town in anything less than a custom-tailored suit. Today, it was charcoal gray with a silver brocade vest. Peanut thought it made Niles look like a riverboat gambler, but he was too polite to say so.

"Morning, Peanut. A bit of a chill to the wind today, don't you think?" Niles said.

"Morning, Niles. It does seem a bit cool."

Niles waited until gas was flowing into his tank before he turned around to talk.

"I hear you brought Ruby Dye home last night."

"Nope. Wasn't me. That was Chief Pittman. I was just along for the ride."

Niles frowned. "Yes, well, mere details," he said. "I heard she was brutalized. Was she raped?"

Peanut was momentarily speechless by the callous manner in which the question was asked.

"No, as a matter of fact, she wasn't. But she did take a knife to her assailant and cut him up enough that if he was thinking about his dick, it would have been in fear she was going to cut that off too."

Nile's lips parted in shock, but Peanut was so angry he kept talking.

"He did manage to subdue her enough to get her in his car, but he was bleeding like a stuck pig when he stopped for fuel and she escaped on her own. He left the gas station in handcuffs, so I better not hear the word 'rape' come out of anyone else's mouth. Do you understand me?"

Niles nodded.

The pump went off at Peanut's car. He replaced the nozzle and drove off without looking back.

Still in a mood, he decided to stop at the florist and bring Ruby some flowers. When he walked in, Myra Franklin saw him and waved.

"Morning, Peanut! How can I help you?" she asked.

"I want a dozen red roses with all the trimmings, and in your prettiest vase. If you don't mind, I'll wait and take it with me."

"Sure thing," Myra said.

Waiting meant he was again fielding questions about Ruby. It had become obvious that, while everyone was so grateful she was alive and home, they wanted the grisly details. It pissed him off.

Just when he thought Myra was through trying to dig up gossip, she gave it one more try as she brought the arrangement to the counter for him to pay.

"How does this look, Peanut?"

He was struggling with his composure as he eyed it. It looked like roses in a lead crystal vase, but he supposed she wanted praise.

"It looks perfect, Myra. Ruby is going to love it." He handed her his credit card.

Myra scanned it in and then handed him the receipt to sign.

"About Ruby's face. Do you think she's going to need any plastic surgery? I mean…I heard it was really messed up."

Peanut signed his name and reached for the vase, then paused long enough to deliver a closing argument of true perfection.

"Well, Myra, that's probably the biggest bunch of bullshit I've heard about this incident yet. She has a black eye and a cut lip. Any kid playing baseball could get hurt worse than that. I hope you told whoever is spreading such outright gossip to shut the hell up. That's beyond rude. Don't you agree?"

Myra's mouth opened, but no sound came out.

"I'd better get home," Peanut added. "Can't have my girl alone for too long."

He saw the shock wave roll through Myra as his words sank in. He'd just called Ruby his girl. That should feed the gossip mill for a while. At least they'd be talking about something true for a change.

He set the vase of flowers against the console in the passenger seat, holding on to it with one hand while he drove with the other all the way home.

He hoped the flowers cheered Ruby up, because he had seen how shocked she'd been by how public her kidnapping had become. The yellow crime-scene tape, the investigators from the county sheriff's office coming to fingerprint and retrieve DNA samples, the public shame of being attacked by her ex-husband—as if she'd brought this horror upon herself and given Blessings a black mark as well. He hadn't expected that reaction, and he wanted her happy again.

Ruby's phone began ringing within minutes of Peanut's departure. LilyAnn Dalton was the first caller to welcome her home.

"Ruby, honey, I'm guessing you're not up to chit-chat, but I wanted you to know how much Mike and I love you. We prayed hard to get you home, and you are. Mike wanted me to tell you that when you feel up to it, there's a free massage waiting for you at the gym. Honey Andrews, the masseuse, said to tell you to just give her a call, and she'll schedule you right in."

"Thank you, LilyAnn, and tell Mike thank you too. I'll be looking forward to that when I feel a little better."

"Is there anything I can do? Can I bring food?"

"I'm good. Staying at Peanut's home until I feel a little stronger. As for food, I have a couple of stitches in my lip so I'm on liquids for a while."

"You're at Peanut's house?"

"Yes, I am."

"As in 'with him'?"

"As in."

LilyAnn giggled. "That's just about the best news I've heard in months. Is this under wraps or stuff to share?"

"My life is an open book," Ruby said.

"Call me if you need anything. Love you," LilyAnn said.

"Love you too," Ruby said, and disconnected.

Fifteen minutes later, the deluge of calls began.

If it hadn't been so painful, Ruby would have laughed. Every customer she had, every friend, every female member of her church inquired first about her health, and then wanted to know if it was true she was recuperating at Peanut Butterman's house.

After an hour of calls, she began letting them go to voicemail. She was tired, talked out, and thirsty so she went to the kitchen for a drink. And after applying some lip gloss to her lips a couple of times, the stitches weren't hurting like they had before. She had ice in a glass and a straw in her hand when Peanut came in the back door carrying a sack of groceries and a vase of flowers.

He paused just inside the door, smiling. "You have no idea how happy it makes me to walk into this house and see you here," he said.

"I am happy to be here too," Ruby said.

He set the groceries on the counter and then held up the roses. "Ruby-red roses for my Ruby."

"Oh, Peanut. They're beautiful, and you're spoiling me."

He set the vase on the counter, then leaned down until their foreheads were touching.

"Lady, you haven't seen anything yet. I'm saving my best moves for when you're well enough to handle them."

Ruby sighed. The fact that she was fantasizing about getting naked with him made her ache.

"You are a dangerous man. You make me feel. I haven't let myself go there in so long, and now you're all I think about. I hope all this is what you call courting, because by the time I am well, the formalities should already be out of the way."

Peanut's heart skipped, just knowing she wanted to make love to him as much as he wanted her. He cupped her face, looking past the bruising to the Ruby he knew and loved.

"I think that can be arranged," he said gently. "I wouldn't want to keep you waiting any longer than necessary, since that almost sounded like a woman in need."

Ruby wasn't wasting another moment of her life hiding anything, including how she felt about him. "I wasn't in need until you stirred everything up, including me."

He slid his hands around her neck, then pulled her close.

"We have time, baby. This will all happen when it's supposed to."

"I know."

He looked over her shoulder at the empty glass.

"What do you want to drink? I'll make it for you. Are you getting hungry, honey? You've only had the milk shake. I bought soups. Let me get them out of the sack, and you pick the one that looks good, okay?"

"I was going to have water."

"How about some sweet tea? I always have that made."

"Sounds wonderful," she said.

He poured some in her glass, then pointed to the kitchen table. "You sit, enjoy your drink. I'm going to put up the groceries."

After he set the soups out on display, she chose tomato because it would be easy to drink through a straw.

A short while later, they were having lunch in the kitchen. After all the meals they'd shared over the past year and a half, this almost felt normal.

"Thank you for taking care of me right now, Peanut. But after I get my house cleaned up, I'll go home."

He frowned. "I don't want to think of that."

"But it's what has to happen, and you know it," Ruby said. "I need us to be on equal ground when we do this. It is a frightening thing to feel helpless. I don't ever want to feel like I can't take care of myself. I want you to love me because I'm me, not because I need protection."

"I understand everything you said and why, but you need to know that, from a male point of view, taking care of the woman he loves is part of how a man shows that. So if I get all overprotective, just know it's because I love you, not because I think you're needy. Okay?"

She nodded.

"Okay then," he said. "I bought ice cream. Do you want another shake, or would you want to try to eat some? The cold might feel good on your mouth."

"Yes, I'd like to try eating it. Just a little dip, and if I can't make it happen, then you'll just have to eat it for me," she said.

He grinned. "Just like I finish your pie, and your cake, and the other half of your cookie? Yeah, I can do that."

One side of her mouth tilted upward in a slight grin.

"Gotta keep this fine, fit body in running condition," he added, and got another handful of chips from the bag to finish off his ham-and-cheese sandwich.

She laughed and then grabbed her mouth.

"Damn. I'm sorry. Lawyer face, lawyer face," he said, and patted her hand. "And speaking of lawyers, that reminds me… I have a pending court case in a few days, so I'm going in to the office after lunch to get the file and work on it here."

"I don't need you to—"

He held up a hand.

"But I need to, Ruby. I nearly lost you. I won't ever take that for granted again."

She lowered her head, humbled by someone so steadfast.

Peanut got up from the table and brought back one big bowl of chocolate ice cream and two spoons. "Saving dishes," he said, and handed her a spoon.

Her eyes twinkled. "You are such a man," she said.

"Thank you for noticing." Then he pointed at the bowl with his spoon. "Ladies first."

She took a little spoonful and eased it between her lips, savoring the sweet chocolate on her tongue.

"Ummmm," she said, and got another spoonful before Peanut dug into the ice cream and took his first bite.

After they finished, Peanut loaded the dishwasher and then grabbed the car keys. "I won't be long, sweetheart. Are you okay for a bit?"

"Yes. I'm going to lie down."

"Then rest well. I'll check in on you when I get back," he said, and kissed the palms of her hands.

She shuddered at the feel of his lips on her skin, then watched him drive away before she lay down to rest.

—~~—

Peanut drove straight to his office to find Betty Purejoy, his secretary, out to a late lunch. She'd left a note on the door that she'd be back at two p.m., so he unlocked the door and went inside.

His desk was neat—which meant Betty had been in—so he booted up his computer, sent the files he'd been working on to his laptop, and then signed off. He was getting ready to leave when the office phone rang. He debated about letting it go to voicemail, but then his conscience wouldn't let him.

"Butterman Law Office. This is Peanut."

"Mr. Butterman, this is Doctor Bennett at NextStep Memory Care in Savannah. I understand Elmer Mathis is your client."

"Yes, sir, he is," Peanut said.

"I am sorry to tell you Mr. Mathis passed away this morning, and part of his instructions were to contact you first and that you would know why."

"How old was he?" Peanut asked.

"He was eighty-seven years old and had just cele-brated his four-year anniversary with us when he passed. I also understand you are to notify his heirs."

Peanut sighed. This was not going to be a pleasant event. "Yes, sir. You do have the information on where to send his body, do you not?"

"We do. He didn't want a funeral, and we've already notified the funeral home in Savannah. They'll be picking up the body shortly. They'll notify his heir when the body will be transported to Blessings to be interred."

"Tell them Melissa Dean is the person to call," Peanut added.

"Yes, we know Melissa well and have her information. She's been a faithful friend to Elmer."

"She's a good woman. She was his housekeeper for ten years before he was sent to your facility," Peanut said.

"She didn't miss a week coming to see him. Drove all the way to Savannah on her day off. Once a month, she cut his toenails and fingernails and had lunch with him. Even after he didn't know who she was, she still came."

"Does she know he passed?" Peanut asked.

"Oh, she was with him. She'd asked Hospice to notify her. Said she didn't want him dying alone."

"Okay," Peanut said. "Then I'll notify her later about the reading of the will."

"Thank you, Mr. Butterman. You have my sympathies."

Peanut heard the disconnect and then hung up. He sat a moment, thinking about a woman who'd given so many years of her time and life to an old man alone. The fact that she'd cared enough to be with him in his last hours moved Peanut. And in the same breath, it made him think of Ruby. Good. Faithful. Loving. She and Melissa Dean were women cut from the same cloth.

And then he heard the door to his office opening and his secretary calling out, "Mr. Butterman? Are you here?"

"In here, Betty."

"What's going on?" she said.

"Will you please pull the file we have on Elmer Mathis? He passed away this morning."

"Oh, bless his heart. He's been lost a long time. Thank God he's not suffering that anymore."

"Agreed," Peanut said.

Betty went to the file cabinets, pulled Elmer's file, and handed it over.

"You're sure there's nothing you need me to do?"

"Do I have free time for a reading of the will?"

Betty scanned his schedule. "Um…this Friday and next Monday are both open."

"Then schedule Friday at ten a.m. for the Mathis estate. I'm calling the heirs this afternoon. Today is Monday. That gives them plenty of time to make travel arrangements. Unless they've moved, they all live in-state."

"Yes, sir," Betty said, and entered the date in his schedule. "Got it," she said.

"Thanks, just keep regular hours here, and notify me if there's any kind of an emergency."

Betty nodded. "Yes, sir, I will. How's Ruby? Is there anything I could do to help?"

"She'll heal. I imagine it will take longer to get over the actual act of being abducted than the physical injuries she suffered."

"God bless her. You tell her she's become my new heroine. I am in awe of how she survived and escaped that."

Peanut smiled. "I sure will, and while I'm thinking about it, I suppose you should know that we are officially a couple."

Betty's eyes widened, and then she clapped her hands and laughed. "I knew it! I knew it! I told my husband a month ago that you were attracted to Ruby Dye, and he didn't believe it."

Peanut shrugged. "I'm gone on her. What can I say?"

"Well, congratulations, boss. You have good taste."

"Thanks. I think so," Peanut said. "So, I'm headed home. Thanks for holding down the fort here."

"No problem," Betty said. "My best to Ruby."

Peanut nodded as he left with his laptop and the Mathis file and headed home, but he couldn't get the reading of Elmer Mathis's will out of his mind. He had a feeling this was going to be a messy one.

—◆◆◆—

Loretta Baird was at her favorite spa getting a pedicure. She'd already had a massage and a manicure and was checking her email when her phone signaled a call. She started to let it go to voicemail and then changed her mind.

"Hello."

"May I speak to Loretta Baird, please? My name's Butterman. I'm the lawyer for Elmer Mathis."

Loretta frowned. "I'm Loretta Baird."

"Ms. Baird, I'm sorry to inform you that your uncle, Elmer Mathis, passed away this morning at his care center in Savannah."

"Oh really? That's too bad," Loretta said.

Peanut's eyebrows rose. Suddenly Elmer's final wishes were beginning to make sense.

"Yes, ma'am," Peanut said. "The reading of the will takes place in my office at ten a.m. this coming Friday in Blessings, Georgia. If you are unable to attend, a letter informing you of the will's contents will be mailed to you. Are you still at the same address in Atlanta?"

Loretta's heart skipped a beat.

"Yes, but I'll be there. Uh...can you tell me what he was worth?"

Peanut frowned. "No, ma'am, I cannot."

"Oh well, no matter. I'll see you Friday," she said, and he heard her squeal "Score! Yay me!" before the call disconnected.

Peanut sighed. Nothing like loving family.

He made similar calls informing her sisters—Betsy Lowe, who also lived in Atlanta, and then Wilma Smith, who lived in Savannah.

By the time he'd made the last call, he was thoroughly disgusted. None of them had expressed sympathy or regret, but all three had asked what Elmer was worth.

There was only one more woman to notify regarding the reading of the will—Melissa Dean. He entered her phone number, listened to the rings, and was preparing himself to leave a voicemail when she answered.

"Hello, this is Melissa," she said.

"Good afternoon, Melissa. This is Peanut Butterman."

"Hello, Mr. Butterman."

He heard both surprise and question in her voice and set out to clarify the call. "First, my condolences on Mr. Mathis's passing. I know you were his caregiver."

Melissa's quick breath and then shaky voice told him everything.

"Yes, I was, and thank you. Even though he hadn't known me for almost a year now, I will miss him."

"I'm calling to inform you that you are named in his will. The reading will be this coming Friday. Ten o'clock in my office."

"Well, my goodness," she said, and then started to cry. "I'm sorry. This just makes it all so final."

"Yes, ma'am. So, see you then?"

"Yes, of course, and thank you for the call."

"You're welcome, Melissa."

Now that all of the heirs had been notified, Peanut got up to check on Ruby. She'd been asleep when he came home, and another peek into her bedroom showed she was still sleeping, so he went back to his office, booted up his laptop, and got back to work.

Chapter 5

AFTER A MEETING WITH HIS COURT-APPOINTED LAWYER, Jarrod Dye saw that his situation was right where he'd guessed it would be. Pleading out was his only option for possible leniency, and he blamed Ruby for all of this. If she hadn't cut him up and made him lose control, none of this would have happened. Because of her, he'd be an old man before he got out—if he survived prison. The longer he thought about it, the angrier he became, so when his lawyer, Allen Young, was getting ready to leave, Jarrod casually asked if Allen would call his brother to let him know where Jarrod was.

Young thought nothing of the request and agreed.

Jarrod wrote down his brother Gary's name and number, then made a couple of notes.

> *Tell him what's happening and where I'll likely be for the rest of my life. And tell him Ruby is just fine.*

The lawyer slipped the phone number into his briefcase, gathered up the rest of his notes, and left the interrogation room while his client was being taken back to his cell.

Jarrod had one last chance to make Ruby sorry for what she'd done, but it wouldn't happen if the lawyer didn't call Jarrod's brother. And even if Young did call

Gary, his brother had to read past the obvious to what Jarrod was asking him to do. Right now, it was all maybes and what-ifs, but Jarrod needed something to pin his future on, and revenge was as good as it would get.

Allen Young, Esquire, considered his latest court-appointed client a done deal. The perp wanted to plead out, which meant no trial, which meant Allen wouldn't have to deal with him long.

He thought about Dye's request to call his brother and decided to get that out of the way before he forgot, so he took the note out of his briefcase and made the call.

—⁓—

Gary Dye was two years older than Jarrod, but they looked so much alike that from time to time people thought they were twins. Both were barely five-ten, with sparse brown hair, and thin to the point of skinny. Gary was in his metal shop finishing a welding job when he felt his cell phone vibrating in his pocket. He turned off the torch, flipped his helmet up, and put his phone on speaker as he answered.

"Dye's Welding," he said.

"May I speak to Gary Dye?"

"I'm Gary. Who are you?" Gary asked.

"This is Allen Young. I'm your brother's lawyer."

Gary frowned. "Why does Jarrod need a lawyer?"

Young proceeded to explain the charges and Jarrod's decision to admit his guilt and plead out.

Gary was stunned. "You're shittin' me," he muttered.

"No, sir. I'm sorry to say it's all true. Jarrod asked me to notify you that he'll likely be spending the rest of his life in prison, and to tell you that Ruby is just fine."

Gary inhaled sharply, then quickly recovered. "I'm real sorry Jarrod did this, and glad to hear she's fine. I appreciate the call."

"No problem," Young said, and disconnected.

Gary set the phone aside, then took off his welding helmet, then went to get a cold drink, but his thoughts were churning.

The lawyer said Jarrod had abducted his ex-wife from a little town called Blessings, Georgia, and while Jarrod could likely die in prison, Ruby was just fine.

But not for damned long. Not if Gary had anything to do about it. He needed to make a little trip to this Blessings, Georgia, and rearrange Ruby's future too. It wasn't going to bother him. He had never liked her anyway.

─∿∿∿─

Peanut was nearly through with the opening statement for next week's trial. Even though a good portion of his business was done out of court as a mediator, he was ready to defend his client, May Temple, who worked at the Blue Ivy Bar at the edge of town.

The charges didn't amount to much. May was being sued by her landlord, Niles Holland, for failure to pay her rent. But the kicker was that May was countersuing, claiming the property was unlivable because the landlord continually refused to fix what was broken. And she'd given Holland fair warning with a certified letter stating she wasn't paying rent until he fixed everything.

As far as Peanut was concerned, it was an open-and-shut case. May had receipts for every month's rent up until three months ago. He had a copy of the letter May had sent Niles, the certified receipt of delivery, and

pictures of the flooded bathroom. Also pictures of a hole
in her ceiling from a leak in the apartment above hers,
and a front door that would no longer lock, which had
resulted in May being robbed while she was at work.

Peanut hadn't been bothered about going up against
Niles until Niles had made the insulting comment about
Ruby. Now Peanut was more than ready to make Niles
own up and do the right thing. He was logging off the
computer when Ruby walked into his office.

"There's my Unsinkable Molly Brown," Peanut said
as he swung around in his chair and patted his leg.

Ruby gave him a little sideways smile as she slid into
his lap, then surprised him with a kiss on the cheek.

"Thank you, love," he said, and returned the favor. "I
take it you had a good rest."

"I did," she said, and slid her arm around his neck,
then laid her head on his shoulder.

Peanut held her close as he rested his chin on the top
of her head. "I got a phone call while I was at the office.
Elmer Mathis passed away this morning."

Ruby sat up, her expression already mirroring her sadness. "Oh, bless his heart. He had a terrible battle with
Alzheimer's. At least he's no longer trapped in that body."

"Yes, this would be one of those times when the
news was a blessing, instead of shock and sadness,"
Peanut said.

"He doesn't have any family anymore, does he?"
Ruby asked.

Peanut hesitated. He couldn't reveal specifics
because of lawyer-client confidentiality, but relatives'
names wouldn't fall under that rule unless the client had
specifically asked for their names not to be mentioned.

THE COLOR OF LOVE

"He has three nieces. I notified them earlier."

"Oh…that's good, then," Ruby said.

Peanut changed the subject. "I have a suggestion. It's about your house."

"What is it?" Ruby asked.

"Laurel Lorde cleans my house. I want to ask her to schedule yours as well. The longer that mess sits, the harder it will be to clean, and you can't get anything in the open wounds on your hands."

Ruby frowned. "I don't want her to see it like that."

"Honey, that's just a little blood and fingerprint powder. I don't think it will faze her."

"What if it reminds her of her first husband's suicide?" Ruby asked.

"She has a small child. She's bound to be mopping up bloody scrapes and nose bleeds now and then."

Ruby was silent for a few moments, considering it. "If she's willing, I would like to know everything is back in place. Except my bedspread, of course. I have an old one I can use until I get a chance to buy another."

"Great. I'll call her later, and I will feel her out first. If I think I hear reluctance, I'll nix it right then, okay?"

"Yes, okay," Ruby said. "And thank you for thinking of me."

"You're always at the top of my list," Peanut said.

Ruby hesitated. "As many years as we've known each other, I don't know a lot about your family."

"And I know nothing about yours," Peanut said. "So I'll go first. As you know by my name, my parents had a weird sense of humor. They thought it was hysterical to name me P. Nutt Butterman."

"What does the *P* stand for?" Ruby asked.

Peanut rolled his eyes. "Not a damn thing. They thought that was funny too. I used to accuse them of smoking pot when they named me. Mom never denied it, but she would always get this indignant look on her face. God, I miss them."

Ruby slipped her hand in his. "Do you have other family?" she asked.

"Not that I know of. What about you? What was your maiden name?" Peanut asked.

"I was Ruby Jo Morris. My parents disowned me when I got pregnant. Mom died from breast cancer the first year I was married, and Dad remarried within a year and moved away. As far as I'm concerned, he's dead too. I know I want nothing to do with him."

"I'm sorry, honey," Peanut said.

Ruby shrugged. "Don't be. I have lots of family. Good family. The people in Blessings are my family."

"If the whole town is invited, we're going to have one really big wedding," he said.

Ruby sighed. "I still can't believe this is real."

Peanut cupped her cheek. "If you'd loved me as long as I've loved you, you'd have no problem believing," he said.

Her eyes narrowed, refusing to let that slide. "Well, if you hadn't kept it to yourself for so long, I wouldn't be behind your timeline."

He threw his head back and laughed.

"Damn...you nailed me with that one, and I didn't see it coming. Remind me never to go up against you in court."

"No problem," she said, and made him laugh again.

"What's your favorite food?" Ruby asked.

"A big rib-eye steak with a baked potato and any kind of salad. What about you?" he asked.

"Chicken and dressing," Ruby said. "What's your favorite kind of movie to watch?"

"Oh, definitely war movies…I'm a bit of a history buff," he said.

"My forever favorite is *Avatar*, and I don't even know what genre that falls into," Ruby said. "All I know is that the first three times I saw it, I wished I was nine feet tall and blue and lived on Pandora."

"Well, I'm really glad you live in Blessings, because I can't imagine this town without you," he said.

"Oh, Peanut…I want to make love to you. This won't feel real until we do."

His heart skipped. He wanted nothing more.

"You have no idea how much I want that, too, but right now you are still hurt enough that I'm almost afraid to touch you."

She sighed. "I know, but I wanted you to know how I feel."

He wrapped his arms around her, then laid her hand over his heart.

"And this is how I feel," he said.

The hard thud of his heartbeat against her palm was heady. Knowing she affected him like this made her ache for more.

When she suddenly shivered, Peanut kissed her.

Ruby leaned into the kiss, ignoring the pull on the stitches in her lips.

When his phone rang, she moaned softly.

"Dang it," she said, then got up and moved away so he could answer it.

It was immediately obvious to her that it was business when he began to talk, and she left the office so he'd have privacy.

━━⁓━━

Vesta and Vera were working until dark every evening to make sure Ruby's clients weren't put at a disadvantage by her absence. Mabel Jean had stepped up to shampoo clients when she wasn't busy with someone's nails.

The Curl Up and Dye was still the place to go in Blessings for the latest news, and the most popular subject was still Ruby Dye.

Rachel Goodhope, who ran the bed-and-breakfast, came in for her appointment carrying a plate of lemon bars.

"I know you girls are having to work overtime to pick up Ruby's clients, and guessed you were going to be really hungry before you could close up and go home. I wanted to bring you a little something, so enjoy!" she said.

"Oh golly, lemon bars," Mabel Jean said. "I love anything lemon. Can I get you some coffee, Rachel?"

"No, thank you," Rachel said, as she set the plate beside the coffee station, then turned around. "So, who's doing me?" she asked.

"I am," Vesta said. "Vera has an appointment due any minute."

"I sure appreciate you guys working me in," Rachel said, and sat down in Vesta's chair long enough for Vesta to put a cape around her shoulders before she moved Rachel to the shampoo station. "How's Ruby?" she asked.

"Healing. Glad to be home."

"I can only imagine," Rachel said. "Is there anything she needs? Anything I can do?"

Vesta kept working as she talked. "I think Peanut has that covered."

"Peanut? How did he get involved?" Rachel asked.

"Oh, haven't you heard?" Vesta asked. "They're a couple."

Rachel's eyes widened. "Seriously? That is so awesome," she said.

Before the conversation could go further, the bell over the door signaled the arrival of Vera's next appointment.

By night, nearly everyone in Blessings knew about Ruby and Peanut, and as Peanut had hoped, news about Ruby's current condition became way less important than finding out she and Peanut were a couple.

Right after dinner, Ruby went to take a shower. She was tired and thinking about going to bed early.

Peanut used the time to call Laurel. Just when he thought it would go to voicemail, the call was answered.

"Hello. This is Jake."

"Jake, this is Peanut Butterman. Is Laurel available?"

"She's putting Bonnie to bed. I'll have her call you back in a few."

"Maybe I should ask your opinion before I talk to her."

"About what?" Jake asked.

"I wanted to see if she would be willing to clean up Ruby Dye's house. The kitchen, hall, and bathroom are somewhat bloody, and there is fingerprint powder all over the place. Ruby thought cleaning it might remind Laurel of her first husband's suicide. Do you think I should let it go?"

Jake hesitated a moment. "You know…that's not something I feel I should answer. This will totally be Laurel's call. Oh…wait. Here she comes now."

Peanut heard Laurel's footsteps and then her say, "Who is it?" and heard Jake say, "It's Peanut."

"Hello, Peanut!"

"Hi, Laurel. Thanks for the extra work you put in here."

"Oh, you're very welcome. How's Ruby?"

"She's doing great. Still banged up but in pretty good spirits, considering."

"That's wonderful. Is there anything I can do to help?"

"That's mostly why I called," Peanut said. "I wanted to see how you would feel about cleaning up Ruby's house. You need to know that besides the fingerprint powder all over the place, there's blood in the kitchen, the hall, and her bedroom. I want you to be honest with me. If doing that cleaning would upset you, all you have to—"

"I'd be happy to do that," Laurel said. "Why would you think I wouldn't?"

Peanut cleared his throat. "Well, Ruby was afraid it might remind you too much of—"

"Oh, you're talking about Adam's suicide? I cleaned up stuff from that incident that a wife should never have seen of her husband. Blood in Ruby's house won't faze me. When do you want it done?"

"As soon as you can work it into your schedule. It's

a big job, and whatever you need to charge is fine. Just send me the bill."

"It will be my welcome home gift to Ruby, and I'm happy to do it."

"You're the best," Peanut said. "The key to her front door is under the mat. Just put it back there after you're done, and thank you a thousand times. Oh…there's an old bedspread somewhere in the house that you can put on her bed. The kidnapper rolled her up in the one that was there to carry her out, so it's long gone."

Laurel shuddered. "Oh my God. I still can't believe she endured all that. I'll get to it next."

"Thank you, Laurel."

"You're welcome. Have a good evening."

Peanut hung up, satisfied that another piece of Ruby's world would be put back in place.

―――∿∿―――

Wilma was on a conference call with her sisters, Betsy and Loretta, trying to coordinate travel plans to Blessings.

"Loretta, you and Betsy could drive to Savannah Wednesday and stay with me, and we could all go down to Blessings on Thursday. There's a quaint little bed-and-breakfast we could stay in and then not have to rush around Friday morning getting to the lawyer's office," Wilma said.

"Oh crap. That's going to take up three, maybe four days," Loretta said.

"Stop whining, Loretta," Betsy said. "I'm the oldest, and I remember Uncle Elmer's house. It was really pretty in its day. Even if it needs some cleaning and painting, it should be worth a lot of money. It sits on several lots, so the grounds around it were big too. Land is always worth money, and we're going to rake in the dough."

"Do you remember Uncle Elmer?" Wilma asked.

"Sort of, but he doesn't matter," Betsy said.

"I remember Mama telling us to take care of him when she was dying," Wilma added.

Loretta snorted. "Well, I never went to see him," she said.

"Neither did I," Betsy said.

They both heard Wilma sigh. "We didn't honor Mama's last wishes. It makes me feel bad to think we let her twin brother die alone," Wilma said.

"Oh, shut up, Wilma. You're always a bleeding heart. Anyway…make reservations at the bed-and-breakfast, and we'll be at your house Wednesday evening. We can all go out to dinner and make this a fun sister trip," Loretta said.

"Okay. See you Wednesday," Betsy said.

"See you," Loretta echoed.

"Take care," Wilma added, and then ended the conference call.

Back in Atlanta, Loretta got up from the sofa and gave her living room a close look. She liked her condo. It was in the right neighborhood and it was paid for, but it was due some updates. This windfall was going to come in handy.

What Wilma had said about them not honoring their mama's dying words niggled at Loretta's conscience, but she had been ignoring it for years, and this was not the time to start paying attention.

<center>~~~</center>

Rachel Goodhope was getting some bread dough ready to rise overnight. She had guests in two rooms, and by doing this, she'd have a jump start on making breakfast for them in the morning. She covered the yeast dough with plastic wrap and then set the big crockery bowl in the refrigerator and turned to face the mess she still had to clean up.

A few minutes later, she was elbow deep in hot water and soapy suds when her phone rang. She wiped her hands as she went to answer.

"Blessings Bed and Breakfast. Rachel speaking."

"Rachel, my name is Wilma Smith. I would like to book three rooms for Thursday night."

"Certainly," Rachel said. "Please hold a moment so I can get to the office. I'm in another part of the inn right now."

"Of course," Wilma said. "I'm sorry to be calling so late, but this just came up."

"No problem. Just a few seconds, and I'll be back on the line," Rachel said. She put the call on hold and ran down the hall to the office. "This is Rachel. Are you still there?" she asked.

"Yes, ma'am," Wilma said.

"All right then. You said three rooms?"

"Yes, please."

"May I please have the names for reservation purposes?"

"Wilma Smith, Loretta Baird, and Betsy Lowe. We're sisters," Wilma added, then rolled her eyes, wondering why she always felt the need to explain herself.

"That's wonderful! A little sisters' get-together then," Rachel said. "I'll need a credit card to hold the overnight reservations."

Wilma gave her the number, then while she was waiting for Rachel to speak, she felt the need to keep talking.

"We're actually coming into Blessings to attend the reading of our uncle Elmer Mathis's will. We'll be checking out Friday morning and returning to our respective homes afterward."

Rachel frowned to herself. "Oh…I hadn't heard that he'd passed. My sympathies on your loss. We all thought the world of Elmer."

"Yes, well, that's wonderful," Wilma said. "So we'll be seeing you early Thursday afternoon."

"Fantastic," Rachel said. "I serve breakfast from six a.m. to eleven a.m. The kitchen is closed after that, but there's a wonderful restaurant here in Blessings called Granny's Country Kitchen. It's the perfect place for a meal."

"Thank you. I'm sure we'll manage," Wilma said. "See you then."

"Yes, ma'am. We'll be looking forward to your arrival," Rachel said.

After she disconnected, she posted the rooms into her online register, then returned to the kitchen to finish cleaning. To her delight, her husband, Bud, was almost through.

"Who was on the phone so late?" he asked.

"A late reservation for three rooms with a Thursday arrival, and thank you for cleaning up my mess," Rachel said.

"Your mess is my mess," he said.

Rachel hugged him. "You are a jewel, and I love you."

Bud grinned. "Well, thank you, honey! I should do dishes more often, I think. You go on up. Take yourself a good, long soaking bath. You've earned it."

Rachel sighed. It had been a long day. "Thank you, darling. Don't forget to lock up."

Chapter 6

MELISSA DEAN WAS GETTING READY TO CLOCK OUT AT Bloomer's Hardware when her boss, Fred Bloomer, called her into his office.

"I'll be right there," she said.

She hung up her canvas work apron and headed for the office.

"What's up?" she asked, smiling at him as she walked in.

"Shut the door, please," Fred said.

The hair stood up on the back of Melissa's arms as she watched him taking an envelope from a desk drawer.

Fred barely looked at her as he dropped the envelope into her hand.

"I'm sorry, Melissa. I didn't want this to happen, but times are hard and business has been falling off. I'm going to have to let you go. I've given you an extra month's salary to tide you over until you find another job."

Melissa stared at the envelope he'd dropped into her hand and then looked up.

"Since I count out the drawer and make the deposit every night, I happen to know you just lied to me," she said, trying desperately not to cry. "I should have known when your nephew showed up last month that I was going to be fired."

"Now, I didn't fire you, I—"

Melissa raised her hand.

"Don't lie on top of it. I've worked here nineteen years. One more year, and I would have qualified for retirement. How fortunate for you that good old Tommy showed up in time. I thought better of you, Fred, and will not be using you for a reference, and I will tell people in town why I was let go."

"Now see here... You can't—"

"Yes, I can and will. It's to protect my reputation, you know. I can't have people thinking I did something awful to get fired after all these years. Oh...and just so you know...Tommy slips twenties out of the till. You'd better start paying attention to sales receipts and counting out your own money. I've been making him put it back, but now you're on your own."

Fred paled. "Why didn't you tell—"

"*Because* he's your nephew," Melissa said, then turned around and walked out.

She made it all the way to her car before she burst into tears, then took off out of town, driving aimlessly as she gathered her thoughts. It was after eight p.m. before she got home, but she'd come to terms with this day.

She was at a crossroads.

It wasn't the first time she'd had that experience. The day her husband, Andy, died had been the worst day of her life, so putting things into perspective, this was just another crossroads, not the end of the world.

Right now, the truth was that she was sad about losing Elmer Mathis and worried about her financial situation. The Mathis estate had always paid her for keeping Elmer's house clean. Now she was about to lose that monthly deposit into her checking account that helped pay her rent. She didn't want to become homeless as well as out of work.

There weren't a lot of jobs in Blessings for women her age. Forty-seven wasn't old, but after Andy's death, Melissa had let the gray in her hair take over, and she couldn't remember the last time she'd bought a tube of lipstick.

Back in her house, she dropped her purse and car keys on the hall table and went to her room to change out of her work clothes, then went back to the kitchen in a bathrobe to fix some supper.

The events of the day had taken away her appetite, but she needed to stay busy, and making herself an omelet was the only thing she had the energy left to do.

She began breaking eggs in a bowl, then turned on the burner to heat up a pan. As she prepared the food, she thought again of Peanut Butterman's phone call requesting her presence at the reading of Elmer's will. She'd watched Elmer take his last breath before daylight this morning and had cried all the way home from Savannah, then changed into her work clothes and clocked in on time at the store. She hadn't talked about it, and now she was glad she hadn't. The last thing she wanted was having someone feel sorry for her.

She tilted the omelet out onto a plate, peppered it, and ate it standing up at the sink, then chased it with a longneck bottle of beer that she kept for the nights when missing Andy was too painful to ignore.

After cleaning up the kitchen, she went back to her bedroom and ran herself a bubble bath. She clipped her ponytail on top of her head, then stepped into the bubbles and sank into the old claw-foot tub until they were at her chin, and closed her eyes.

Almost instantly, Andy's face appeared.

"Yes, my feelings are hurt, but I'm okay. Because I had you, I will always be okay."

And then she cried until the water cooled and her fingertips were wrinkled.

Ruby was asleep, but her legs were jerking and her feet were kicking. She was once again locked in a nightmare that wouldn't go away.

Jarrod hadn't come home from work, and it was just after midnight. Ruby was sitting in the living room in the dark, afraid to go to bed, when she heard a car in the driveway. She leaped up and peered through a curtain. She could see from the porch light that it was Jarrod. When she saw him stagger as he got out of his truck, she knew he was drunk. Then she saw the pistol in his hand.

"Oh my God, oh my God," Ruby moaned.

She unlocked the door to keep him from kicking it in and then ran. She had to hide until he passed out or she would die, but where? There was nowhere to hide in this house without him finding her. Her only chance was to get out of the house, so she headed for the back door in the kitchen, praying she could get out before he came in.

But she wasn't fast enough. Jarrod bolted into the house, slamming the door behind him. Despite the lack of lights, he caught a glimpse of her running toward the kitchen.

"Come back here, you bitch!" Jarrod roared as he staggered after her, waving the .22 pistol in his hand.

Ruby's heart was hammering so hard she could barely breathe, but she didn't dare stop. Even when his footsteps followed her exit, she kept running.

Her hand was on the doorknob when he caught her, grabbing her by her hair.

"Where do you think you're going?" he shouted, and threw her to the floor.

Ruby rolled onto her back and started begging.

"No, Jarrod, no. Don't hurt me. Please, don't hurt me."

He waved the pistol in her face, and then to prove it was loaded, fired into the floor near her head.

Ruby screamed aloud in her sleep, just as she had that night, and then kept on screaming.

Peanut heard Ruby scream and was out of bed within seconds and running. She was still screaming and begging in a voice he didn't recognize when he turned on the lights and called out her name.

"Ruby!"

She sat up with a gasp, saw Peanut coming toward her, and flew out of bed and into his arms.

"I've got you. I've got you," he said.

Ruby's arms went around his neck, her feet dangling off the floor.

"You're safe, baby, you're safe," Peanut said. He backed them up and sat in the easy chair beside the window.

Ruby curled up in his arms, shaking.

"Talk to me," Peanut said. "Don't keep it inside. Let it go."

"Ugly, so ugly," Ruby said.

Peanut pushed her back enough that she could see his face.

"Look at me! Do you see disgust? Do you see judgment? You matter to me. I love you. I am so angry right now at whoever caused this dream that I would be hard-pressed not to take a whip to him, so let me guess. Jarrod Dye?"

She nodded.

Peanut pulled her close again. "Now talk to me, and remember I am your safe place to fall."

Ruby took a deep breath and then shuddered. "Oh my God, Peanut."

He kissed the top of her head, then looked down at his long, bare legs and realized that all he had on were gym shorts. But since it didn't seem to bother Ruby, he wasn't going to let it bother him.

Ruby reached for his arm, needing to hold onto him, as if saying it aloud gave power to the horror.

Peanut heard her take a deep breath, and then the words came tumbling out.

"Jarrod didn't come home after work, which scared me. I knew he would come home drunk, so I was afraid to sleep. I sat up in the dark waiting, and when I heard him drive up, I looked out. I saw him stagger, then I saw the gun in his hand and I ran."

Peanut was reeling. He would never have imagined she'd endured such a life.

"He caught me before I could get out the back door. He shot the gun into the floor beside my head to prove he was in charge and then started shouting. A neighbor heard the gunshot, me screaming, and then Jarrod shouting that he was going to kill me. If the neighbor hadn't called the police, I probably wouldn't be here. I filed for divorce while Jarrod was in jail on assault charges, and I hid. He didn't know where I was, but I showed up in court to testify against him. He went to prison.

"The divorce was granted, and I left Nashville in the dark of night. It was an accident that I wound up in Georgia, but I say to myself every day that it was God Who led me to Blessings. I never saw Jarrod again until the other day, and I've never told this to anyone… until you."

Peanut was so enraged for her that it was all he could do to talk in a calm, rational voice. But he did, because she needed calm and rational.

He tilted her face to meet a very brief and gentle kiss. He needed that more than she probably did.

"First, know that everything between us stays between us. Second, remember that he'll likely be in prison for most, if not all, of the rest of his life for the charges on this stunt, okay?"

Despite his calm voice, Ruby's gaze was locked on the fury in his eyes, and she felt a sense of satisfaction that the man who loved her was this enraged on her behalf.

"Yes, okay," she said.

Peanut glanced at the clock. It was after two a.m. "Do you think you can go back to sleep?"

She shrugged. "I don't know. I had nightmares last night too. I think it's going to take time to get past this."

"Well, hell, Ruby. That is not okay with me."

He stood up as if she weighed nothing in his arms and laid her back down in bed, then went to turn out the light.

Ruby had a glimpse of his long, bare body and the tight buns beneath the gym shorts before the lights went out. When he crawled into bed behind her, she shivered.

"It's just me, and I'm not going to make a move beyond holding you in my arms. You have demons, Ruby. Sometimes my job requires me to slay demons for people, even the ones disguised in human form. I am good at my job." He pulled the covers up over the both of them and spooned himself against her backside. "I'm here. I'll know if you start dreaming again, and I'll whisper the magic words in your ear that will drive those demons away."

"What are the magic words?" Ruby whispered.

"I love you."

"Oh, Peanut, I love you too. So much."

"Good for me to know," he said, and kissed the side of her neck. "Now we sleep."

She closed her eyes, but the tears still found their way out. The last thing she remembered was the steady rise and fall of Peanut's chest against her back and the warmth of his body.

When she woke, it was morning and she was alone. She threw back the covers and, as she was heading into the bathroom, smelled coffee brewing in the kitchen.

She dressed quickly, then paused in front of the mirror. The swelling in her lips was almost gone, but the stitches were still evident. The swelling was down in her eye, while the bruises on her face were turning brilliant shades of green and purple. She ran a brush through her hair and then looked down at her hands. A couple more days, and she'd be healed enough to get back to work. But was she willing to let the world see her like this?

Shrugging it off, she followed her nose to the kitchen and found Peanut frying bacon, barefoot, in a pair of jeans and a long-sleeved T-shirt. Her heart did a little flip. How could she not have noticed what a hunk he was all these years? But then she realized she hadn't been ready to look.

"Good morning, Peanut," she said.

He turned toward her with a smile.

"Good morning, sweetheart. Hey! The swelling is really going down in your face, especially your lips. Want to try a bite of solid food and see how that works?"

"Yes, if it's bacon," she said.

He leaned over and kissed her square on the mouth, but so gently that if she hadn't gotten an up-close sniff of some wonderful aftershave cologne, she might not have known that he'd done it.

"Bacon is the boss, right? I knew you were the woman for me. Help yourself to bacon and coffee. As soon as I get these last pieces out of the pan, I'll scramble some eggs."

"Yum," Ruby said, and rolled her eyes at the deliciousness of that first bite of bacon.

"Okay?" he asked. "Doesn't hurt your mouth?"

"Not enough to make me stop eating," she said, and poured herself a cup of coffee.

"The paper is on the table. Sit and relax while I finish up here."

Ruby slid into a seat at the table, opened up the paper with one hand while she finished off the bacon with the other. She glanced through the pages without reading, saving all of that for later, and was about to set the paper aside when she noticed a story on the inside back page.

She read it all the way through, frowning, then folded the paper back up and pushed it aside as Peanut carried their plates to the table.

"Looks so good. I can't thank you enough for all of this," Ruby said.

"I wouldn't have had it any other way," Peanut said. "Do you want to try any toast?"

"Not today," she said. "I'll see how this goes first."

He began buttering a piece of toast for himself. "See anything interesting in the paper?" he asked.

She frowned. "I saw a story about child abuse buried on the inside of the last page. Why wasn't that the lead headline? Physical and sexual abuse is an epidemic in this country."

Peanut watched her take a bite of her eggs before he spoke.

"Maybe for the same reason you don't want people to see you like this," he said.

Ruby blinked, then swallowed her bite of eggs. She sat there for so long Peanut was afraid that he'd hurt her feelings, and just when he was about to apologize, she started talking.

"You're right! You're absolutely right! It's shame. That's why! Victims shame themselves subconsciously, while others shame them outright."

She poked another bite of eggs in her mouth, but she was still frowning.

Peanut didn't know for sure what to say, but something told him that what he'd said had just lit another fire under Ruby Dye.

"What are you going to do today?" Ruby asked.

"Oh, just stick around here with you."

"Well, I think I'll go shopping, and I don't want you along for moral support."

His mouth dropped. "But are you—"

She pointed her fork at him. "Yes."

He grinned. "I am so going to love spending the rest of my life with you."

"I would hope so," she said, and then forked up another bite of eggs. "These are good, by the way. I'm a good cook too."

"Ruby, I already know that. I've been eating at your house off and on for the last six months, remember?"

She grinned. "Poor Peanut. All those committee meetings," she said, laughed, and then winced. "Ouch. Eating is good. Laughing still hurts."

"Where are you going?" Peanut asked.

"I'm starting off at the shop. They always need supplies. I can run errands. And then I would love to meet you for lunch at Granny's. That should take care of my first public outing, and I'm not going to shy away from the stares *or* the likely rude questions, but I will make people ashamed they asked if their questions are ugly."

Peanut was watching the way her eyes flashed and her jaw set when she got angry. He couldn't wait to see the expression on her face when they finally made love.

"Just let me know when it's time to arrive at Granny's, and I'll be there."

"Thank you for understanding," she said.

"I will always 'get you' Ruby. You are my heart," he said, and laid a hand over hers.

Ruby got up, slid into his lap long enough to hug him. "I love you. I've never said that to a man before."

Peanut's heart swelled. "Then thank you for trusting me enough to take a chance."

"Easy peasy," she said, and grinned. "Now finish your breakfast before it gets cold," she ordered, and slid back into her chair.

"Yes, ma'am," Peanut said, and dug into his food.

———

While Ruby woke up to a new kind of joy, Melissa Dean was waking up to the reality of her crossroads. She'd gone to bed last night feeling a little defeated.

And then she woke up.

Today was the day she took her first step on a new path. But she wasn't going to take the old Melissa with her on this journey, and to get rid of her, she needed to pay a visit to the Curl Up and Dye.

It was just after eight a.m. when she sat down with her first cup of coffee and picked up her phone to Google the number, then called it. As she was listening to it ring, she wondered if she had called too early, but then someone answered the phone.

"Curl Up and Dye, Vera speaking."

"Good morning, Vera. This is Melissa Dean."

"Hi, honey. What can I do for you?"

"I need to be fixed. My hair's a mess. I'm a mess. Can you help?"

Vera heard way more than the need for an appointment in Melissa's voice.

"As it happens, Vesta's nine o'clock just called to cancel. If you can get here by then, you've got the appointment."

"Oh my gosh! That's wonderful! I didn't dream it would be this soon. Yes, yes, thank you. I'll be there."

"Good. See you soon," Vera said, and hung up.

Melissa disconnected, then slapped the table with delight just as her toast popped up from the toaster. She jumped up to get it, buttered it, and gulped it down without tasting it, too anxious about the upcoming appointment.

She dressed quickly, then realized as she was about to leave that she hadn't even looked at herself in a mirror, so she turned around and went back to her bathroom. She stared a moment, then jammed her finger against her own reflection.

"You are part of my past. I appreciate your participation, but you are about to be put to rest."

Minutes later, she was out the door.

⁓

Because of the cool day, Ruby chose jeans, a soft blue cable-knit sweater, and a little black leather jacket to go with her black leather half-boots.

She fixed her hair, still eyeing the strawberry blonde color, and wondered if she should think about changing that sometime in the future. She didn't own enough makeup to cover the bruises, so she chose to let them shine. Adding some clear lip gloss to her mouth to keep the skin soft, she stood back to get a look at the entire outfit just as Peanut walked in.

"You look gorgeous," he said.

She shook her head. "You always say the right thing at the right time."

"I speak my truth," he said.

Ruby turned back around to the mirror. "What do you think about this hair color?" she asked. "I know I change it a lot. Does that bother you? Is there a color you like better than another?"

Peanut walked up behind her. He stood a moment, towering over her, then reached over her shoulders and pulled her hair away from her face.

"That's what I love. That face. You. You are the color of love to me, Ruby. I don't care what you do to your hair."

Ruby was suddenly in tears. "Oh, Peanut. You did it again. Thank you for waiting for me to find you."

Peanut put his arms around her, his hands resting lightly on the tops of her breasts.

"Love you. Whatever you do today, you'll do what you do best, which is make waves, pretty girl."

Ruby was dabbing at tears. "Okay, I'm ready for you to take me home so I can get my car. The keys are in my purse. I don't need to go inside."

"I'm ready," he said, and grabbed his jacket as he followed her out.

A few minutes later, he let her out at the curb, then watched her go straight to her car without a hitch in her step. As soon as her car started, he drove away.

Ruby buckled her seat belt and then adjusted the rearview mirror before she backed out of the drive and headed for her shop. It felt good to be in control of her life again.

Melissa walked into the salon, smiling as the little bell over the door signaled her arrival.

Vesta came hurrying up front.

"Melissa! So glad to see you," Vesta said. "You can hang your jacket up there, and then follow me back."

Melissa was already getting excited as she followed Vesta back to her station.

"Have a seat here, and let's talk about what you're wanting before we go to the shampoo station, okay?"

Melissa sat, eyeing all that was going on as Vesta put a cape over her clothes and snapped it at the neck.

Vera was blow-drying LilyAnn Dalton's hair and listening to her talk about her husband, Mike, with such love in her voice it made Melissa ache, remembering that's how she'd been about Andy.

Then Vesta took the ponytail holder out of Melissa's hair, tossed it on the station, and began finger-combing Melissa's hair to get a feel for the length and texture.

"So what are we doing today?" Vesta asked.

"We are changing me," Melissa said. "Cut it, color it, and make me look younger than my forty-seven years because I'm gonna need a new job."

The workroom momentarily went silent as that statement sank in.

"What happened?" Vesta cried.

"Fred let me go."

"Oh my lord!" LilyAnn said. "Has he gone and lost his mind?"

Melissa shrugged. "Nephew needed a job, and Fred didn't need two clerks."

Vera rolled her eyes. "I'm sorry, honey."

Melissa shrugged. "I was sorry for myself last night. That was the end of one thing, but today is a beginning of another."

"Do you have a hairstyle in mind?" Vesta asked.

"Just not this," Melissa said. "Cut it to fit my face. Color it to fit my complexion."

And on that, Ruby walked in the back door.

"Good morning, ladies. A little chilly out today. Hello, LilyAnn. How's that hunky husband of yours? Why, Melissa Dean, it's good to see you. Are we cutting, coloring, or both?"

There was a brief moment of shocked silence, and then LilyAnn took a deep breath.

"I am so glad to see you upright and talking," she said, and started to cry.

"No crying allowed," Ruby said. "I'm alive."

Melissa held out a hand and Ruby clasped it, revealing the healing cuts and spreading bruises on her hands.

"Just want you to know that you are my new favorite super-heroine. Kicked ass and saved yourself, I hear. I need tips on saving myself. I got fired yesterday, so keep me informed if you hear of any local jobs. Not in the mood to drive out of town to work."

And just like that, the shock passed and everyone went back to work, talking over each other, laughing or shrieking in dismay, whatever the story demanded.

Ruby let the energy of their voices flow through her, helping to heal her wounded spirit. She sat in the chair at her station, watching Vesta shampoo Melissa's hair, then eyeing the chin-length bob she began to cut. When Ruby saw the hair color Melissa had chosen, she gave her a thumbs-up.

"That dark brown is going to look gorgeous with your big, green eyes."

"It's my natural hair color," Melissa said.

Ruby heard the excitement in her voice.

"Change is good," she said, then stood up. "Girls, are there any errands that need running? How are we on toilet paper and paper towels? Do you need anything? I'm here to work."

Vesta grinned. "Good for you. We do need toilet paper, but when do we not? Mabel Jean isn't coming in until afternoon, but we're completely out of paper towels for her. You can check the till. We might need change."

Vera turned off the dryer long enough to be heard. "I meant to bring some sodas for the client refrigerator and forgot."

Ruby waved an okay and ran up to the front to check the till. She pulled out a hundred dollars in twenties, then came back with a lift in her step.

"I've got you covered," she said. "I'll be back soon. Ladies, if you're gone before I return, enjoy your hairdos."

"Thank you, Ruby!" said LilyAnn.

Ruby waved and walked out the back door as abruptly as she had entered.

The twins looked at each other, then grinned.

"I don't know what happened, but she's done a one-eighty from the woman who was in here before," Vesta said.

Vera shrugged.

"Ruby is just finding her spirit again. Now, Melissa, let's get this color on and see what mischief we can stir up for you."

Chapter 7

RUBY DROVE TO THE PIGGLY WIGGLY FIRST AND GRABBED a shopping cart as she entered the store. She went straight for the paper towel aisle, tossed in a couple of rolls, then moved to the toilet paper display. Doing these tasks felt so normal that she'd almost forgotten her appearance until she heard someone gasp. She had a moment of panic and then set her jaw as she turned around.

Precious Peters was standing a few feet away with a look of horror on her face.

Ruby sighed. *And here we go.*

"Morning, Precious. How are things at the travel agency?"

"Oh my God, Ruby. Your face."

Ruby waved her hand as if it were nothing. "Black eyes and three stitches in my lip? You should see the other guy."

Precious blinked. "I'm sorry?"

"That means my kidnapper looks worse," Ruby said. "Have you had many trips to book this winter?"

Precious couldn't focus enough to follow the change of subject. "Uh... I..."

"Really?" Ruby said. "I would have thought there would be more. Well, gotta hustle. Don't want to be late meeting Peanut for lunch. Later."

She tossed in some toilet paper, and then headed for the soda aisle. Of all the people to see next, they were the three women she'd banned from her beauty shop for maligning Mercy Dane before Mercy and Lon Pittman were married. The fact that they'd finally made amends to Mercy and were back on the reservation books at Ruby's salon was beside the point. They were perennial busybodies.

She saw the shock on their faces and braced herself and went for the old "best defense is a good offense."

"Hi, Betina. Molly, I see your roots. You need to make an appointment to get your color done. Angel... have you been cutting your own bangs again?"

Molly grabbed at the top of her head as Angel covered her forehead with her hands. Betina just stared.

"You look..."

"Careful what you say to me. I'm not feeling kindly toward idiots today. Never saw so many shocked looks over a pair of black eyes in my life."

Betina paled, trying to imagine the pain of getting stitches in her lip, then sighed and hugged Ruby.

"Really glad to see you. We all prayed."

"Then I thank you, because I needed all the help I could get to stay alive."

Angel started crying. "I'm sorry he hurt you," she sobbed.

Ruby grinned. "You're not half as sorry as he is."

Molly gasped. "What do you mean?"

"I have three little stitches in my lower lip. I quit counting how many they put in him."

"You did that...to him?"

Ruby rolled her eyes. "Well, yes. Wouldn't you try to save your own life? Listen, I need to hurry. The girls at the shop are waiting for me, so I should finish my errands." Then she pointed at Molly and Angel. "I'll be back to work in a few days. Make an appointment."

"Yes, we will," they echoed.

Ruby pushed past them to the end of the aisle where the six-packs of sodas were shelved and picked up three different brands, then headed to checkout. The lines were long and people were staring, so she lifted her chin and went to the self-checkout. By the time she got the purchases inside her car, it was five minutes to eleven — just enough time to go through the drive-through at the bank for change.

The line at the drive-through was short. Ruby put the car in park then pulled out the twenty-dollar bills and left them in her lap.

One car drove away, and now there were only two ahead of her. Buzz Higdon in his old pickup had just pulled up to the window. She grinned. Buzz had yet to master the speaker and yelled loud enough throughout his transactions that she could hear him shouting two cars back with her windows rolled up.

Then Buzz drove away, and there was only one car between her and the window. She wasn't paying much attention until she realized people were gathering inside the teller cage, looking at her and pointing.

She waved.

They scattered like quail after a gunshot.

The car ahead of her moved, and she pulled up to the teller's window and waited for the drawer to open.

When it did, she put the money in the drawer.

"Hi, Randall. I need some change for the shop. A bundle of ones, and the rest in fives or tens."

"Yes, ma'am. Right away," he said.

Randall Meeks shifted the knot in his tie and made himself look away as he reached for the bills to complete the transaction.

Ruby looked past him to the tellers standing about five feet away, all staring at her.

She waved again.

They waved back, then ducked their heads and went back to work.

She sighed. This wasn't nearly as hard as she'd imagined. When Randall opened the drawer with her change, she removed the envelope.

"Can I do anything else for you, Ruby?" Randall asked.

She grinned. "Just tell your coworkers I'm fine."

He flushed. "Yes, ma'am, and glad to hear it."

She drove back to the shop, unloaded the bags, and was returning the money to the drawer when Mabel Jean came in the back door.

She broke into a big grin when she saw Ruby and came running to give her a hug.

"You don't know how good it is to see you back here where you belong!" Mabel Jean said.

Ruby hugged her back. "It's good to be here, honey. How's it going?"

"Oh good, good. I had a dentist appointment this morning, and I feel like I'm drooling."

Ruby laughed and didn't mind one bit when her stitches pulled.

"Bless your heart. You're numb, and I'm sore. We could go on the road with that show, right?"

Mabel Jean giggled, and then went to hang up her coat while Ruby strolled back to the work area.

Vesta was coloring Sue Beamon's hair her usual

shade of pale lilac. No matter how many times the stylists had politely recommended a different color for Sue's hair, she was steadfast in her choice of what Vera called "old lady purple."

Vera was on break, waiting for her next appointment to arrive.

"Want a cookie, Ruby?" Vera asked, as she held out a container with homemade cookies. "Oatmeal raisin."

"Ummm, sounds good, but I'm having lunch with Peanut shortly so I don't want to ruin my appetite."

Vera grinned. "Oh, I sure wouldn't want to ruin anything between the two of you."

"You are so bad," Ruby said, grinning.

Vera waggled her eyebrows and took another bite of her cookie as Ruby left.

Ruby got back in her car and sent Peanut a text.

On my way to Granny's. I'll save you a seat.

Then she drove away.

Peanut sighed with relief when the text finally came, and he headed for the car in long strides. He was proud of Ruby for having the guts to do this. If someone was rude to her in front of him, all bets were off. Then he saw her the moment he walked into Granny's and let out a sigh of relief.

Lovey was sitting beside her in the booth in typical Lovey style, talking more with her hands than her mouth. He grinned. Lovey always said if anyone ever tied her up, she wouldn't be able to speak.

The room was already filling up, and no one was even pretending not to stare, which didn't sit well with him. He decided to give them something to look at and shifted into jury mode as he walked into the room, purposefully walking between them and Ruby to break their stares. The moment they glanced up, he gave them a hard look and kept moving.

Lovey got up after he reached the booth.

"Meatloaf on special today. I know it's one of your favorites."

"My favorite is sitting right there," Peanut said, and pointed at Ruby.

Lovey giggled.

Peanut leaned over and kissed Ruby full on the lips, and then took the seat across from her.

"Hello, darlin'," he said. "Have you had a good morning?"

Ruby's whole body had gone into relax mode the moment she'd seen him enter.

"Yes, I have. I'll tell you all about it when we get home."

And that's how the rest of Blessings found out that Peanut and Ruby were a thing. He'd kissed her in front of God and everybody, and then she'd admitted she was staying at his house. Her face had suddenly taken a big back seat to her love life.

Peanut winked.

Ruby grinned.

"I'm having meatloaf and mashed potatoes," Ruby said. "Easy to eat."

"I'm having the same thing," Peanut said. "That and some of Mercy's heavenly biscuits."

"Ummm, dripping in butter," Ruby added.

One of Lovey's waitresses was out today. Wendy and Lila were the only ones on duty and having to hustle to keep up. When Wendy saw Ruby and Peanut were in her area, she caught Peanut's attention and called out from a couple of tables away, "I'll be right with you."

Myra Franklin, who owned the flower shop, was a table away and across the aisle with her back to their booth, but that obviously hadn't interfered with her hearing.

"They just want meatloaf and mashed potatoes, and some of Mercy's biscuits," Myra said, and then the minute she said it, she realized she'd let everyone know she'd been eavesdropping. She blushed as the customers exploded with laughter.

Everyone laughed, but Ruby and Peanut laughed the most, and when Peanut gave Wendy a thumbs-up to indicate Myra was right, they laughed again.

That set the tone for the room, and it never changed. Ruby was still Ruby, but with black eyes and a boyfriend.

Life in Blessings was moving on.

———

Melissa came out of the Curl Up and Dye with a dark-chocolate mocha color on hair that Vesta had cut into a shoulder-length bob. The thick, shiny strands swung as she walked, and the makeup, compliments of Mabel Jean, gave her the confidence she so needed.

She went straight to Kitty Carlton's Unique Boutique and came out with one outfit in a zipper bag. She was going to wear it to the reading of the will in honor of Elmer and then spend the rest of that day applying for new jobs.

She already knew jobs these days were mostly applied for online, but this was Blessings, where face-to-face still sold the hire. Since she'd been making deposits and keeping books for the hardware store for years, she was going to apply first at both banks.

Heads were turning as she walked to her car, and Melissa knew most of them didn't know who she was. She grinned. She should have done this years ago. Unwilling to go home and waste the look, she stopped at the pharmacy to buy a lipstick, then decided to spend a bit more and treat herself to a piece of Mercy Pittman's pie at Granny's.

She walked in just as Peanut and Ruby were being served, then looked around for a place to sit. Ruby saw her and gave her a thumbs-up.

"You look amazing, Melissa! Good choice!"

Melissa grinned, and then saw a friend from church sitting alone on the other side of the room and started toward her.

The looks of shock and surprise were worth a lot to Melissa's ego, but worth even more for the gossips to share around town. Ruby Dye had a boyfriend, and Melissa Dean had gotten herself a makeover.

The single men in that room suddenly took notice, a few even sucking in their gut as she passed them.

One man even winked. "Looking good, Melissa," he said.

"Oh, shut up, Roscoe. You've been looking at me in the hardware store for years and never even said hello. And you're married. Eat your lunch," she muttered.

Roscoe grinned and flushed while his friends at the table began teasing him about the put-down.

"Hey, Jane, mind if I join you?" Melissa asked.

Jane Farris looked up, her eyes widening as she realized who was talking to her.

"Melissa? My word! Yes, sit, sit. I don't have to be back at Before and After until time for school to be out."

Melissa sat. She was looking for jobs, but she sure didn't want to run a day care like Jane.

Jane grinned as she leaned across the table and patted Melissa's hand. "Tell me everything! What prompted all of this?" she asked.

"I'm job hunting. Fred let me go yesterday."

Jane gasped, as did people at neighboring tables, but Melissa didn't care. Fred was the one who should be ashamed.

"Why?" Jane asked.

"He needed a job for his nephew. It happens." Then she pointed at Jane's dessert. "That looks so good. What kind is it?"

"Oh, coconut cream," Jane said. "It's my favorite, and Mercy makes the best pie crust I ever ate in my life. I can't believe a woman that young is such an amazing baker, you know?"

Melissa grinned. "Everyone has a gift, but in Mercy's case, I think she has several. She is something special, isn't she?"

Jane nodded. "Want a bite of my pie?"

"No way! I want a piece of my own," Melissa said, and flagged down a passing waitress. "A piece of coconut cream pie and a glass of sweet iced tea, when you get a chance."

Wendy gave her a grin and a thumbs-up as she disappeared into the kitchen.

"I'm sorry about your job, and I'm sure sorry about Elmer Mathis's passing. I know how close you two were."

"Thank you," Melissa said. "I knew it was inevitable, and I'm glad he's no longer trapped by the Alzheimer's he was suffering, but I sure will miss him."

"Do you know anything about a service?" Jane asked.

"I know he's not having one. He didn't want anything but to be laid to rest beside his wife, Cora."

"I understand that," Jane said, and then Wendy came out with a piece of pie and set it at Melissa's place.

"Iced tea coming up, and you look like a million bucks," she said, and winked.

Melissa dug into her pie, happy to be sharing food with a friend. She stayed, visiting with Jane after her pie was gone, then realized she had nowhere else to go. She intended to pick up some job applications, so she might as well do that right now.

"I had no idea what time it was. I should be going. Thanks for the company, Jane. I'll see you in church," Melissa said. She left a tip on the table and paid for her pie on the way out.

Once she was in the car, she refreshed her lipstick, then drove straight to the bank, secretly delighting in the double-takes she was getting.

She stopped at the first desk.

"Could I have a job application, please?"

The woman looked up. "Melissa?"

She grinned. "Yes, it's me. Uh, the job application?"

"You don't work at the hardware store anymore?"

"Nope. Fred let me go."

The woman gasped. "But why?"

"His nephew has my job."

The woman rolled her eyes. "I'm sorry." She opened a drawer and pulled out an application. "Bring it back to me when you're done."

"Thank you so much," Melissa said, and walked out as abruptly as she'd come in.

But she knew Blessings. It would be all over town by dark that Fred Bloomer had fired her because of nepotism, and she was looking for a job. It was self-preservation. She wasn't hiding Fred's bad behavior at the expense of her own well-being. She had to work to survive.

She stopped in at the other bank and repeated the process, then decided to go home. A job at either of these banks would be her first choice, so she decided to wait on any more job applications to see if either bank offered her a job.

Melissa went home with more optimism than when she'd left and settled in with a cup of hot tea and the applications. She filled in her name, and then stopped. It had been such a long time since she'd done this. Right after Andy died. And now she was having to start over.

Crossroads.

Life was always full of crossroads.

--~~--

Ruby ate until she was too full to swallow another bite, then pushed her plate aside.

"Aren't you going to eat that?" Peanut asked.

"No. Help yourself," she said, and then laughed when he did. "Do you ever get full?"

Peanut shrugged, as he scooped up the mashed potatoes and leftover meatloaf and transferred them to his plate.

"Can't remember it, if I have," he said, and grinned.

Ruby couldn't help thinking she was just beginning to live again, and that all the years she'd spent here had been the time she'd needed to heal and trust.

"Want some pie?" Peanut asked.

"Too full, but you have some. I'm in no hurry since no one is waiting for me at the salon."

Wendy came by to refill their glasses. "Anybody want dessert?" she asked.

Peanut held up his hand. "What kind of cobblers did Mercy make today?" he asked.

"Apple and peach."

"Peach, please, with a scoop of vanilla ice cream."

"You got it. Anything for you, Miss Ruby?"

"I'm having a bite of his," Ruby said.

"Then you better bring a couple of spoons with that cobbler. I'm thinking one bite won't be enough," Peanut said.

"Coming up," Wendy said, and off she went to turn in the order.

Ruby leaned across the table and lowered her voice. "Thank you," she whispered.

Peanut leaned forward. "For sharing dessert?"

"For loving me," Ruby whispered, then saw a gleam in his eyes.

He lowered his voice. "You haven't even scratched the surface of my passion, Ruby Dye."

Her face was still flushed and her heart still racing when Wendy came back with dessert.

———

Gary Dye didn't own a gun, but he knew people who did. One phone call, and a guy he did work for showed up with a burner, asking two hundred dollars for it.

Gary handed it over. "This never happened, understand?"

"Well, hell, man. Do I look like I advertise my business?"

Gary never cracked a smile. "Just so you know," he said.

The man put the money in his wallet and drove off as Gary locked the gun up in his safe. He wasn't sure when he'd have time to get away, but he wanted to make sure he was prepared to leave when the opportunity arose.

After a quick glance at the clock, he went back to work. He should have this job finished by this evening. A couple more welding jobs were already booked, but after that, he was heading to Georgia.

———

Peanut and Ruby parted ways at Granny's. He went to check in at the office, and Ruby decided to drive by her house to pick up the mail. But as she came up the street toward her house, she saw a car in the drive, then realized it was Laurel Lorde's.

God bless Peanut. Laurel was cleaning her house, but Ruby wasn't going in. The next time she set foot in that house, she wanted every vestige of Jarrod Dye's existence removed.

She jumped out to get the mail from the mailbox on the porch. Even though the front door was closed, she could smell lemon oil and Pine-Sol, scents that made her happy. She grabbed the two days' worth of mail and then drove back to Peanut's.

The wind was picking up as she got out, which made her realize she hadn't been paying attention to the weather. A quick glance up at the sky showed dark, gathering clouds, which were a sure sign it was likely to rain.

Ruby parked under the far side of the portico, leaving plenty of room for Peanut's car next to the house, then grabbed her things as she ran toward the house. The wind gave a final tug at her hair as she opened the door, but the moment she was inside, the feeling of sanctuary returned.

She loved his house.

It felt like him—safe and strong.

Ruby took off her jacket and then tossed the mail on the counter. Another gust of wind rattled a window, which made her frown. Must be a loose pane of glass. She needed to mention it to Peanut when he got home.

The thought of a hot cup of coffee sounded good, so she started a pot brewing and then began opening her mail. Setting aside the envelopes with bills to be paid, she unfolded a flyer. As she read, her eyes widened in delight. There was a picture of a tall, skinny boy standing beside a big bloodhound in the middle of the page, both as solemn as a photo on a wanted poster.

LOST SUMTHIN'?
FOR TWENTY-FIVE BUCKS, BOOGER CAN FIND IT.
I'M CHARLIE.
CALL ME.

A phone number was handwritten below the block letters.

Ruby laughed out loud.

She'd never seen the boy before, but he was adorable.

She poured herself a cup of coffee and then carried her mail to the table to finish going through it, leaving the flyer out to show Peanut.

When he came home about an hour later, she met him at the back door.

"I went by the house to pick up my mail. Laurel was cleaning. Thank you for following up on that for me."

Peanut was happy to see her so upbeat. "You're more than welcome."

Then she took him by the hand.

"You have to see this," she said as she led him toward the table, then handed him the flyer.

He stared at the picture, but he wasn't laughing like Ruby had. He was frowning.

"I know this boy from somewhere."

"Does he go to school here? I've never seen him in town."

"I can't remember. Maybe I'll think of it later," he said, and then laid the flyer aside and rubbed his hands together, trying to warm them. "Feels like it's going to rain," he said.

"You need to warm up. I made coffee," Ruby said.

Peanut turned around to pour himself a cup and then stopped, turned back around, and looked at the photo again.

"Oh man...this might be Marty Conroy's boy."

"Who?"

"Uh, a man I represented in court once."

"Where is he now?" Ruby asked.

"Dead. Blew himself up making meth. I wonder what this kid is doing down here trying to drum up business in Blessings. I'll need to look into this," Peanut said.

Ruby picked the flyer back up.

"It's a pretty good slogan and one heck of a dog's name," she said, smiling. "'For twenty-five bucks, Booger can find it.'"

Peanut grinned.

"Of that I have no doubt. Bloodhounds can find anything or anybody if they have a trail to follow." He picked up the flyer. "Mind if I keep this? I'm going to call this number later."

"Sure, keep it," Ruby said. "I won't be needing it. I know where I am."

Peanut swooped her up into his arms. "You're with me, that's where," he said, and then he kissed her.

The kiss went from playful to still, then softly searching before Peanut pulled back.

"Did that hurt you?" he asked, gently rubbing a thumb below her lower lip.

"Not enough that I was needing you to stop."

He sighed. "Patience is not my best virtue."

The wind blew hard against the window, rattling it again.

"There's a loose pane somewhere in that window," Ruby said.

"I hear it, but I'll deal with it later," he said, and gently cupped the side of her cheek. "Want to lie down and rest before dinner?"

"I want to lie down," Ruby said, "but I'm not tired."

Peanut's eyes narrowed, thinking about making love but at the same time afraid of hurting her.

"What if I hurt you?"

"What if you don't?" Ruby whispered.

"Then I'd say we would make magic."

Ruby held out her hand. "I haven't made love before. I've had sex. They're two different things. If you can pretend my two black eyes are something sexier, like a Mardi Gras mask, then abracadabra, my love."

Chapter 8

IT SHOULD HAVE BEEN AWKWARD, TWO PEOPLE WHO'D never even made out undressing in front of each other to make love. But age and maturity added a level of confidence that might have been missing had they been younger.

There was no panic or hasty discarding of clothes, no worry about being caught, no fear of getting pregnant. Just a man and a woman in love, moving to the next step in their relationship.

Peanut pulled back the covers on his bed and then slipped in beside her. Her body held no surprises. She was as she seemed, a beautiful woman in full bloom. His greatest wish was to give her joy, to translate the love he had for her into an ecstasy she'd never known. He wanted to sink into the warmth of her, to make slow, sweet love to her as he went out of his mind from the pleasure, and there was nothing stopping it from happening now.

Propped up on one elbow as he lay beside her, he slowly trailed one hand along the valleys and curves, marking territory, laying trails, watching the changing expressions on her face to remember which places on her body were more sensitive than others.

They didn't speak. There was no need. They'd been talking for three days now about loving. Now was the moment for making it real.

~~~

Ruby's gaze was locked on Peanut's face when he first touched her. She had wondered if the transition from friends to lovers would be hard, and now she knew. To lie down beside this man was the most natural thing she'd ever done. She'd already let him into her heart, and now it was time to let him into her body.

As she watched him stretch out beside her, she wondered why she'd ever thought of him as skinny. The muscle mass on his body was there, well-toned and long and lean, like him.

When he dipped his head and kissed the hollow in her throat, she combed her fingers through his hair and closed her eyes, giving herself up to whatever came next.

As it turned out, it was sex on the grandest scale she'd ever known. Twice, he took her over the edge before he moved between her legs. After that, it was another time for rebuilding just to reach that one little moment when her world went up in a wave of heat.

After it happened, they didn't move.

Ruby couldn't, and Peanut didn't want to, but as time ticked on, it was inevitable that they must.

Ruby's arms were still around his neck.

Peanut was still deep within her body and looking down into her eyes. The love he saw both awed and humbled him. She was, for him, the right woman to love.

"This was pretty much every dream I've ever had about making love to a woman all rolled into one epic event. The fact that I get to do this with you for the rest of our lives is the best thing that's ever happened to me.

I loved you, and now I made love with you. Perfect in every way."

He brushed a very gentle kiss across her mouth.

Ruby was at peace. This was the man meant for her to love, and if she had to, she'd walk the hard path just to find him all over again. Loving him, making love with him, had healed every broken place in her spirit.

"I love you too. Thank you for looking my way."

He sighed. It was time to move.

"I'm getting up. Just remember to hold my place for the next time," he said.

Ruby smiled, watching as he got off the bed and then strode into his bathroom. She got up, gathered up her clothes and went across the hall to her room. A few minutes later, they met in the hall and walked to the kitchen with his hand on her shoulder and hers against the middle of his back.

"Hungry?" he asked.

"Yes."

He grinned. "You should have eaten what you left on your plate at noon."

She swatted his arm. "Don't make fun of me. Where's that soup you bought the other day?"

He pointed.

She headed toward the pantry as he began taking out stuff to make sandwiches.

—⁂—

Outside, the rain that had been threatening Blessings earlier had finally arrived. While it was welcoming to some, it was not to twelve-year-old Charlie Conroy.

The old house they'd moved into three months ago

was across the alley from the Blue Ivy Bar. The city had turned off the utilities three days ago for lack of payment, and the roof had a leak right over the kitchen table. Charlie had set a bucket beneath the leak and put his five-year-old sister, Patricia—a.k.a. Pitty-Pat—in bed with his mama to stay warm. Until the rain let up, it was all he could do.

His old bloodhound, Booger, was lying next to an unlit heating stove, almost as if he knew this would be a place of warmth—only it wasn't.

Charlie counted the money he had in his pocket, and then counted it again, as if by magic the money might have multiplied unobserved. But it had not. Any way he counted, it was still thirty-four dollars—not enough to pay the rent next month. Not enough to get the power back on. Not enough to get Mama some medicine for her cough and still keep them fed. If it hadn't been for May, the bartender just across the alley, he wouldn't have been able to distribute his flyers.

He kept Mama's phone in his pocket now because that was the number on the flyers. Mama didn't know it was missing from her purse because there was no one left who would be calling, and it was a burner phone. Once the minutes were used up on it, it would be of no use.

From where he was sitting, he could see straight into the bedroom to where Mama and Pitty-Pat were sleeping.

He thought about getting under the covers of his own bed, and then looked away. He was the man of the house now. Someone had to keep them safe.

Along about midnight, someone tried to get in their house, and Booger came up off the floor baying like he had something treed. Charlie was holding his baseball bat as he looked out a window in time to see someone stumbling down the alley. He relaxed, guessing the guy was drunk and looking for a place out of the rain. He glanced down at the bat and then stood it back in the corner. There was a time when he'd been the best batter on his team up in the hills. Now it was the only weapon he had.

He sat down beside Booger, his hand on the folds in the big dog's face, and scratched him between the eyes. Booger whined.

"Like that, don't ya, boy?"

Booger licked his hand, and the room got quiet again. Charlie scooted closer to his dog for warmth, and sometime afterward he fell asleep curled up next to old Booger's back.

The next time he woke up, it was morning and the phone in his pocket was ringing.

Ruby was stirring oatmeal at the stove. Peanut was running enough bread through the toaster to feed the high school football team, but this morning he could do no wrong in her eyes.

In the past, she had been awakened by noise, alarms, and before she'd lost the baby, by nausea, but she'd never been awakened quite like she had this morning and hoped it was just the start of many mornings in Peanut Butterman's bed.

"Think this is enough?" Peanut asked, holding up a small platter.

"I'm not even sure I can handle one, so if it looks good to you, then I'd say yes."

"Good," he said, and set it on the table. "Now the butter and jam. Is the oatmeal almost ready?"

She gave it a final stir and turned off the flame beneath.

"It is exactly ready," she said, and poured it up into the bowls next to the stove.

"Sugar and cream," Peanut muttered, still adding condiments to the table.

Still unsure of the strength of her grip, Ruby carried the bowls to the table one at a time, then scooted into her chair. Peanut was bringing coffee when her cell phone rang. She started to let it go to voicemail, then noticed it was the number from her salon.

"It's the shop. I'd better take this in case there's a problem," she said.

Peanut gave her a thumbs-up as he began buttering toast.

"Hello," Ruby said.

"Oh, Ruby, this is Vera. We just got news here at the shop that Gertie Lafferty has gone missing from the old folks' home. They don't know how long she's been gone and can't find her anywhere. Chief Pittman is organizing a search party at the nursing home as we speak."

"Oh no! That's terrible," Ruby said. "I'll see if there's anything we can do, and thanks for calling."

Peanut looked up just as Ruby disconnected. "What's wrong?"

"Gertie Lafferty is missing from the old folks' home. They don't know how long she's been gone. Chief Pittman is organizing search parties."

Peanut frowned. "What about that flyer you got yesterday...the one about Charlie and his bloodhound?"

Ruby nodded. "Good call, Peanut. Maybe someone has already thought of that."

"You eat. It takes you longer to eat around stitches. I can inhale mine in minutes. I'll call the chief to ask."

Ruby went about adding sugar and then a splash of cream to her oatmeal. It tasted good, and the warmth was easy on her mouth, but now she was worried about Gertie. The little woman wasn't quite five feet tall and in her late eighties. Lord only knew what had prompted her to wander off.

Since Peanut had the chief's private number on his cell, he called it rather than going through the department.

The chief answered on the first ring. "This is Lon. We're kind of in the middle of something right now, Peanut. Can I call you back?"

"Your *something* is why I'm calling. There's a kid named Charlie who put flyers in mailboxes yesterday about hiring out his bloodhound to find what was lost."

"Oh, Mercy showed me that last night. Do you know who he is?"

"Pretty sure he's Marty Conroy's son. There's a number to call. It's pretty damn cold out. It might not hurt to add that bloodhound to the search. If he can't pull it off, it doesn't change what you're already doing, but if the dog finds her fast, it might be the difference between life and death for Gertie."

There was a moment of silence. "Do you have that number handy?" Lon asked.

Peanut got the flyer from the sideboard. "Yes, it's right here. Are you ready?" he asked.

"Yes, go ahead," Lon said, and wrote it down. "Thanks. I'll give him a call right now."

Charlie answered on the second ring, thinking to himself that this had to be good.

"Hello. This is Charlie."

"Charlie, this is Chief Pittman. Someone told me you have a bloodhound for hire."

Charlie's heart skipped a beat. "Yes, sir, I sure do. Booger can find anything or anyone."

"Well, we have an elderly lady from the nursing home who's gone missing. Would you be available to bring Booger to the police station to help us out?"

"Yes, sir. It'll take me a bit to get there. We live on the outskirts of town behind the Blue Ivy Bar."

"Then stay there and I'll come get you and your hound, okay?"

"We'll be waiting for you," Charlie said, then hung up and threw his arms around his dog's neck. "This is it, Booger! This is our chance!"

Alice Conroy had been awake for over an hour, staring up at the water-stained ceiling with her daughter tucked close against her. She'd been born into hard times, and her entire life had been more of the same. When she heard the phone ring, she threw back the covers to get up, then heard Charlie answer. She pulled the covers back up over Pitty-Pat and then sat on the side of the bed, frowning as she listened to the one-sided conversation. After he hung up, she got up and went into the kitchen.

"Who were you talking to?" she asked.

Charlie eyed his mother's pale face and sleep-tumbled

hair, then glanced at her nervously as she covered her
mouth to cough. She needed medicine, but all he could
do was button the top button on her coat, then put a hand
on her shoulder.

"It was the police chief. Me and Booger are gonna
help find a lost lady from the nursing home, and they'll
pay me twenty-five dollars to do it."

Alice frowned. "I don't understand. How would he
know to even call you?"

"Because yesterday I put flyers in mailboxes all
over town advertising me and Booger's services for
finding stuff that's lost. The price and everything was
on the flyer."

All of a sudden, Alice panicked.

"Oh, Charlie! How did you pay to make flyers? Did
you spend all our money?"

He shook his head. "'Course not. Miss May at the
Blue Ivy helped. She took a picture of me and Booger on
her phone, then helped me make and print off the flyers
from the copier in her office."

Alice stared at her twelve-year-old son as if she'd
never seen him before.

"What made you think to do something like this?"

"Well, Mama, we got ourselves a situation here, and
since I'm the man of the family, I figured it's up to me
to get us out of it as fast as I can."

Her heart sank. He needed to be in school, not out
trying to earn a living—and of all things, hiring out
that hound. She couldn't believe he'd even thought to
do that.

"I'm sorry, Charlie. I'm so sorry we have fallen on
hard times, but now that it's quit raining, I'm going to

see about signing up for food stamps and welfare today. I never thought we'd be struggling like this, but then I never thought your daddy would go and die, neither."

Charlie frowned. "I don't want to talk about Daddy. If he hadn't been making meth, he'd still be alive and this wouldn't be happening. Wait till I get back, and I'll walk to town with you and Pitty-Pat."

Alice nodded.

"There's still bread and peanut butter, and water in that empty milk jug. I got it from the hydrant at the Blue Ivy," Charlie said. "No milk for Sissy, though."

"We'll manage. You get yourself something to eat before you go."

"I don't have time, Mama. The chief will be here any minute."

He was starting to turn away when Alice grabbed his arm.

"Thank you, Son."

He nodded.

"It's okay, Mama. We'll get back on our feet. You wait and see."

———

Gertie Lafferty's long, gray braid was as sodden as her nightgown and bathrobe. Wet leaves were caught in her hair, and mud was all over her from the countless times she'd stumbled and fallen.

She'd been dreaming about picking blackberries with Bennie, when all of a sudden he took the berries from her hands and disappeared. His absence was what woke her.

To say she was confused to find herself in the woods

was beside the point. She was wet, cold, and hungry. She wanted her morning coffee and someone to help her change clothes, but she wasn't sure where she was or how she came to be there. She didn't like being dirty, and tried to get up to wash her hands, but when she tried to stand, her legs were too shaky to hold her.

She needed help. Bennie would help. He'd taken good care of her their whole married life, and she took good care of him. She glanced up through the bare limbs to the sky. It was time for her to get home and start breakfast. Bennie must be wondering where she'd gone.

"Bennie! Bennie! Come help me up!" Gertie called, and then waited. The only thing she heard was water dripping off the leaves onto the forest floor. "Help me, Bennie! I need help!"

The silence scared her. She rolled over on her hands and knees, and as she tried to push herself up, her hands slipped on the wet leaves. She fell headfirst against the trunk of the tree in front of her, then didn't move.

—∿∿—

Chief Pittman drove through town with lights flashing, then pulled into the alley behind the bar to the small clapboard house.

There was no smoke coming out of the fireplace, no lights on anywhere inside. When he saw the front door open and a tall, gangly boy and a huge bloodhound emerging, Lon jumped out to open the back door of his cruiser.

As he did, a woman followed them out. She was blue from cold and shivering. She coughed, then couldn't stop. Then the boy approached and held out his hand.

"I'm Charlie Conroy, sir. Thank you for calling."

Lon wondered how desperate they were and then decided to deal with that later. "You can put your dog in the back and ride up front with me."

"Yes, sir," Charlie said. He loaded up Booger, then got into the front seat.

Lon turned around."Mrs. Conroy, I'm Chief Pittman. Thank you for allowing your boy to help us. I'll have him back as soon as possible, okay?"

"Yes, it's okay," she said.

And then another little voice piped up, and Lon saw a tiny girl standing in the doorway, also wearing her coat over her clothes. She was crying.

"Mommy, Mommy, I'm cold."

"I have to go," Alice said. She ran back to the doorway, picked up the little girl, and disappeared into the house, shutting the door behind her as she went.

Lon got in. The boy was already buckled up.

"We're going straight to the nursing home."

"Yes, sir," Charlie said, his heartbeat jumping as the chief drove away.

"So what's going on at your house? Don't you have any heat?"

"We don't have any utilities, sir. We got cut off."

"When was this?" Lon asked.

"Oh, a few days ago, but I'll get the money earned to get them back on."

"Is this why you put out the flyers?" Lon asked.

Charlie nodded.

"That was very industrious. How old are you?" Lon said.

"I'm twelve, but I am the man of the family now,"

Charlie said, and then turned his head as they passed the school, looking at it with a mixture of longing and despair.

Another two blocks, and they pulled up in front of the nursing home. One of Lon's deputies was already there gathering info, while the other one on duty was back at the station. People had begun gathering here as the news had spread, ready to help search.

"Here we go," Lon said as he parked. "You get your hound and follow me."

"Yes, sir," Charlie said, and leaped out, grabbed Booger's leash, and took off after the chief.

Nathan Rose, the nursing home administrator, was trying not to panic as he explained what he knew to Deputy Ralph.

"We've never had this happen before," Nathan said. "We lock the doors at night and everything. Wanda is the one who discovered Gertie's absence."

Ralph eyed the aide in purple scrubs. She looked to be in her late twenties, and she also looked scared to death, like someone was going to lay the blame for this on her.

"So, Wanda, how did you know she was missing?" Ralph asked.

"She wasn't in her bed when I came on duty at six a.m., so I went looking for her, assuming she'd just fallen asleep somewhere else inside the building. They do that sometimes, but I couldn't find her. That's when we all began to search. She's not here."

"Were there any unlocked doors?" Ralph asked.

Wanda's shoulders slumped. "The one from the kitchen leading out into the back alley. There's an extra lock up high. She's so little, I don't know how she reached to open it."

"Either someone helped her, or it was unintentionally left unlocked," Nathan said. "It's the only explanation."

"Have you notified her next of kin?" the deputy asked.

"She doesn't have any," Nathan said. "She brought herself here three years back and hasn't had a visitor from outside Blessings since."

At that point, the chief walked up and didn't waste time explaining.

"Nathan, I need something that belongs to Gertie... something that would have her scent on it...like her shoes...or a piece of her clothing...something that hasn't been washed yet."

Nathan saw the boy and the bloodhound and didn't ask questions.

"Wanda, you heard him. Bring something that will have Gertie's scent on it."

Wanda turned and ran into the building as the deputy recognized the boy.

"Hey, that's the kid from the flyer," he said, then glanced at Lon. "Good call, Chief."

"If it works, we can all thank Peanut Butterman. It was his suggestion."

Charlie had outgrown his coat months ago and had been wearing his daddy's clothes all winter, but he didn't have a coat. It had burned up in the explosion. He shivered slightly as he waited, thinking nothing of the discomfort because it had become the norm, but Lon saw it.

"Be right back," he said, and jogged toward his cruiser, popped the trunk, and then came back with a heavy, fleece-lined flannel jacket. "Put this on," he said, as he handed it to Charlie.

Charlie's eyes widened.

"I might get it dirty."

"Son, it'll wash," Lon said. "Put it on."

Charlie didn't argue. The warmth that enveloped him was so welcome it brought tears to his eyes.

"I thank you," Charlie whispered.

Lon patted the boy's shoulder as Wanda came running back holding a pair of cotton socks.

"Gertie wore these yesterday. They were still in her shoes. Will they work?"

Lon glanced at Charlie, who nodded.

"They'll do just fine," Charlie said, then glanced at Lon. "Are you ready, Chief?"

Lon glanced around at the small crowd of people who'd gathered to help search.

"We're going to try this first before we send everyone out in different directions. If some of you want to go home, you're welcome. But if there are any who want to follow us and the hound, then fan out in a grid behind him and do your best to keep up."

A few waved and headed back to their cars, but a good dozen of them stayed.

Lon heard one searcher call out, "That hound won't track. I reckon the rain has washed out her tracks and scent."

"We'll see," Lon said, and watched as Charlie Conroy got down on one knee and shoved the socks up under Booger's nose.

As he did, the hound began to whine, as if sensing he'd just been given a task.

"Hunt, Booger! Hunt!" Charlie said.

The massive bloodhound lifted his head, sniffing the air, then put his nose to the ground and moved toward the back of the building with Charlie hanging onto the leash. The moment they reached the back door, Booger bayed.

"He's on the scent," Charlie cried, and off they went, through two blocks of housing, across the baseball field, and then up into the woods, with the cops and the searchers behind them.

Chapter 9

THEY'D BEEN ON THE MARCH FOR NEARLY A HALF HOUR when Booger stopped going forward and began moving in wide, spreading circles.

Charlie saw the tracks and frowned. Something wasn't right.

"Stop!" he shouted, adding, "Wait here," as he loosened his grasp on Booger's leash to allow the dog more lead as he began to circle an area about the size of a football field.

Charlie could hear grumbling from the searchers around him, saying the dog was no good, that he couldn't even follow a scent and didn't know what he was doing. The talk made Charlie nervous, afraid that his first chance to make money was going to go bust before it began. But he could see what some of the others could not. Booger was following the scent just fine. It was Miss Gertie who didn't know what she was doing.

Finally, someone near Charlie even shouted at him. "Hey, kid. You sure that dog knows what he's doing?"

Charlie's face turned red with anger. Even though he'd been taught to mind his elders, he was nearly a man, and a man had to stand up for himself.

"It's not the dog that's lost, mister. It's Miss Gertie. If you don't believe me, come look at the footprints Booger is following. She walked in circles here, likely realizing she was lost," he shouted, and then he took a tighter grip on the leash as Booger suddenly plunged ahead, dragging Charlie with him and leaving the rest struggling to catch up.

The loudmouth in the crowd was startled that the boy had called him out and started to grumble again until someone told him to shut up or go home.

They were back on the move again. It was now three hours past the moment they had discovered Gertie Lafferty missing from her room in the nursing home. Not knowing how long she'd been gone before that was frightening. Time was not on their side.

Lon had seen enough hunting dogs in his day to know a good dog when he saw one, and old Booger was a dandy. He knew they'd find Gertie. What he didn't know—and what worried him most—was not knowing what shape she'd be in. He kept praying as he went. *Lord, please don't let us find her dead.*

Charlie and Booger were so far ahead now that Lon couldn't see them, and he increased his stride as he jogged through the forest. There were quite a few evergreens, but also a lot of trees that had shed all their leaves, and their dark, naked branches looked like arms reaching for someone to pick them up. He couldn't see or hear Charlie or the dog anymore and was about to break out in a run when he heard the hound bugle. He knew that sound.

"They found her!" Lon yelled, and started running.

―∼∼―

The moment Charlie saw the little body crumpled next to a tree, he wanted to cry. Booger began to bugle. He'd treed his prey, so to speak… He'd found Miss Gertie.

"Good boy! Good boy!" Charlie said, praising Booger and petting him as he tied the hound's leash to a nearby tree, then ran to the old woman's side.

Her whole face was bloody, and for a moment Charlie thought some animal had been at her to cause all that blood, and she was most likely dead. Then he noticed the cut on her forehead just below the hairline and the blood on the trunk of the tree. She'd fallen, and that's where she'd hit her head.

He felt for a pulse and was so excited when he felt one that he jumped straight up and started shouting, "She's here! She's alive!" over and over until he saw Chief Pittman coming through the trees at a lope. "Over here, Chief!" Charlie yelled, waving his arms. "She has a pulse, Chief. She's alive."

Lon reached them in seconds, thumping Charlie on the shoulder over and over.

"Good job, Charlie. You and Booger did a real fine job!" Then he got on his walkie-talkie and called for a stretcher.

The searchers who had been carrying it came running. Ken Yancy was the EMT who'd come with the searchers, and once he reached Gertie's body, he knelt to check for a pulse. It wasn't a strong pulse, but it was there. Ken gauged the angle of her body to the blood on the tree, then looked up at the kid who'd found her.

"Did you move her at all, son?"

"No, sir," Charlie said. "Just felt her neck for a pulse."

"Good," Ken said, and unhooked the cervical collar he'd fastened to his belt. "Okay, Chief, I need two people to slide that stretcher up against her back while I hold her. Looks like she went headfirst into that tree when she fell, so I need to get this collar on her, and then we'll turn her."

Charlie was riding an adrenaline crash and starting to shake. He kept swallowing back tears, praying the old woman didn't die.

A few minutes later, they had an IV in Gertie's arm, a pressure bandage on the head wound, and a blanket tucked over her as they started back. Ken radioed his partner to bring the ambulance to the edge of the tree line at the back of the baseball field and said they'd meet him there.

Charlie was walking beside the Chief as they moved quickly back toward Blessings.

"She was really cold," Charlie said.

"They'll get her warmed up at the hospital," Lon said. "You and your dog sure earned your money today. You both made a name for yourself, and I hope it brings you all the money you need. As soon as we get back to my cruiser, I'll get you home and see about getting you and your family some help. I don't like to see people doing without in Blessings. It's not how we roll here."

Once again, Charlie felt like crying. The relief of having even a small part of the burden of his family on someone else's shoulders was overwhelming.

"I sure thank you," he said gruffly, and then cleared his throat, not wanting the chief to think he was the cry-baby sort.

—◦◦◦—

They came out of the woods to find the ambulance waiting. The EMTs loaded Gertie and took off through town with the lights flashing and the siren screaming.

Deputy Ralph was also there to pick up the chief, along with Charlie and his dog. He dropped them off at the nursing home and went back on duty patrolling Blessings, as Lon reclaimed his cruiser and took Charlie and Booger home.

The chief pulled up in front of the house and parked, then got his wallet and counted out twenty-five dollars.

"Here you go, Charlie, and thank you again for your help."

Charlie palmed the money gratefully. "If you have any other emergencies we can help you with, keep us in mind."

"Is it okay with you if I go in and talk to your mother?" Lon asked.

Charlie hesitated.

"I won't insult her," Lon said. "I just want to help."

"Yes, all right," Charlie said. "Come with me."

Lon got out and followed Charlie and the dog to the house. Charlie knocked.

"We only have one key," he explained, and then the door opened, and Alice was there with her daughter in her arms.

"Thank you for bringing him back, Chief," Alice said.

"Yes, ma'am," Lon said. "He did great. We found Mrs. Lafferty alive, thanks to Charlie and his dog."

Alice smiled and then coughed, then kept coughing until Charlie took his little sister out of her arms.

"Come in, Chief," Charlie said.

Alice gasped. She didn't want anyone to see what a state they were in. "No, wait! I don't—"

"It's okay, Mama," Charlie said. "Chief Pittman wants to talk to you."

Alice clutched at her coat collar, as if holding it tight against her throat would stop the coughing. She was scared they were going to call DHS on her for neglect.

"Please, Chief, please don't take my kids from me. I can't live without my babies," she whispered, and started to cry.

"I came to help, Mrs. Conroy. Not make matters worse."

"Oh lord, lord," Alice cried, and sank into a chair near her sofa.

Charlie tweaked his little sister's nose until she grinned.

"Chief, this is my sister, Patricia, but we call her Pitty-Pat. Honey, this is the police chief. His name is Chief Pittman."

Lon grinned. "Hello, Pitty-Pat. You have very pretty blue eyes."

She hid her face against her brother's shoulder.

Lon had been thinking about this ever since he'd picked up the boy and his dog, and now he sat down near Alice to lay out his plan.

"I will have your utilities turned on before noon today," he said.

Charlie panicked. "But we can't pay for them yet."

"Let me worry about that," Lon said. "Mrs. Conroy, do you have food?"

Alice looked helplessly at Charlie.

"I'm not sure. I've been sick," she said.

Charlie sighed. "Barely."

Lon nodded. "That's okay. Just know that some people will be coming by with groceries today."

"Uh, Chief...we've only got one skillet to cook with, so make sure whatever they bring can be cooked in that. Everything we had burned up when Daddy blew up the house."

Lon paled. "Even your clothes?"

"Yes, sir. We went down to the Salvation Army and got a couple of outfits apiece, so we're managing."

Lon took a deep breath and then made himself get back on track. "I'll contact the County Department of Human Services to get you setup for some financial assistance. You definitely qualify. And rest assured, I'm not reporting your behavior. Just your situation."

"I don't know how to thank you," Alice said.

Charlie's legs were beginning to shake, so he sat down. He'd gone a long way this morning on a very empty belly.

"Thank you, Chief. Thank you so much," Charlie said.

"It's part of my job, and I'm glad I can help," Lon said. "So, I'd better get back to the office and get the ball rolling on all of this. Have faith, ma'am. We don't abandon our own here in Blessings. Just stay seated. I'll see myself out."

They watched the chief leave and then looked at each other in disbelief.

"It's gonna be okay, Mama," Charlie said. "Why don't you take Pitty-Pat and go back to bed so you two can get warm? I'm here. I can handle stuff."

Alice began wiping her tears as she stood. "Maybe I will lie down just for a bit. I don't feel good."

Charlie was scared for her, but trying not to show it. Mama couldn't die too. God wouldn't do that to them—would He?

--- ∿ ---

Lon had already called the gas company and was calling the city utilities department on the way back to the office.

"Utility Department, this is Rita."

"Rita, this is Chief Pittman. I need a favor."

"Yes, sir, what can I do?"

"I need the utilities turned on at 440 Milway ASAP."

"Just a moment while I check the—"

"No," Lon said. "I know they were turned off because the family owed money, and I'm asking you to turn them back on now. I will be down to pay what's owed before the day is over."

"Yes, sir. I'll get the order written up right now."

"I need them on before noon. A woman and two kids are living there without power. She's sick, and they're cold and hungry. Understand?"

"Yes, sir. Right away."

"Thank you," Lon said, and then finally called Peanut.

Peanut had been waiting for news. When his phone rang and he saw it was from the chief, he answered abruptly, hoping the news wasn't bad.

"Peanut, it's me. Thanks for the heads-up about the bloodhound. That kid and his dog found Miss Gertie more than a mile up in the trees behind the park."

Peanut frowned. "Please tell me she was alive," he said.

"She had a pulse. She also had a big gash on her head when she fell against a tree. She's definitely suffering from exposure. Can't say what the outcome will be, but that's not why I'm calling. I need your help."

"Yes, sure, what do you need?" Peanut asked.

"That kid, Charlie Conroy…he and his mother and little sister are in the old house behind the Blue Ivy Bar.

Their utilities got cut off days ago. They're cold and
mostly out of food, and his mother is sick. I've already
dealt with getting the utilities turned back on, but I
need some help with DHS, and I know you work with
them often."

"Yes, there are people I could call," Peanut said.

"I know this is clearly not protocol, but is there any
way you can get someone to their house to help them
sign up for assistance and whatever else that welfare can
do for a situation like this?"

"I'll make it happen," Peanut said.

Ruby walked in and slid onto the side of Peanut's
desk. "Is it Gertie?"

"They found her," he whispered. "We're talking
about Charlie and his family. Hang on, Chief. I'm putting this on speaker phone so Ruby can hear too. Is there
anything else you need?"

"I need people willing to donate groceries and cold or
flu meds—particularly cough medicine—and get them
to the Conroy house. Alice Conroy is sick with either the
cold from hell or a case of the flu. They have a single
skillet to cook in and next to no clothes. God only knows
what else they're doing without since everything they
owned burned up with their house."

"I can tend to all that," Ruby said. "Where do they
live?"

"The old house behind the Blue Ivy bar. It's 440
Milway."

"I know which one you're talking about," Ruby said.

"The utilities are off, but I'm having them turned on.
Hopefully they'll be back on by the time the groceries
arrive."

"Okay, Chief. If you need anything further, you can call my cell. I can make this happen. Talk to you later," Ruby said, and bolted out of the office.

Peanut grinned. "Well, she's gone. You gave her a mission, and you know Ruby. She'll get the food there. In the meantime, I'm calling County. I'll let you know how it goes later."

"Thanks, Peanut. Your help is much appreciated. I need to go check on Miss Gertie. Call if you need me."

"Will do," Peanut said, as the chief disconnected. He searched his contacts for the number to DHS, then made the call.

———

Ruby was on her phone on her way to the Piggly Wiggly. She'd already called Lovey, who was donating cooked food from Granny's along with money, and she was talking to Rachel Goodhope as she drove.

"Yes, it's a terrible situation they're in, and I'm upset I didn't know about this sooner."

"I'll do anything you ask," Rachel said. "Do you just need money donated, or can I come help you shop?"

"Come help me shop," Ruby said. "I'm going to call Mabel Jean. If she doesn't have any appointments scheduled, she can help too. Oh…if you have any old kitchen pots and pans you don't use anymore, or one or two you can spare, they have a skillet and that's all. Everything they owned burned up in a fire."

"I'll go through my stuff and bring enough for them to cook a meal in. As for the groceries, I'll call you once I'm inside," Rachel said. "You come find me and tell me what to do."

"I will, and thanks," Ruby said, then put in a call to the shop. Within minutes, Mabel Jean was headed to the Piggly Wiggly to meet her.

—∿∿—

Alice Conroy had no idea what was coming as she crawled back into bed and tucked Pitty-Pat in beside her. All she knew was that because an elderly lady had wandered away from the nursing home, their own lives were about to change for the better.

"I'm still hungry, Mama," Pitty-Pat whispered.

"More food is coming, honey. We ate our peanut butter sandwich, remember? Just close your eyes and help Mama rest."

"I'll help," Pitty-Pat said as she backed into the curve of her mother's body and closed her eyes.

Charlie went to the cabinet to see what food was on hand. There were four slices of bread, a half jar of peanut butter, and one can of dog food.

He opened the dog food and dumped it in Booger's feeding bowl, then scratched him behind the ears as he gulped it down in two bites.

"I'm sorry there's not more," Charlie said.

As soon as the bowl was empty, he took it outside, filled it with water from the hydrant on the outer wall of the bar, and then ran back.

Booger lapped at the water until he had quenched his thirst and then plopped down near the cold stove.

Charlie took one slice of bread, spread a very thin layer of peanut butter on it, then ate it slowly to make it last. He knew the chief had said groceries would come, but until they were here, he trusted nothing.

Once he finished eating, he got their broom and began to sweep. He closed the door to his mother's bedroom so stirring the dust wouldn't make her cough more, and then got to work. The longer he swept, the better he felt—like he was sweeping away their troubles along with the dust. When he was finished, he put the broom away and then began dusting the house, because sweeping had left a thin layer of dust on top of the dust that was already there.

He was straightening up in the living room when someone knocked. He hurried to the door, and when he opened it, a man from the gas company was on the step.

"I just turned the gas back on, so I need to relight the pilot lights in your cook stove, heating unit, and water heater."

"Thank you," Charlie said, and led him to the kitchen and then into the short, dark hall where the water heater and heating unit were housed. "Sorry it's dark. I don't have a flashlight."

"Don't worry, I have one," the man said.

Within minutes, both of the pilots were lit.

"Oh…the water is on too," the man said. "A guy left here in a city truck as I was pulling up. Now all you need is your electric and—"

At that very moment, the lights came on. The gas man grinned. "Ask and ye shall receive, right, son?"

Charlie nodded, so grateful for power he couldn't speak as he followed the man back to the front door.

"Now then, you guys are all set up. Have a good day, okay?"

Charlie nodded again, then closed the door and sat down and cried.

The central heat was on. The lights worked, and they had both hot and cold water. It was a miracle. He was so excited about the water that he got the mop and mop bucket and began cleaning the floors, starting from the kitchen, working all the way through the living room, then down the hall and into his bedroom.

He tossed the mop water out the back door and was coming inside when he heard another knock at the door.

He ran to answer.

The three women standing on the doorstep with their arms full of groceries were strangers, and one of them, a small blonde with stitches in her lip and two black eyes, seemed to be in charge. He tried not to stare.

"Hello, Charlie. I'm Ruby Dye. I own the hair salon down on Main Street. This is Mabel Jean Doolittle, she works there with me, and this other lady is Rachel Goodhope, who runs the bed-and-breakfast. We have some groceries for you. May we come in?"

"Yes, ma'am," Charlie said. He stepped aside as they walked in, then led them to the kitchen.

"There are more bags in the cars, Charlie. If you don't mind, it would be a big help if you started bringing them in too," Ruby said.

He looked out, saw three cars, and paused. "Which car, ma'am?"

Ruby grinned. "Oh, all of them. Trust me, there's a lot to carry in here."

Before Charlie could get out the door, his mother emerged from her bedroom, saw all the women, and grabbed at her sleep-tousled hair. "I thought I heard voices," she said.

"Yes, ma'am, you sure did, and I'll bet it sounded like a

henhouse full of chickens," Ruby said, then went through the introductions again, then began to explain. "We brought food. Charlie, get busy carrying sacks. Alice, this is your house and your kitchen. We'll bring things in, and then you put it all where you want it to go. How's that?"

Alice nodded, too wide-eyed to speak. It wasn't until they all went back for more that she realized the power was on and the house was clean. It even smelled clean, although all Charlie would have had to clean with was water. It was the most wonderful thing in the world to feel heat and have water and light.

She began emptying sacks and putting away food, some in the refrigerator humming near the kitchen counter, and the rest in her very empty pantry. They'd even brought a big bag of dog food for Booger. When the sacks kept coming, and she saw what they'd brought, she was in shock. *How did they know? God in heaven, how did they know?* And Charlie. She hadn't seen him smile in months, and now he was grinning and talking with the ladies as if he'd known them all his life.

Finally, all the sacks were inside, and Mabel Jean and Rachel had said their goodbyes and left to go back to work. Ruby brought in the last sack, which was the food Lovey had donated from Granny's Country Kitchen. Ruby set it on their kitchen table and then turned around.

"This is already cooked. Lovey Cooper sent it. She owns Granny's Country Kitchen. And before you dig in, take the medicine we brought."

"Yes, yes, I should do that," Alice said, and went to get a glass of water.

The bedroom door opened again as Alice was swallowing pills.

Pitty-Pat saw a strange woman standing beside her mother and was too scared to come in. "Mama?"

"Hi, baby. Come meet Miss Ruby."

The little girl came in and then scooted behind her mother's leg. "Her face is funny," she said.

Alice gasped. "Patricia, that's not a nice thing to say!"

Before the little girl could burst into the tears Ruby saw coming, she laughed.

"No, it's okay, and I totally agree with you. Right now my face is a mess, but it will heal and then I'll be myself again."

Alice sighed. "I'm sorry. Kids are so brutally honest."

"No, it's fine," Ruby said.

"Were you in an accident?" Alice asked.

Ruby shook her head. "I'm the woman who was kidnapped last Sunday."

Alice gasped. "I didn't know about that. Really kidnapped?"

"Yes, but I'm alive and home, and he's in jail—forever, I hope."

Alice was in shock, trying to imagine the horror of such a thing happening to her. "That's wonderful. I'm so glad you're okay," she said.

"Yes, it is wonderful," Ruby said. "And I need to let you and your family sit down to a meal. Enjoy, get well, and the first time you're downtown, stop by the Curl Up and Dye and say hello. First family haircuts will be on me."

"I will, oh, I will," Alice said. "I can't thank you enough. People are so good here. I'm grateful. Very, very grateful."

"It's our pleasure," Ruby said. "You and Patricia take

care." And then she glanced at Charlie. "It has been a true honor to meet you, Charlie. You and Booger rock."

Charlie smiled. "Thank you, Miss Ruby. Thank you!"

"You're welcome, Charlie. Give Booger an extra scoop of dog food for the fine job he did finding Miss Gertie."

"Yes, ma'am, I sure will," Charlie said, and let Ruby out before locking the door behind her. When he turned around, his mother was already taking out the food from Granny's.

"It's fried chicken," Alice said. "And biscuits, and mashed potatoes, and green beans. Oh my lord! And pie! There's a whole fruit pie."

Charlie took down the three plates from the cabinet that May from the Blue Ivy Bar had given them, and got out the mismatched forks and spoons he'd pulled out of the ashes of their old home.

"Fill 'em up, Mama, and let's eat. I'm starved."

"I'm starved too," Pitty-Pat said.

Alice sat down, too shaky to stand, but she was more than able to fill her children's plates. Coming to Blessings had been the smartest thing she'd done in years. There were angels in this town—real angels masquerading as humans. Of that she was convinced.

Chapter 10

PEANUT HAD KNOWN JEWEL EASLEY SINCE GRADE SCHOOL and had worked with her whenever a case involved a family with underage children. She was a by-the-book caseworker for the County Department of Human Services and a woman with a good heart. He wasn't sure how she'd react to what he was going to ask, but he'd soon find out.

He called her cell, hoping she was in the office and not out on a visitation somewhere.

"Hello, this is Jewel."

"Hi, Jewel. Peanut Butterman here. Are you busy, or can we talk?"

"I'm just leaving a visitation, so talk away."

"Good. I need a favor."

She chuckled. "When do you not?"

"Yes, well…this is a big one."

She sighed. "I'm listening."

"How do you handle emergency services for a family in dire need?"

"How dire?"

"A widow and two kids here in Blessings have been living in a house with no utilities, no food, and she's sick."

"Oh good grief, Peanut. It's winter. Are you serious?"

"Unfortunately, yes," Peanut said.

"Where's the husband?"

"Blew himself up making meth and burned their

house down in the process. I don't know how they got to Blessings, but they're here and destitute."

Jewel cursed softly. "Drugs. Drugs. Drugs. If this epidemic did not exist, my job would be so much simpler."

"Yeah," Peanut said. "Just so you know…we just found out about them today. The chief has already had their utilities turned back on. Knowing him, he's paid whatever it took to make that happen, but that won't help next month when payment is due again."

"And food?"

"That's being taken care of as well, but again, when it's gone, they have no money for more."

"You said the mother is sick. Do you know what with?"

"The chief just said she was sick. I'm sorry, I don't know details."

"It doesn't matter," Jewel said. "You already know I won't be able to sleep tonight. I will consider your phone call an official report of a family in need, which I will write up, and since I am less than an hour away from Blessings, I will put on my caseworker hat and make the necessary official interview happen. That way I can get them in the system and get the ball rolling on how to help them."

"Thank you, Jewel. I really owe you for this."

"What's the woman's name and address?" she asked.

"Alice Conroy, living at 440 Milway in Blessings. It's at the far end of town on the street behind the Blue Ivy Bar. The power should be on by the time you get there, and if I know my girl, there will be food on their shelves."

Jewel gasped. "Oh my God! You have a girl? When did all that happen?"

"Not so long ago."

"Do I know her?"

"Ever been to the hair salon here in Blessings?"

"Well, who hasn't? Oh wait! Is it Ruby? It's Ruby Dye, isn't it? She is a cutie. I've wondered for years why she was still single. Way to go, Peanut."

He grinned. "Thanks. Please let me know if there's a problem getting Alice Conroy and kids into the system. I need to know they're going to be okay."

"Yes, I will," Jewel said. "Now I have to get off the phone so I can turn my car around, because at the moment I am going the wrong way."

Peanut laughed. "You rock," he said.

"Yes, I do, and don't forget it." She disconnected.

He was still grinning as he sent the chief a text to let him know what was happening.

—◊◊◊—

Gertie Lafferty had stitches in her head and a spreading bruise across the top of her face. They were treating her for hypothermia and mild frostbite on her fingers and ears—and hoping nothing turned into pneumonia. She had yet to regain consciousness, but she was hanging on, and that's all Lon Pittman could ask of someone her age who'd undergone such physical trauma. They still didn't know why she'd left the nursing home, but in the long run, it didn't matter. She had been lost, and now she was found.

Lon was on his way to deal with unpaid utilities when he got Peanut's text. Knowing that was being taken care of was one more burden off his shoulders.

—◊◊◊—

Ruby left the Conroy home full of purpose. She wanted to get back to work, to be useful in the world again. Helping them had been the best medicine she could have taken to heal the emotional damage Jarrod had caused. She was driving without thought when she realized how close she was to her home. Before she could talk herself out of it, she turned down the street toward home and pulled up in the drive.

But the fear she was expecting didn't happen as she walked in. Everything was clean and in its place. There was a bouquet of fresh flowers on the dining room table, and the air smelled like lemon oil. God bless Laurel Lorde for her diligence to detail! The house was still home.

Ruby went straight to the kitchen where the initial knife fight had taken place, but there was no feeling of fear. As she moved down the hall to the bedroom, she was all but certain that would be the trigger to a flash-back like she'd had before. To her relief, there was none. Even the old bedspread on her bed was a welcome and familiar sight. It was from the time before the abduction, and if not for the marks on her face and hands, it was almost as if the incident had never happened.

"I'm home," she said aloud, and walked back through the house, announcing her return in every room to let the house know she was here.

Now it was a matter of leaving Peanut—which had to happen because she wanted their relationship to breathe and grow, rather than having happened from desperation.

She paused in the kitchen long enough to check the contents of her refrigerator, making note of what she was out of, or what was out of date, and then headed for the front door.

"I'll be back," she said, then let herself out.

—⁓—

Thanks to the wisdom of the women who'd brought all the groceries, Alice Conroy was doing laundry. Not only had they brought food, but they'd brought things for the bathroom, and cleaning supplies, including soap to do laundry.

The cough medicine she took had helped a little, but she was still running a fever and had taken some medicine for that as well. The sound of Charlie and Pitty-Pat playing in the living room, laughing over a card game, brought tears to her eyes. She couldn't remember the last time she'd heard them laughing.

She was putting her first load of laundry into the dryer and getting ready to start the second load when there was a knock at their door.

"I'll get it," Charlie called out.

She could hear his footsteps thumping as he ran to answer. She tossed the last handful of wet clothes into the dryer, started it up, then put soap in the washer and started the next load. It wasn't as if they had all that much laundry to do, because they didn't have many extra clothes to wash, but Alice took pride in being clean.

She heard a woman's voice in the living room, and then Charlie asking her to sit down. Within seconds, Charlie was back at the door.

"Mama, it's a lady from DHS," he whispered.

Alice's heart skipped a beat. Chief Pittman had sworn he wouldn't turn her in on neglect, so she had to trust that someone else was here to help.

"Okay, I'll be right there. Unless the lady wants to

talk to you and Pitty-Pat, do me a favor and keep your sister occupied in your room," she said.

"Yes, ma'am," Charlie said, and bolted.

Alice paused a moment to smooth down her hair and straighten her clothing.

"Lord, please let this be one more step into a better life," she said, and headed for the living room.

The woman on the sofa looked to be in her late thirties or early forties with short brown hair and kind eyes. She stood up when Alice walked into the room and immediately held out her hand.

"Mrs. Conroy, I'm Jewel Easley. I'm a DHS caseworker for this county. I got a call that you and your family are having some difficulties. Can we talk?"

Alice shook the woman's hand and then sat down on the other end of the sofa.

"Yes, ma'am, we do need a hand up. I've never been on welfare before, and I'm sorry to have to be asking for it now."

Jewel pulled some paperwork to make notes. "So, I saw your children. Are those the only two you have?"

Alice nodded.

"Okay, then tell me a little about the circumstances that got you to this place in your life," Jewel said.

Alice folded her shaky hands in her lap, took a deep breath, and started talking. She went all the way from her husband's addiction to meth to him cooking and selling it, then to him blowing up their house and himself, which had led to them winding up in Blessings.

She ended with Charlie's desperate attempt to raise money for them, and how he and Booger had helped find a missing lady earlier this morning. By the time

Alice was finished talking, Pitty-Pat was in her lap and Charlie was sitting quietly nearby, because he hadn't been able to let his mother confess their fears alone.

Jewel had seen and heard plenty of stories during her job as a caseworker, but she'd never heard one quite like this, where the child in a destitute family had been the one to take the initiative to be the money earner. She glanced at the boy, then at the dog at his feet, and smiled.

"Good dog you have there," she said.

Charlie nodded. "Yes, ma'am. So can you help us?"

Jewel's heart tugged again. It was the boy who asked the hard question, not the mother.

"Yes, I can help your family, Charlie. Everything has to go through proper channels, but I'll push everything through from my end. You will receive a SNAP card in the mail to buy food. Money will be reloaded onto that card every month, and your mother will get a direct deposit in the bank every month for your other needs, including rent and utilities."

Alice broke down in sobs, which sent her cough into overdrive.

Jewel frowned. "You also qualify for Medicaid, which means when you or the kids are sick, you can get treatment and medicine."

"We sure thank you," Charlie said. "When I get older, I'll get a real job to help out."

Jewel felt obliged to add, "Just don't quit school, Charlie Conroy. You have the makings of a really good man, but you'll need that education. You and your sister too. Understand?"

"Yes, ma'am. As soon as I get some clothes for me and my sister, we'll get enrolled in school here."

Jewel nodded, then made a mental note to mention the clothes situation to Peanut when she called him back.

"For the record, let me have your shoe and clothing sizes. I'll pass them on to people who can help," she said. "Alice, can you help me with that?"

Alice wiped her eyes, blew her nose, and nodded, then quietly gave Jewel the sizes for all of them.

"Okay, I think that's it," Jewel said. "I will stop by periodically. If you have a problem, call the number on the card I gave you."

"Yes, ma'am," Alice said.

Jewel stood up, and then so did Charlie.

He opened the door for her. Towering over Jewel's height although he was only twelve, he shook her hand and thanked her for coming, which sealed him in Jewel's heart forever.

She left with a lump in her throat and called Peanut to inform him the Conroy family was set with DHS, but they still needed clothes. She gave Peanut the sizes and hung up, then said a prayer for the family's well-being as she drove out of town.

———~~~———

Ruby parked next to Peanut's car, thinking to herself how much she was going to miss being under the same roof with him, and then grabbed her purse and hurried inside.

She left it on the sideboard and went through the house room by room until she found him. The smile on his face when he saw her come into the room tugged at her heart.

"There's my girl!" Peanut said as he got up from his

desk to give her a big hug. "Did you get the Conroy family fixed up with groceries?"

"Yes, but I'll continue to drop by little things like bread, milk, and eggs until I know they're getting assistance through DHS," she said.

"My friend, Jewel Easley, who is a caseworker at DHS, has already started that process rolling," Peanut said.

"Oh, I know Jewel!" Ruby said.

"She knows you too," Peanut said. "She gave me a verbal high five because I had the good sense to snap you up off the open dating market."

Ruby smiled, but Peanut noticed she seemed preoccupied.

"I have another mission for you," he said. "Jewel gave me clothes sizes. Do you think we could organize some kind of clothing drive like we did for Dori Grant and her baby after her granddad's house burned?"

"Absolutely. I'll call the preacher and get permission to use the church as a drop-off site, then have Lovey put a notice on the bulletin board at Granny's, and I'll put a few signs in some of the businesses on Main Street, including ours."

"You're the best," Peanut said.

"Can we talk a minute?"

Peanut frowned. *Here it comes.* He knew she was bothered and was about to find out why.

"Of course, let's get out of this office, though. My coffee cup is empty."

He grabbed his empty cup as he left. Once they were in the kitchen, he set the cup aside as he turned to face her. "So talk to me," he said.

"Come sit," Ruby said. "I'm exhausted, and this isn't an easy thing to say."

His gut knotted. "You don't get to back out of loving me."

She reached for his hand. "It's not that at all," she said.

"Then what?" he asked.

"It's time I went home," she said.

He frowned. "I was just getting spoiled by knowing you were here. Tell me why so soon."

"I came here out of desperation. I want us to happen by choice…because we finally can't bear another day apart. We'll still be in each other's pockets. We'll still do everything we've been doing, but without pretending we weren't attracted to each other."

He sighed. "I can't say I want to hear this, but I honor your feelings and understand the wisdom." He tilted her chin. "I do so desperately want to kiss you senseless. When do those damn stitches come out?"

Ruby sighed. "About seven to ten days, and tomorrow is Thursday so that's barely four days, counting from Monday."

"Okay then. You're well worth the wait, and now I have a date upon which to focus."

She grinned. "I sure do love you," she said.

He cupped the side of her cheek, looking past the purple and green bruises to the wide brown eyes of the woman he loved and letting the beauty of those words settle deep within his heart.

"I sure do love you too, Ruby Dye. Since my belly is growling, and it's a bit early to get naked and make love, what say you and I order in? Do you think you can handle pizza, or would you rather have pasta?"

"You order whatever you want most, and I'll have baked ziti with meat sauce, not Alfredo sauce."

"Deal," he said, and reached for his cell phone, but it was still on his desk.

"Be right back," he said, and left the kitchen at a lope.

Ruby sighed. That hurt even more than she'd expected. It was going to be a painful break for her too.

He came running back, slipped his arm around her waist, and pulled her into a quick hug.

"One baked ziti with meat sauce coming up," he said. "And you do know, if you don't want—"

She laughed. "Yes…if I don't want to eat it all, you'll eat my leftovers," she said.

He gave her a thumbs-up and then made the call as she went to change clothes.

Their dinner was peppered with conversation ranging from Gertie Lafferty's rescue to the Conroy family to Ruby's imminent return to work. What they didn't talk about, but what was uppermost on their minds, was how much they were going to miss the closeness of falling asleep in each other's arms.

Even though it felt like it, tonight wasn't the end of anything. It was the beginning of the courtship of Ruby Dye.

It was late before they finally went to bed, and when they did, they fell into each other's arms and made love as if it was never going to happen again.

Ruby cried.

Peanut held her, resisting the urge to beg her to stay. They fell asleep, and woke to a bright, sunshiny day.

They had breakfast together, refusing to discuss the

inevitable, and when Peanut left for the office, Ruby packed up her things and went home.

By mid-afternoon, Peanut had his office set up for the reading of Elmer Mathis's will. There was no way to guess how the news would be received, but come ten a.m. tomorrow morning, he was going to find out.

Rachel Goodhope had just carried a fresh arrangement of flowers out to put on the table in the entryway and was about to go back to the kitchen when she caught a glimpse of three women coming up the walk, each pulling a small travel bag.

"Ahhh, Elmer Mathis's nieces have arrived."

She waited for them to ring the bell and then went to the door with a smile. "Welcome to Blessings Bed and Breakfast! I'm Rachel. Please come in."

Loretta Baird entered first, talking in an assertive, almost strident tone of voice. "I'm Loretta. The blonde is my sister, Betsy Lowe, and the chubby one is Wilma Smith, the youngest."

Betsy frowned. "Seriously, Loretta, that's no way to introduce anyone. Sorry, Wilma," she said.

Wilma shrugged, embarrassed she'd become the topic of conversation. "It's okay," she mumbled, then smiled at Rachel. "You have a very pretty place. I love the landscaping out front."

Rachel smiled. "My husband does the gardening. He's at a meeting tonight, but you'll see him in the morning at breakfast. Follow me, and I'll show the three of you to your rooms."

"Are they all upstairs?" Loretta asked.

"Yes, the downstairs is our family home. The upstairs bedrooms are for our guests, but there is an elevator for handicap access."

"I'll take that," Loretta stated.

"I'm fine with the stairs," Wilma said.

"So am I," Betsy said.

"Then up you go," Rachel said. "Just wait for us at the top of the landing. I'll take Loretta up in the elevator."

Loretta lifted her chin, handed the handle of her overnight bag to Rachel, and waited.

Rachel had been in the business long enough to have seen all kinds of behavior from their guests, so Loretta Baird's attitude didn't faze her.

"This way, ma'am," Rachel said, and walked off, pulling the little bag behind her.

Loretta eyed her sisters and then smirked as she walked away.

Rachel was at the elevator, waiting for Loretta to step inside, then she followed her guest and punched the button to take them up.

The car moved smoothly, and the trip was short. Rachel emerged first and then waited for Loretta to get out before catching up with the other sisters.

"You'll be at the far end of the hall. Your rooms are close to each other. Two are side by side, and one is across the hall."

"I don't want to be down that hall. I want one at the front," Loretta demanded.

"Sorry, those two are reserved for families with children. This way, please," Rachel said, and led the way, refusing to discuss it further.

"I have Mrs. Baird in the blue room, Mrs. Smith in the yellow room, and Mrs. Lowe in the lilac room."

"I don't know if I want to be in a blue—"

Betsy turned to Loretta and glared. "Loretta Fay, you need to shut up. We're not moving in. We're here one night, and then we'll all be going home."

Loretta glared back at her, but she didn't argue further.

Rachel opened the first door, then handed her a room key.

"Make yourself comfortable," Rachel said. "There is a sitting area, as well as refreshments on the sideboard, and cable television. As I mentioned, the only meal served here is breakfast, but Granny's Country Kitchen down on Main Street is a wonderful place to eat. The woman who does the baking is becoming famous for her breads and pies."

"I love a good piece of pie," Betsy said. "Sounds perfect."

Loretta sniffed as she walked into the room. Rachel set Loretta's bag inside the door and then let the other sisters into their rooms.

"If you have an emergency and need me, just dial nine on the phone by your bed. Everything you'll need is in your room. Enjoy your evening. We lock the door at eleven p.m., so if you're out later than that, you'll have to call to have us let you in."

"Why on earth would you lock up so early?" Loretta snapped.

"Granny's stays open later than everything else in Blessings, and Lovey quits serving at ten p.m., so unless you're leaving town, you won't have anywhere else to go."

"Oh," Loretta said, and then closed her door in Rachel's face.

Rachel ignored the snub.

"Ladies, welcome to Blessings," she said, and calmly walked back down the stairs.

Wilma looked at Betsy, who rolled her eyes and shook her head. They were used to Loretta, but there were times, like today, when she was a true embarrassment.

"What time do you want to get together for dinner?" Wilma asked.

"Oh, how about six o'clock?" Betsy said.

"I won't eat a bite before seven!" Loretta yelled.

"If you want to talk to me, open the damn door or shut your mouth," Betsy said.

The door swung inward. "Seven o'clock," Loretta said.

"Fine. It'll already be dark. Hope you know how to get from here back to Main Street. And I thought you wanted to drive by Uncle Elmer's house and look it over. Can't see a dang thing in the dark," Betsy said.

Loretta glared.

Wilma went into her room and closed the door. She'd let them fight this out. Decisions were not on Wilma's radar.

Chapter 11

GARY DYE TOSSED HIS OVERNIGHT BAG ONTO THE FRONT floorboard of his car and then patted his pocket to make sure his wallet was there, and it was. He'd already been to Jarrod's girlfriend's house to pick up his things and had found Ruby's address among them. That was all the information he needed. All he had to do now was drive to Georgia. It didn't bother him that he was going there to kill a woman. It didn't occur to him that he might get caught like Jarrod had. Jarrod's whole life had been one knee-jerk reaction after another. Gary considered himself smarter since he'd already gotten away with murder once when he was a teenager. He'd rolled a drunk for his wallet. The drunk woke up and saw him, so Gary slit his throat, and with no witness to the crime, he was never brought to justice. The success of that crime had given him a sense of empowerment—like he could do whatever he wanted and get away with it.

As for Ruby, he had a silencer on his handgun. She'd be dead and he'd be gone before anyone found the body. But it had to happen quickly, before people realized there was a stranger in town.

He glanced at the time. It would be dark soon. He could drive all night and be there by morning, find a place to stay, and get a few hours' sleep. That was his plan, and he was sticking to it.

He buckled up and drove away.

—◇◇◇—

The sisters finally decided to check out Uncle Elmer's property and then go to dinner afterward. Only one problem… None of them knew the address. They were halfway down the stairs when they saw Rachel moving through the downstairs foyer.

"Rachel! Rachel!" Betsy called out.

Rachel stopped and looked up. "Good evening, ladies. On your way out to dinner, I see."

"Yes, ma'am," Betsy said. "But we have a bit of a dilemma and were wondering if you could tell us how to get to Elmer Mathis's property. We didn't ask the lawyer for an address when he notified us."

"Oh. You've never been there?" Rachel asked as they reached the ground floor.

"I was there once, years ago," Betsy said. "But I was little."

"Okay then. Of course I know where it is, but I'm trying to think of the best way to tell you. I think, just stay on the road as you leave the bed-and-breakfast until you get to Downing Street. Turn left, go two…no, go three blocks down, and it will be the big red two-story brick with white columns along the verandah."

"Okay, got it," Betsy said. "Thank you so much. We won't be late coming back."

"Enjoy," Rachel said, and then watched them leave before going back to work.

The sisters were chattering among themselves, each planning what they wanted to do with their share of the inheritance, when they reached Downing Street.

"Turn left here," Betsy said.

Loretta glared. "I heard her. I'm already turning," she said.

"Soo-rrr-yyy," Betsy drawled.

Wilma sighed. "Can we please just get along for more than five minutes at a time?"

No one answered her, so she leaned back and shut her mouth. The house was easy to spot. The only two-story dark-red brick on the block, with a wide verandah and small, white columns.

"Not as grand as I expected," Loretta muttered.

"What exactly were you expecting? A version of Tara from *Gone with the Wind*? For crying out loud, Loretta. No one in our family was rich, including us," Wilma muttered.

Loretta's face turned red, but she didn't talk back. Instead, she pulled up in the driveway and parked.

"I want to see what it looks like around back," Loretta said.

Betsy pointed to a sign on the privacy fence. "It says No Trespassers."

"We're not trespassing on our own property," Loretta snapped.

"It's not ours yet," Betsy said.

Loretta shrugged. "I still want to look."

"Fine. You look. I'm staying in the car," Wilma said.

"I'm staying with Wilma," Betsy said.

Loretta got out alone, slammed the door shut behind her, stomped up the steps to peer inside the windows, and then came down off the verandah and headed for the gate.

Before she could get there, a man came out of the house next door and walked to the edge of his property.

"Hey, lady, what are you doing?" he asked.

"I'm going to look at my property!" Loretta snapped.

"This belongs to Elmer Mathis."

"He was our mother's twin brother. He died, and we're inheriting," she said.

The expression on the man's face went from concern to distaste. He looked at the women in the car and then walked back into his house.

Loretta smirked as she opened the gate and then disappeared.

"Do you think we should have gone with her?" Betsy asked.

Wilma shrugged. "I'm not doing anything illegal, regardless of what Loretta wants."

Betsy sighed.

Wilma folded her arms.

It wasn't long before Loretta came back. She got in the car and drove away without saying a word.

"Well?" Betsy asked.

Loretta shrugged, a little disillusioned by Uncle Elmer's property. "It's a large backyard with an overgrown garden. Nothing fancy."

Betsy sighed. "I'm starved. The cafe is on Main Street."

"And that's where I'm headed," Loretta muttered, taking a left turn to get out of the residential area.

A few minutes later, they pulled into the parking lot at Granny's.

"Wow. Look at all the cars," Wilma said.

"I hope we don't have to wait. I don't like to wait," Loretta said.

"We know," Betsy muttered, and got out.

The other two followed and managed to enter the cafe without another fuss.

Lovey was at the register. "Welcome to Granny's," she said. "Three for dinner, or will some more be joining you?"

"Just us, thank you," Betsy said.

"Booth or table?"

"We'll take a booth," Loretta said.

"Follow me," Lovey said, and took them to the only empty booth, which just happened to be behind the one in which Peanut had been seated.

The sisters took note of the man as they sat down.

"Your waitress will be right with you," Lovey said, and headed back to the front.

"The man in the booth behind us is cute," Betsy whispered.

Loretta nodded.

Wilma giggled and lowered her voice. "Too bad we don't live here. I'd date someone like him."

Loretta glanced around the cafe with her upper lip slightly curled. "This place is definitely not a five-star establishment, but I suppose it *is* quaint," she said.

"It smells good in here," Wilma said.

"It does not smell anything like fine dining," Loretta said.

Betsy leaned across the table. "Either stop talking so loudly, or stop talking," she hissed.

Loretta frowned.

Wilma sighed.

And Peanut heard it all, including what they thought about him and the sarcastic tone in one woman's voice. He'd only talked to them once, but he was pretty sure that Elmer Mathis's nieces were already in Blessings. He did not look forward to the face-to-face meeting tomorrow. Then he saw Ruby coming in the door and forgot all about them as he stood, greeting her with a quick kiss on the cheek before they sat down.

"This has been the longest day of my life," Peanut said.

Ruby frowned. "Why, honey?"

"Because I haven't seen you since breakfast."

She grinned. "Well, I'm here now, and I'm starving. How about you?"

"Now darlin', you know I'm always hungry...for one thing or another."

Ruby laughed, and the sound was nothing short of pure delight.

The sisters heard the laugh and shrugged at each other. Loretta pointed to her eyes and then made a disparaging face to indicate what she thought of Ruby's appearance.

Betsy kicked her under the table and frowned.

Wilma put a finger to her lips to indicate silence.

Loretta sighed. Regardless of the little blonde's facial appearance, it was obvious the man was already taken.

Then their waitress arrived with menus and a smile.

"Evening, ladies. My name is Lila. I'll be your waitress. What would you like to drink?"

They ordered sweet tea, two with lemon, one without, then Lila left them studying the menus.

She came back almost immediately with a basket of biscuits and a small bowl of honey butter. "These are our famous heavenly biscuits. I'll be back to get your orders shortly."

Betsy reached for a biscuit.

"You'll ruin your dinner," Loretta snapped.

"You are not my mother," Betsy said. She split the biscuit, spread honey butter on it, and handed half to Wilma, then took a big bite of her half. "Oh my God," she groaned. "This is the best biscuit I've ever had in my life."

"Ditto," Wilma said, licking the butter off her finger and taking another bite.

"Well, for goodness' sake," Loretta said, and buttered one of her own.

She took the first bite and then another, then finished off the biscuit and went for seconds.

"You'll ruin your dinner," Betsy mocked.

"Do shut up," Loretta said, and licked her thumb to get the last bit of butter.

Wilma just kept studying the menu. After a couple of minutes, she had decided. "I'm having the sliced ham dinner. How about you?"

"Oh...uh..." Betsy grabbed her menu. "Chicken. Fried chicken."

Loretta glanced down at her menu. "I'll have fried chicken too," she said. "And more biscuits with dinner."

They giggled.

"We need to save room for pie," Wilma said. "The woman who makes biscuits also makes pies, remember?"

"Right...pie," Betsy said. "Oh my. Pie." Then she giggled again. "Wilma, I feel like I did the night I drank all that champagne at your daughter's wedding."

Loretta glared. "You cannot get drunk on buttered biscuits."

Betsy sighed. "Well, they make me as happy as that champagne did, anyway."

Wilma laughed.

Loretta sighed, and then Lila came back to take their orders. Two fried chicken dinners, one ham dinner, and a refill on biscuits, along with three pieces of coconut cream pie.

Lila left to turn in the orders.

The sisters' introduction to Blessings was just getting started.

Lovey, being Lovey, was always curious about strangers. Visiting with strangers in her cafe was how she'd met her last husband, God rest his soul. She brought the pitcher of sweet tea to their booth and began topping off their glasses.

"Evening, ladies. I'm Lovey Cooper. I own Granny's. How is everything?" she asked.

Betsy giggled. "Everything is wonderful. Best biscuits I ever ate."

Lovey grinned. "Everyone says that. Glad you're enjoying them."

Betsy giggled again.

Wilma rolled her eyes. "Betsy thinks she's drunk. She said the biscuits made her as happy as the night she got drunk on champagne."

Lovey laughed out loud. "Now that's a new one. I'll have to share that with Mercy. She's my baker."

"I'd like to meet that woman," Loretta said. "She has to be a five-star chef from somewhere else."

Lovey resisted the urge to roll her eyes. Why people persisted in thinking it wasn't possible for anyone special to come from small-town America was beyond her.

"I'll see if she has a couple of minutes to come say hello," Lovey said.

"Wonderful," Loretta said, then watched Lovey disappear into the kitchen. She was not expecting the tall, black-haired beauty who came back out with her. "Oh. My. Lord," she whispered.

"What?" Betsy asked, and turned to see what Loretta was looking at. Her eyes widened, and her mouth opened, but she never got anything else said.

"Ladies, this is Mercy Pittman. She's Chief Pittman's wife, and the amazing baker you've been raving about. Mercy, these ladies love your biscuits."

Mercy's dark eyes flashed with delight. "I am happy to hear that," she said.

Loretta was rarely speechless, but the young woman's beauty was startling. "Uh...where did you study? Your culinary skills, I mean," she asked.

Mercy smiled. "At the fourth foster family I was sent to...or maybe it was my fifth. There were enough of them that they all ran together after a while."

The shock on Loretta's face was obvious. "You mean you're not classically trained?"

Mercy laughed. "No, ma'am. I guess I'm just good at what I do. Now if you ladies will excuse me, I think there's another batch of biscuits due to come out of the oven. I wouldn't want to let them burn."

She waved and then headed back to the kitchen.

"She's as stunning from the backside as she is from the front," Betsy said. "And she can bake with the best of them. I would say the chief of police must be one very happy man."

"Enjoy your dinner," Lovey said, and went back to the front of the cafe as Lila came back with their food.

The sisters bickered for a few minutes as condiments

were passed around, and then the booth went quiet as they began to eat. A short while later, Lila brought out the desserts they'd ordered, and the sisters dug into the pie.

"This is just as good as the biscuits," Wilma said. "I wish I could bake like this."

"So maybe you could go to cooking classes with some of your inheritance money," Betsy said.

Wilma smiled. "Maybe so!"

Loretta swallowed her last bite and pushed back her plate with a groan. "If I ate here every day I'd soon be fat as a pig," she said.

"I know," Betsy said. "Me too."

"I'm going to redecorate," Loretta said. "I wish we already knew what we're getting, but there's bound to be money as well as property, or the old man would not have been able to pay for that nursing home he was in. I don't know why that lawyer wouldn't tell us. It's certain he already knows."

"I'm going to travel," Betsy said.

"I just want to pay bills," Wilma said.

Lila came back by to leave their bill. "Thank you, ladies, for coming to Granny's," she said.

"Do we pay you?" Betsy asked.

Lila pointed up front to the register. "You pay Lovey," she said, and moved to Peanut and Ruby's booth to refill their drinks.

Peanut watched the women as they passed by on their way up front.

As soon as Lila was gone, Ruby leaned over the table. "Who are those women?"

"Elmer Mathis's nieces," he replied.

"Really?"

Ruby turned around in the booth for a second look. They were still at the register, arguing with each other as they paid their tabs.

"I don't remember seeing them before," Ruby said as she turned back around.

"That's because they didn't visit," Peanut said, then changed the subject. "Did you get settled in okay?"

She shrugged. "Sort of. I wound up going to the shop, then stayed too late to go to the Piggly Wiggly so I'll have to do that in the morning."

"I'll be in my office early for the reading of the will. Can I take you to lunch afterward?"

"No, but you can come by the house for lunch," Ruby said.

Peanut grinned.

"That's even better. Thank you for the invitation," he said, then eyed the bowl of potato soup that she'd ordered. "You ate most of your soup. Would you like dessert?"

"I couldn't eat a whole piece of pie," she said.

He grinned. "How about I order the dessert and two forks?"

"Yes, please," Ruby said.

Peanut waved Lila down. "The usual," he said.

"One dessert, two forks," Lila said, and giggled. "What'll it be tonight. Pie or cobbler?"

"Surprise us," Peanut said.

Ruby leaned back in the booth, watching the play of emotions on Peanut's face, and thought about how it had felt when they made love.

Lila came back almost immediately with their dessert—chocolate cream pie and two forks. "I thought this might be easier for you, Ruby...until you get the stitches out of your lip."

"That is so thoughtful of you, Lila. Thank you," Peanut said.

Ruby's fingers automatically went to her lip. It was healing. "Yes, thank you," she said.

"Welcome," Lila said. "Enjoy."

Ruby picked up her fork, cut the first bite, and then aimed it at Peanut's mouth.

"First bite and last bite will be yours tonight."

He didn't argue.

Ruby was laughing at him when she was struck by such a sense of sadness that tears suddenly welled. The feeling scared her, but she quickly blinked back the tears.

"Now my bite," she said, and dug in.

But the chocolate was bitter in her mouth, and it was all she could do to swallow it. She chased it with a drink of sweet tea and then let Peanut eat what was left.

Even after he walked her to her car and gave her a sweet goodbye kiss, she couldn't shake the feeling.

"Love you, darlin'," Peanut said. "Drive safe going home."

She had hold of both sides of his jacket as he bent down to kiss her goodbye.

"I love you too. Remember that. I love you too."

He laughed. "I'm not likely to forget, since it took me so long to get the guts to tell you how I felt."

"Right," she said, and laughed it off. Then she got in her car and drove out of the parking lot.

She glanced up into her rearview mirror and saw Peanut's car behind her. He turned off Main before her, and as his lights disappeared, the sadness struck her again.

She cried the rest of the way home.

———∿∿∿———

It was just before daylight when Gary Dye drove into Blessings, looking for the local motel. He'd seen a billboard with their name on it a couple miles back and was more than ready for a few hours of sleep.

The little town was just beginning to wake up. Lights were on in a cafe called Granny's, and the gas stations were open for business. There was a light on outside the police station, and one he could see inside through a frosted-glass window. He wouldn't be here long enough to worry about the cops.

When he saw the Curl Up and Dye hair salon, his heart skipped a beat. He knew Ruby used to be a stylist so that had to be hers! He sneered. She must have thought she was being cute by using his family name for a damn beauty shop. He'd soon put a stop to that.

A few minutes later, he drove up to the motel where he went into the office and signed a fake name. When the clerk asked for an ID, he gave her a long, silent look and shoved two one-hundred-dollar bills across the counter.

She took the money and gave him a room key.

"Two-thirteen, upstairs and to your left."

He grabbed the key without comment and headed for his room with dragging steps. He unlocked the door, then immediately locked it behind him before tossing his travel bag onto the table. He hung his coat over the chair and went to wash up.

The room was nothing fancy but clean enough, and he was tired. He checked the locks once more, took his pistol out of his bag, and laid it beside the bed, then took off his shoes and stretched out.

The mattress was lumpy. The coverlet smelled slightly of smoke despite the No Smoking signs all over. He fell asleep wondering how much Ruby's appearance had changed, and if he would recognize her.

Chapter 12

RUBY WOKE EARLY AFTER A RESTLESS NIGHT AND TOLD herself it was because she was home alone once more. But that wasn't the truth. She was still uneasy, which wasn't like her. So after breakfast, she called the pastor to get permission to use the church as a drop-off point for the clothing drive, to which he readily agreed. Then she made a flyer on her laptop about the clothing drive for the Conroy family, adding clothes and shoe sizes. She chose a bold typeface in an easily readable font, printed out fifty copies, and put them in a folder along with a roll of Scotch tape to take with her.

The next thing was her grocery list. She went through the refrigerator and the pantry as she wrote what was missing, then added some extras to make a special lunch for her and Peanut at noon, then she headed to the Piggly Wiggly.

As soon as she got permission, her first flyer went up on their public bulletin board, and after doing her shopping, Ruby stopped at Granny's to leave a flyer, and then at businesses along Main before she went to her salon.

She sailed in the back door with the folder and her tape dispenser and surprised the twins at work.

"I can't stay," she said. "I have groceries in the car. But I need to put one of these flyers on the front door, and then I'm going to leave the rest by the register for anyone to take."

"What's it for?" Vera asked.

"A clothing drive for a family in town. They lost everything when their house burned down."

"I didn't know about any fire," Vesta said.

Both of the clients in their chairs were curious as well.

"Remember the boy who put out the flyer about his dog?"

"Yes! That was the cutest thing," Vera said.

"As it turned out, it wasn't all that humorous. They have been suffering great hardship since moving here, and we didn't know. He was trying to earn money to feed his mother and little sister. Mabel Jean helped me shop for food yesterday, remember? Anyway…we've got most everything else covered for them except clothing. The sizes are on the flyer, and so is the drop-off point."

She went up front, taped the flyer to the front door, and then left the others by the register.

"I plan on coming back to work in a couple more days. I think my hands are healed enough now."

"I can shampoo for you for a while if that would help," Mabel Jean said.

"And I might just take you up on that," Ruby said. "So, got to go. I should get the food in the refrigerator. Call me if you need me," she said, and went out the door.

———∿∿∿———

Melissa Dean was up early as well, but from a little spurt of anticipation. As soon as the reading of the will was over, she was going to drop off the two job applications at the banks and then go home and pray for a miracle. She knew her landlord would let her slide for a month or so on rent until she could find a job, but she didn't want to be one of those middle-aged women who suddenly found themselves homeless. The thought terrified her.

Still, she took pleasure in fixing her new hairstyle, putting on a little makeup, and then dressing in her new outfit.

It was the first time in years that she'd actually worn a dress, and she felt half naked because her legs were showing above her knees. She had good legs to go with her slender body, but it still felt strange. When it was nearing time, Melissa gave herself one last glance, and decided the blue long-sleeved sheath had been a good choice. Satisfied with the new look, she put on her coat, grabbed her things, and left the house.

Rachel had hot homemade cinnamon rolls coming out of the oven just as the sisters came downstairs for breakfast. They were dressed for their meeting and looked very well put-together and in good moods.

"Good morning, ladies. Please have a seat."

They sat, appreciative of the hot coffee Bud was pouring into the delicate cups at their place settings.

"Good morning, ladies. Enjoy," he said.

"Everything smells wonderful," Wilma said.

Rachel beamed. She did take pride in what came out of her kitchen.

"Thank you," she said. "The chafing dishes are on the sideboard. Please help yourself, and let me know if there's anything else you need."

Betsy was the first to jump up and serve herself a freshly baked cinnamon roll. She picked up a small crystal bowl filled with fresh fruit, added fluffy yellow scrambled eggs with crispy strips of sugar-cured bacon to her plate, and went back to their table.

Loretta was right behind her and turned her plate upside down to see what company had produced it.

"I love this china pattern," she said, then filled her plate as well and carried it back to the table.

Wilma quickly joined her sisters, and they ate quietly for a few minutes until their immediate hunger had been sated. When they began their second cups of coffee, they started discussing the upcoming meeting.

"I wonder what the lawyer will be like," Betsy said.

Loretta shrugged. "Can't amount to much, seeing as how he practices law in such a dinky little town."

"I think Blessings is charming," Wilma said. "It feels like it would be a nice place to live."

"Well, you're not living here in Uncle Elmer's house unless you want to buy us out," Loretta snapped.

Wilma sighed. "It was a comment, Loretta. A simple comment. I have no intention of moving."

"Oh. Well, just so you know," Loretta said.

Betsy got up to get another cinnamon roll. "Anybody else want seconds on the cinnamon rolls?" she asked.

"I'll have another," Loretta said.

Wilma shook her head. "No, thank you."

And the meal moved on until they were finished.

"We need to get our bags in the car and get moving," Loretta said. "Don't want to be late. Rachel, is there anything we need to sign to check out?" she asked.

"Just stop by the desk on your way out. I'll have your final bills ready when you drop off your keys."

"Will do," Loretta said, and the trio got up together and left.

Rachel could hear them talking all the way up the stairs and then down the hall.

She cleared the table and was already at the desk when they came down with their bags, all except Loretta, who persisted in using the elevator to transport hers.

They gathered at the desk and handed over their keys.

"Do you want to leave the charge on the one credit card?" Rachel asked.

"No, we'll each pay for our room," Wilma said, knowing that her sisters would stick her with the bill if she didn't speak up because she was the one who'd reserved the rooms.

Loretta and Betsy pulled out their own cards, and Rachel printed a bill for each of them.

"Have a safe journey home, and thank you for staying at the Blessings Bed and Breakfast."

"You have a nice place," Wilma said, and then they were gone.

Rachel went to clean off the sideboard and put the dining room back in order as the sisters drove off to find the law office of P. Nutt Butterman, Esquire.

—∿—

Peanut was getting dressed for work, but all he could think about was how much he missed Ruby. He missed her spirit in his house, the sound of her voice, the hurried sound of her footsteps.

"But you're having lunch with her, so get a grip," he muttered as he stood in front of the mirror to put on his necktie.

Once he was satisfied with the knot, he put on his suit coat, glanced down to make sure his boots were shiny, and grabbed his briefcase on the way out the door.

Betty was already in the office when he got there. She handed him a stack of messages and a cup of coffee.

"Morning, Peanut. None of the messages are urgent except one. It's on top."

"Who's it from?" he asked.

"Niles Holland."

He frowned. "He knows better than to contact me. I'm representing his renter, not him. Please call him back and tell him that whatever he wants me to know comes through his lawyer," Peanut said.

"Yes, sir," Betty said. "I have everything laid out on your desk for your ten o'clock appointment and four chairs for the heirs. Will you need more than that?"

"No, just for the four women mentioned," he said.

"I thought some of them might be bringing spouses."

"I saw Elmer's nieces at Granny's last night, and they were alone. If we need more chairs, we'll get them later."

"Okay then," she said.

Peanut took everything into his office and sat down to drink at least a half cup of his coffee before he was ready to face the day.

———

The sisters were the first to arrive at Peanut's office and stopped at Betty's desk.

"We're here for the reading of our uncle's will. Mr. Butterman is expecting us."

"Yes, ma'am. One moment please." She called Peanut's intercom. "Mr. Mathis's nieces are here."

"What about Melissa?" he asked.

"Not yet," Betty said.

"Okay. Send them in."

Betty walked them to his door, knocked once, and then walked in with them behind her.

"Come in, ladies. Please have a seat."

The sisters froze in the doorway. It was the good-looking man from the cafe. He was the lawyer?

"Ladies?" Peanut said, gesturing toward the empty chairs.

They stumbled over each other to get inside and take a seat.

"I'm Loretta Baird. This is my sister, Betsy Lowe, and our youngest sister, Wilma Smith."

Peanut shook each of their hands. "It's a pleasure to meet you. Elmer was highly thought of here in Blessings. He will be missed."

"Yes, yes," Loretta said. "He was a dear man."

Betsy and Wilma gave Loretta a look, which she chose to ignore.

Peanut returned to his seat. "We'll start as soon as the other heir arrives."

"What do you mean, other heir? We're his only blood kin!" Loretta cried.

"Yes, ma'am, that you are. But blood kin do not automatically inherit. It is an individual's privilege to name anyone he or she so chooses to inherit their worldly goods, as I'm sure you know," he said.

Loretta's neck was red, and the flush was spreading up her cheeks. Her eyes had narrowed to little more than slits, and her nostrils were flaring with every breath.

Betsy was stunned. She hadn't seen this coming.

Wilma saw the look on Loretta's face and said nothing.

There was another knock at the door.

The sisters turned in unison to see what they already viewed as their competition.

"Melissa is here," Betty said, and stepped aside as Melissa Dean entered.

Peanut eyed her new look with appreciation, unaware of what brought it on.

"Good morning, Melissa. Have a seat. Now we're ready to begin."

Melissa slipped into the empty chair.

"Who's she?" Loretta asked.

"I was about to introduce everyone, Mrs. Baird. Melissa Dean, these are Elmer's nieces, Loretta Baird, Betsy Lowe, and Wilma Smith. They're sisters. Ladies, this is Melissa Dean, the woman who has been looking after your uncle since the death of his wife, Cora, fourteen years ago. She has continued to maintain his property for him since his move to the nursing home, and has visited him weekly for the past four years. Melissa was with him when he passed."

"My sympathies on your loss," Melissa said. "He was the dearest man, and I will miss him."

The sisters' mouths opened, and then, wisely, they shut them without uttering a word.

"Nice to meet you," Melissa added.

They blinked.

She sensed their hostility but didn't let it bother her. They'd been notified when their Aunt Cora died, and she'd seen the hurt on Elmer's face when they didn't show. Even though they were related to Elmer, they meant nothing to Melissa.

Peanut opened the folder and began to read.

The first couple of pages were standard wording; the next page listed the entirety of Elmer's holdings. As Peanut began reading them off, the sisters leaned forward, hanging on his every word.

He listed the house on four lots, a business called Mathis Dry Cleaners—still in operation and pulling in the income that had been paying for their uncle's care—and a checking account and a savings account together worth nearly two hundred thousand dollars.

The sisters exhaled as one when Peanut finished, and leaned back with smiles on their faces.

Peanut paused.

"I now have a personal letter that I am to read to his nieces, should they happen to appear. Melissa, this does not include you, so bear with me."

"Yes, sir," she said, expecting little more than a nominal sum as Elmer's way of a thank-you.

Peanut picked up a separate piece of paper.

"This is the original letter in Mr. Mathis's handwriting. It was written fourteen years ago, the week after his wife's death. I have a copy for each of you, along with a copy of the will."

He cleared his throat and began.

"Loretta, Betsy, and Wilma. You are the daughters of my twin sister, Ella, whom I loved with all of my heart. She and my love, Cora, were the dearest women in my life.

"When Ella found out she was dying, she confided in me that she'd instructed each of you to be sure to see to my welfare, and that I should rest assured that if I outlived my Cora, I would not wind up old and alone."

Wilma covered her face and started to weep, quietly but already suffering the guilt.

Betsy was ashen, and Loretta's shocked expression appeared to have frozen on her face.

"To my dismay, you did not live up to your mother's expectations, and when you ignored my dear Cora's passing after being notified, I realized you were not capable of living up to my expectations either.

"Therefore, I am officially relieving you of your guilt, along with any claims you think you deserve with regards to my property. You are each awarded one dollar, and not another cent more.

"Elmer Lee Mathis"

Peanut laid the paper aside.

"It was signed in my presence, in front of four separate witnesses from Blessings, including his doctor, who can testify he was sound of mind and body at that time; his banker; his pastor; and the manager of his dry cleaners. My secretary, Betty Purejoy, notarized it, and it has been in my file ever since."

He handed each of them an envelope. "Your copies are in there, along with your inheritance."

Melissa Dean was in shock. She was already starting to shake when Peanut picked up the will once more.

"Now I'll continue with the reading. *'I bequeath everything I own, save the three dollars awarded to my thankless kin, to a most kind and faithful woman, Melissa Dean. Thank you for your years of kindness, care, and devotion. It has not gone unnoticed.'"*

"Oh my God," Melissa whispered.

Loretta shrieked. "We'll fight this!"

Peanut arched an eyebrow. "Well, you'd just be

wasting money, because there's nothing to fight, Mrs. Baird. Mr. Mathis was of sound mind and body when he had me draw up this will. And unless you can show proof that his claims of neglect are untrue, you don't have a leg to stand on."

Wilma stood. "It's true. We neglected him. We ignored our mother's dying wish. We forgot he existed, and I'm ashamed that I did it. This dollar is more than I deserve."

She walked out of the office and didn't look back.

Betsy stood but was too ashamed to look up or speak and slunk out of the office to catch up with Wilma.

Loretta stood up. She was livid and unwilling to admit she'd gotten exactly what she deserved. When she took a step toward where Melissa was sitting, Peanut shot out of his chair. The tone of his voice was nothing short of furious.

"No, ma'am. I do not tolerate discord in this office. What happened to you has nothing to do with her. You dismissed an old man from your life, and that is on you."

Loretta pivoted angrily and strode out of the office with her head up, shaking with rage.

But the minute she joined her sisters in the car, they shut her down.

"I won't stand for this!" Loretta screamed as she jammed the key into the ignition.

"Shut up, Loretta! Shut the hell up!" Betsy shouted.

Loretta gasped. "But we—"

"We broke our vow to Mama. A vow we made on her deathbed," Wilma shouted. "We got exactly what we deserved. If you aren't calm enough to drive us home, then trade seats with me, because I have no intention of falling victim to bad behavior twice today. Now start the car and drive us home."

The truth of their situation finally hit home. Chastened and ashamed, Loretta buckled her seat belt and drove out of Blessings in silence.

But there was one more woman still in Peanut's office who was in shock. She hadn't said a word since his announcement and was still reeling from the news.

Peanut sat down in the chair beside her and grinned. "Are you all right?"

Melissa nodded.

He chuckled. "Surprised you, didn't he?"

She nodded again and burst into tears.

"I thought when Fred Bloomer let me go that I was in serious trouble, and all the while this was waiting for me," Melissa said. "Elmer saved me, Peanut. He saved me for certain. I've never owned a house in my life. Couldn't afford it. My old car is on its last legs, and now I have money in the bank. I have savings. I don't have to turn in my job applications. I am a business owner. Oh my God, I wish I could tell Elmer how much this means to me."

Peanut patted her on the shoulder.

"He already knows. It's why he named you his sole heir. He admired your work ethic and determination, and he loved you like a daughter, but he always said you worked too hard for too little."

Then Peanut gave her a handful of tissues.

"Now wipe your eyes and blow your nose. You need to go to the First State Bank. Herman Lewis knows you're coming. There are papers for you to sign to access Elmer's accounts, which will be transferred into your name. The people at the cleaner's will be relieved to know their jobs are secure. And I have just one more thing to give you."

"What's that?" she asked.

"I know you already have a key to the house, but this key was Elmer's. Now it's yours."

She recognized the old keychain with the tattered rabbit's foot dangling beneath the key. When Peanut dropped it into her palm, she curled her fingers around it and pressed it against her chest.

"Oh good grief! That pitiful rabbit's foot. I begged him for years to put what was left of that rabbit to rest. To bury it in the garden or something, but he would just shake his head and grin."

"Well, now it's yours, along with everything else. Welcome to your new life, Melissa."

She got up and then threw her arms around his neck and hugged him. "Thank you!"

Peanut laughed. "Hey, I'm just the messenger. You can thank Elmer tonight when you say your prayers."

"Oh I will. Sweet lord, so I will."

She left the office, laughing.

Peanut sat down on the corner of his desk, grinning from ear to ear as Betty appeared in the doorway. "That was one of the good ones, wasn't it?" she said.

"Yes, ma'am, it sure was."

He glanced at his watch and then picked up the first message on the stack and handed it back to her. "I've got another hour of work before I go have lunch with Ruby, so time to start returning phone calls."

"I called Mr. Holland. He wasn't trying to influence you after all. He said he was withdrawing his lawsuit against May Temple, fixing everything that is broken, replacing what is worn out, and reimbursing her for the cost of what was stolen. He said he will also be paying your fees on her behalf, assuming she withdraws her countersuit against him. He said you can verify this through his lawyer."

Peanut grinned. "Now that's what I call good news. I'll call his lawyer to verify, then call May and let her know. He's probably coming to realize that May Temple's countersuit against him is the one that's going to hold up in court."

Betty grinned.

"Today it's good guys, two. Bad guys, zero."

———∽∽∽———

Melissa Dean felt like she was floating.

It was all she could do not to giggle as she sat at Herman Lewis's desk at the bank signing papers.

Herman was happy for her and teased her gently when she handed back the last signed papers. "I suppose you won't be turning in that job application now?"

She grinned. "No, sir. I think I'll be devoting my time to running the dry cleaners."

"I'm very happy for you," Herman said. "Congratulations, and thank you for banking with us."

Melissa got up, clutching a small pad of blank checks to tide her over until her printed checks and debit card arrived in the mail. She drove straight to the dry cleaners, waited until the customer at the counter paid and left with his cleaning, and then grabbed the clerk by the hands, smiling from ear to ear.

"Can you call everyone up front for just a second?"

"Yeah…sure, I guess," he said. "What's this about?"

"The new owner."

"Oh God," he muttered, and went to the back, returning moments later with the crew on duty. "This is all of us except Martin, who's out sick."

"I don't know how to say this," she said.

"Oh God, please don't tell us we're fired," one woman said.

Melissa grinned. "To the contrary. Your jobs are secure, and the dry cleaners is staying open."

"Oh thank God," she said. "Who bought it?"

"No one bought it. Elmer named me his heir. I inherited it and his house. A couple of days ago, Fred Bloomer let me go. I got up this morning with very little money and no job, and now this has happened!"

They let out a whoop and cheers, both for themselves and for her, and crowded around her in relief.

Melissa kept laughing and talking and hugging them back. It lasted until the next customer came in to drop off some clothes. The fact that it was Fred Bloomer's wife seemed like kismet.

She saw Melissa and flushed, but Melissa surprised her. "Welcome, Mrs. Bloomer. You are my first official customer."

Mrs. Bloomer gasped. "What? What do you mean?"

"I learned this morning that Elmer Mathis named me his heir. I inherited his holdings, which includes the dry cleaners. Have a nice day."

Her employees were still shouting congratulations as Melissa walked out the door.

Chapter 13

THE SOUND OF SHATTERING GLASS AND A LONG STRING OF curse words were followed by a scream so shrill it woke Gary up.

Thinking someone was breaking into his room, he grabbed his pistol as he leaped from the bed. It took a few seconds for him to realize the noise that woke him was a couple arguing in the room next door.

"Shut the hell up!" he shouted, and pounded on the wall. The shouting stopped.

He glanced at the clock. It was too late for breakfast and too early for lunch, so he decided to settle for a fast-food drive-through. Since he was up, this was as good a time as any to reconnoiter. He combed his fingers through his hair and grabbed his coat, slipped the gun into the inner pocket of his jacket, and took his little travel bag on the off chance he wasn't coming back. He drove until he found a drive-in burger joint and ate like he was starving. Once he finished, his next move was to get a look at how the town was laid out. He needed to know streets—which way they ran, and the quickest way to get out of town.

Gary drove back down Main Street past a Quick Stop. They were all the same. Gas pumps, minimal groceries inside, free air. He grunted. Didn't see free anything much these days.

He passed the Piggly Wiggly, then checked out the

police station and the Curl Up and Dye again. In a town this size, a strange car and a stranger driving it would be noticed. Since he didn't want to advertise that, he headed for the residential area. He had a general idea of where Ruby's house was located from the GPS on his phone, but he wanted eyes on it to be sure. He found the street and then drove until he found the house, but he didn't slow down.

Next, he drove back to Main Street and then took the alley behind the Curl Up and Dye to check on the possibility of taking her out there. There was a big Dumpster just outside the back door that piqued his interest. A possible location for a surprise attack.

Then he drove back past her house to the end of the block and took the alley behind it. Ruby had a yard surrounded by a chain-link fence, and then an odd, narrow alley fenced off beside her house that ran all the way from the street behind her to the street in front of her. He didn't know what it was for, but it was too narrow for vehicles and would do him no good. She did have a small shed at the back corner of her yard. He couldn't get in it, but he could hide behind it in the alley.

He drove out and was getting ready to go back to the motel when he saw a woman in a white SUV turn into the driveway of Ruby's house. He tapped the brakes to see who got out, and when he saw the woman and all the bruises on her face, he almost didn't recognize her.

"Damn, little brother, you put the hurt on her. Shame you didn't finish her off yourself," Gary muttered, and watched as she carried what looked like grocery sacks into the house.

But now that he knew what kind of car she drove, he

took off to the motel. As soon as he got into his room, he used the motel phone to call the hair salon.

The call rang and rang, and just when he thought no one was going to answer, a woman picked up.

"Curl Up and Dye. This is Vera."

"I'm passing through, saw your shop, and was curious what time you open in the morning."

"We open according to how early we book appointments, but usually around eight a.m. Would you like to book an appointment?"

"If I do, I'll call back," he said, and hung up.

He sat a few moments, trying to decide if he wanted to wait until early tomorrow and take her out at the shop, or do it now. She was alone in that house. The longer he stayed in Blessings, the greater the risk. He wasn't going to take the chance of going to her front door. That would put his car and face in plain sight for a lot of neighbors. All he needed was something to get her to come out the back door of her house.

He could knock on the back door, but there was a good chance she'd look out first and recognize him, and that wouldn't fly. What could he do to get her to come out on her own without making any noise? And then it hit him.

He grabbed a washcloth from the shelf to use for a fuse, tossed the room key on the bed, and left.

Ruby came home with a roasted chicken from the deli to make chicken salad for her lunch with Peanut. As soon as she got the groceries put up, she put on a pair of disposable latex gloves to protect her hands and began taking the meat from the bones.

Doing normal things again felt good, and as she worked, she thought about Alice Conroy and her kids. She wondered if Alice was any better or getting sicker. She needed to find out.

As she finished deboning the chicken, she threw away the disposable gloves, washed up, and called the number on the flyer.

It rang a couple of times, and then she heard Charlie's voice. "Hello. This is Charlie."

"Hello, Charlie, this is Ruby Dye. I'm the lady with the black eyes, remember?"

Charlie chuckled. "Yes, ma'am, I remember."

"I called to find out how your mother is feeling. Is she any better?"

"Oh, yes, ma'am. She is feeling some better. Not coughing nearly as much. She's in the kitchen making us some lunch. Do you need to talk to her?"

"I won't bother her, but I want you to take down my phone number so that if any of you need help, you can easily reach me. If I can't help, I will find someone who can, okay?"

"That is so nice of you," Charlie said. "Just a minute, Miss Ruby. I need to find a pen and paper."

"I'll wait," Ruby said.

She heard him shuffling around, and then he was back. "I'm ready. Go ahead."

She gave him the number, and the number to her salon as well. "Just in case," she said.

"I sure appreciate it," Charlie said.

"You're welcome. And please let your mother know that there is an ongoing clothing drive in town to help replace the clothes you lost in the fire. We should have everything gathered up within a couple of days, and then we'll bring them over, okay?"

She heard Charlie sigh. "When I get me and Pitty-Pat some clothes, we get to go enroll in school."

"Well, today is Friday. We're picking up the donations on Sunday, so we should have everything brought to your house by that afternoon if not before. You should have plenty of clothes to choose from come Monday morning. How's that?"

"That is great news," Charlie said. "If I can ever do anything for you, promise to let me know, okay?"

Ruby grinned. "That's a deal, Charlie. Have a nice day."

"Yes, ma'am. Thank you again."

Ruby was still smiling when she disconnected and got back on task to finish the chicken salad. Then she glanced at the clock. Peanut would be here soon. She needed to hurry.

She had just finished the chicken salad and put it in the refrigerator to stay cool when she heard a knock. She shivered a little with anticipation.

He was here!

~~~

"I'm leaving for lunch," Peanut said as he passed Betty's desk. "I called May. She is overjoyed, so there's that. Now we need to file papers to withdraw the countersuit."

"I'm sure May is relieved. She's put up with a lot from him. I'll get the papers drawn up."

"Then I'll sign them when I get back."

"Yes, sir," Betty said. "Tell Ruby I said hello."

"I'll do that," he said, and left the office with a big grin on his face.

The day was milder than it had been in a while. The sun was bright, a nice reminder of the summer to come.

He hurried out of the office building, taking off his tie as he jumped in his car and headed to Ruby's, anxious to see her. He started to stop at the florist and take her some flowers, and then he changed his mind and kept going.

—◇◇◇—

Gary Dye drove up the alley that ran behind Ruby's house but parked a couple of houses down, using that owner's privacy fence to conceal his vehicle. He grabbed his gear and jogged back to her house, taking care to use the shed to shield his presence, and began putting together his version of a little firebomb, unaware Ruby had a guest already pulling into her drive.

—◇◇◇—

Peanut parked behind Ruby's car. He was elated at the thought of seeing her when he reached the front door and knocked.

Ruby came to the door smiling. He slid his arms around her as he stepped inside, then brushed a kiss across her lips.

"I hope you don't greet all your guests like this," he said, as he nuzzled the spot below her right ear.

She laughed.

"So, something sure smells good," he said.

"Lunch is almost ready. Follow me."

Peanut took off his coat, rolled up his sleeves, and headed to the kitchen.

"Chicken salad sandwiches," she said as she took plates down from the cabinet.

"Sounds good," he said, and went to the sink to wash his hands.

When Ruby turned around to get the sack of fresh croissants to make the sandwiches, she saw smoke drifting past the window, and seconds later, she heard sirens.

———

Gary Dye was satisfied with the little firebomb. It was a silent message to come out of the house, and he'd already seen Ruby moving back and forth through the window nearest the back door. She should see the smoke any time now.

He palmed his gun, ready to jump out from behind the shed the moment she came through the door. One shot, and he'd be in his car and gone before anyone saw the smoke.

———

Myra Franklin had gone home with what felt like the beginnings of a migraine, leaving her husband in charge at the flower shop. She took her meds, then went upstairs to her bedroom to lie down. She was getting ready to pull the shades when she glanced out and saw a man in the alley behind her house. He didn't look like anyone she knew. He wasn't wearing a company uniform, and he was down on his knees behind the shed in Ruby Dye's backyard. She couldn't tell what he was doing, but it looked suspicious.

With Ruby's recent kidnapping fresh in her mind, Myra thought better safe than sorry and was about to call the police and have them check it out when she saw the man stand up and throw something into Ruby's backyard. It took a second for her to realize what he'd thrown was on fire.

Myra gasped, ran over to the table to get her cell and dialed 911, and then ran back to the window.

Avery immediately answered the call.

"Nine-one-one. What is your emergency?"

"Someone threw a bomb into Ruby Dye's backyard and set it on fire! He's in the alley between our houses. Hurry. The fire is spreading! I don't know what he—" And then she gasped. "Oh my God. He has a gun! I can see it in his hand. Hurry. Hurry."

"Yes, ma'am, dispatching police and fire now. Stay on the line with me until the police arrive."

Myra moaned. She didn't want to watch for fear of what was going to happen next, but she was afraid to look away. She could hear Avery dispatching personnel to the scene and began to pray they would get there in time.

—∞—

Lon Pittman was on patrol when the call came in. An armed arsonist in the alley behind Ruby Dye's house?

What the hell?

He made a U-turn in the street, hit the lights and siren, and took off through town in a black-and-white blur.

Deputy Ralph was also on duty when he heard the dispatch. He hit his lights and siren, made a U-turn in front of the Blue Ivy Bar, and floored it.

The smoke from the burning grass in Ruby's yard was barely rising about the rooftops when the fire truck shot out of the station with its siren sounding a warning.

People all over town were either running outside or to their windows to look. That many sirens at once signaled danger.

———

Ruby ran to the kitchen window.

"My backyard is on fire!" she cried, and ran out.

Peanut heard the sirens at the same time he heard Ruby shout. He was two steps behind her as she ran out the door and was gaining on her when he saw a man suddenly appear in the alley on the other side of her fence. And then Peanut saw the pistol in the man's hand and leaped.

Ruby saw the man and, for a moment, thought she was having a bad dream. Gary Dye? Why was he here?

And then she was hit from behind in a flying tackle as Peanut grabbed her. At that point, if felt as if everything began happening in slow motion.

She heard a pop as she hit the ground. The impact knocked the breath out of her, and as she was struggling to breathe, she realized Peanut was on top of her and motionless.

Fear rolled through her in waves.

"Peanut! Peanut! Are you okay?"

Nothing.

"Peanut, what's…"

Something wet rolled down the side of her cheek. She touched her face, saw the blood on her fingers, and realized the pop she'd heard had to have been a gunshot. She screamed, and screamed again, then couldn't stop.

Gary Dye was in shock. He could already hear sirens and the smoke was just a wispy gray, barely visible in the air.

"How the hell?" he muttered, and swung his gun toward Ruby, only to see a man running right behind her. This wasn't going as planned, but he shot anyway because he knew they'd both seen him. He fired a heartbeat after the man took her down in a flying tackle. When the bullet meant for Ruby hit the man instead, Gary silently cursed in frustration.

Damn Jarrod and damn Ruby.

If he could start over, he would have ignored his brother's subtle message and let both of them rot. But it was too late to take all of it back, and now he couldn't see anything because of the smoke blowing in his face. Anxious to be gone, he ran away from the smoke to the other end of the yard.

Because he was taking aim, Gary never saw the cop who came running through the gate from the street. He never saw the gun in the cop's hand, and heard the shot only a second before a bullet went through his heart. He was dead before he hit the ground.

Lon Pittman saw him go down and could tell by the way he dropped that he was gone. He saw his deputy's cruiser coming down the alley toward the shooter as he ran toward Ruby. He knew she was alive because she was screaming, but he wasn't so sure about his friend.

He dropped down beside them and grabbed Ruby's arm.

"Ruby! Ruby! We're here! Help is here!" he said.

"Oh my God! Oh help him, please help him," she sobbed.

Lon checked Peanut for a pulse. It was there.

He grabbed his radio.

"This is Chief Pittman! I need ambulances to 312 Porter Avenue, ASAP. I have multiple gunshot victims."

Deputy Ralph came to a sliding halt in the alley beside the body and got out with his weapon drawn, then dropped to check for a pulse.

"He's dead," the deputy yelled, and then called dispatch to get more officers on the scene to work traffic.

The fire truck arrived, but when the firemen realized the blaze was small and there were injured people too close to use water and hoses, they grabbed fire extinguishers instead.

Ruby was covered in Peanut's blood and sobbing when Lon began applying pressure to the wound on Peanut's head, trying to stem the flow of blood.

"Ruby, are you wounded?"

"It should have been me!" she cried, and then began clawing at the grass, trying to pull herself out from under Peanut's body.

"Ruby! Answer me! Are you wounded?"

"No, no, no," she moaned.

Lon motioned to the firemen. "Hey, I need a couple of you guys to help me get Ruby free," Lon said.

Two of them rolled Peanut over just enough for another fireman to pull Ruby out. She got to her knees, then rocked back on her heels and reached for Peanut.

"Is he dead? Please God, don't let him be dead."

"He has a pulse. An ambulance is on the way. Are

you hurting anywhere?" Lon asked. "Your ribs, your chest? You both fell hard."

"No! He saved me and took the shot meant for me. Oh my God, oh my God, this can't be happening," she moaned. She wanted to hold Peanut, but he was too hurt and she was too scared he would die in her arms.

The EMTs came running past neighbors who were rapidly gathering at the gate. They took over for the chief, assessed Peanut's injury, and got him ready to transport.

Lon pulled Ruby to her feet and out of the way. "Can you tell me what happened? Did you know the shooter?"

"His name is Gary Dye. He's Jarrod's older brother," she said, swaying on her feet.

Lon caught her, then put an arm around her shoulders to steady her. "I'm sorry, Ruby."

"Is he dead?" she asked, staring across the black-ened patch in her yard to the body on the other side of the fence.

"Yes."

She shuddered, then realized the EMTs had Peanut on a gurney and were already moving him out of the yard toward the ambulance. "I want to go with him!"

"You can't," Lon said. "I'll take you to the ER."

She pulled away from him, running behind the gurney, past her neighbors who were calling her name, telling her they loved her, telling her they were praying for Peanut, telling her they would take care of things here.

She didn't see them. She didn't hear them. She didn't care about anything but Peanut.

The ride in the police car was a nightmare.

Lon drove with the lights flashing and the siren screaming, echoing the scream inside Ruby's head.

Word was spreading through Blessings faster than the fire Gary Dye had set. Half the people heard that Ruby and Peanut were dead. The other half heard one of them was dead and didn't know which one. But everyone knew that Chief Pittman took out the shooter.

Mercy Pittman was in a panic until she knew that her husband was safe.

Betty Purejoy locked up Peanut's office and went straight to the hospital.

Lovey drove to the ER to be with Ruby, praying the story she'd heard about Peanut's death wasn't true.

Vera and Vesta closed the Curl Up and Dye and headed to the ER, with Mabel Jean in her car right behind them.

The town was in an uproar as people headed to the hospital in shock. A prayer vigil began in the hospital parking lot, and the more people who arrived, the larger it grew.

Chapter 14

LON'S CAR WAS STILL ROLLING TO A STOP WHEN RUBY opened the door. He slammed on the brakes just as she jumped out and disappeared inside the ER.

"Good lord," he muttered as he parked and followed her inside.

He heard her voice before he saw her. She was arguing, telling the nurses around her that she wasn't hurt, and it wasn't her blood.

"Where's Peanut?" she cried, trying to push past them.

"They're already working on him. He's alive, and you need to let them do their job," a nurse said.

Lon put a hand on Ruby's shoulder. "Come with me, Ruby. You can't be with him right now."

She looked at him then, and the stark terror in her eyes nearly broke him.

"But what if he doesn't make it? I need him to hear my voice. I need him to follow it back to me."

Lon sighed. "Wait here a second," he replied, and walked away.

Ruby ignored what he'd said and followed, and when he found the right exam room, she pushed past him.

Peanut was motionless, oblivious to the meds they were shooting into his IV. He was already hooked to a heart monitor, and another machine was taking his blood pressure. He looked even taller than usual because his ankles and feet were hanging off the end of the exam table, and Ruby shuddered as she watched a tech positioning a portable X-ray machine over Peanut's head wound.

Oh God, please, God, don't let him die.

Lon pulled her back out of the way, but she didn't acknowledge his presence. Every ounce of her energy was focused on the man she loved. When the doctor left to view the X-rays, Ruby wanted to go to Peanut's bedside, but there were nurses all around his bed.

And then the doctor came back with the news.

"The bullet didn't fully penetrate the skull, but he has a small brain bleed and swelling. We'll monitor him to make sure it doesn't get worse. For now, he's going to critical care," the doctor said, and when they began wheeling him out of the bay, Ruby panicked and began running beside the bed, her hand on his arm.

"I'm here, Peanut. I'm here. I love you."

"No, ma'am, you can't go any further," someone said, and then they went through double doors and out of her line of sight.

Ruby didn't move. Couldn't move. And she couldn't stop shaking.

"Wake me up. Wake me up," she kept muttering. "This isn't real. Wake me up."

Then she heard Lovey's voice behind her. "It's me, honey. You need to come with me now."

Ruby turned, unaware tears were rolling down her face.

"Oh, Lovey, why doesn't God want me to be happy?"

Lovey grabbed her by the shoulders and pulled her into her arms. "It's not God doing this, baby. It's the devil in those men. God's got this. Peanut is going to wake up, and you two will live happy ever after."

Ruby let the words wash over her, willing them to be true.

———

The parking lot was packed with people standing silently, praying and waiting for word of one of their beloved residents. Peanut Butterman had done so much for so many, and now the people who cared for him were helpless to do anything for him but pray. They slowly learned the same thing Ruby had been told. Brain bleed and swelling, concussion…in critical care. They stayed praying, waiting for word that he had awakened, and were there when night fell.

Ruby was upstairs in the waiting room outside critical care, waiting for news as well.

The twins and Mabel Jean left to get Ruby clean clothes, but when they saw all the food that had been left out at her house, they put it up and cleaned the kitchen before they got her clothes.

Back at the hospital, Lovey took what the girls had brought and stripped Ruby of the bloody clothes and helped her into clean ones.

Ruby knew it was happening, but she couldn't focus enough to talk. She kept reliving the shooting, as if thinking of it enough would change the ending. Now she sat motionless in the waiting room, watching the door for someone to come jump-start her life.

———

It was midnight—the witching hour—when a nurse came into the waiting room.

Ruby wasn't alone, but she was the only one awake.

She stood abruptly, her hands fisted and motionless, as if she was going to have to fight her way to him.

"He's waking up," the nurse said. "You have five minutes."

Lovey woke and grabbed Ruby's arm. "I'm going with you. I won't say a word, but you're not going in there alone."

Ruby nodded, then followed the nurse. They moved past the other patients, ever mindful that Peanut was not the only resident of Blessings in critical condition, and then they walked into his room.

The nurse moved toward his IV to check the drip.

Ruby was trembling.

He was so pale and so still, that for a moment she thought they'd made a mistake. He wasn't waking up. If it hadn't been for all the machines beeping his life signs, she wouldn't have thought he was even breathing.

So she took a breath for him and moved forward. It wasn't until she put a hand on his arm and felt a muscle twitch beneath her palm that she knew he was still in there.

His eyelids twitched.

She stifled a quick sob. "Peanut, sweetheart…I'm here."

He took a deeper breath.

"Can you hear me? I love you, Peanut…so much."

His fingers twitched.

She waited, watching his eyelashes fluttering, fluttering, and then his eyes opening. She saw confusion in his eyes, then his gaze was going from ceiling to floor to the nurse and then to her.

"Hey, you," she said, and made herself smile.

His eyebrows knitted across his forehead. She thought it was from pain. She was wrong.

"Where?" he mumbled.

"You're in the hospital, but you're going to be okay."

The confusion on his face was turning to panic as he stared at the fading bruises on her face. "Who are you?"

She froze.

"How do I know you? Do you know my name?"

Ruby moaned.

The room was beginning to spin when she fainted in Lovey's arms.

Lovey sent a text to the chief, telling him Peanut had awakened without knowing who or where he was—and didn't recognize Ruby—and then she sent the same text to the girls in Ruby's shop. Within half an hour, the news had spread to the prayer vigil in the hospital parking lot. It was bittersweet, knowing Peanut was alive and going to recover, and yet unaware of who he was. The heartbreak for all of them was Ruby. In less than a week, she'd gone from terror to true joy to heartbreak.

One by one, they gathered up their things and started home—some walking, some driving, but all of them with the same guilty thought.

Thank God it wasn't me.

Ruby came to in the waiting room, curled up on a sofa with a pillow beneath her head and a blanket covering her body. Lovey was gone, but Vesta was there with a cup of coffee in her hand, standing at the window over-looking the parking lot below.

For a moment, Ruby couldn't think where she was, and then the dark, sick feeling returned as she remembered.

She pushed the blanket aside and sat up. "Why are you here?" she asked.

Vesta turned. "Because you are."

Ruby's lower lip trembled. "I don't know how to live with this," she said.

Vesta sat down beside her and took her hand.

"You don't live with it, honey. You set it aside and let it live on its own. Given enough time, everything finds its own level. He'll get better, and he'll remember. You'll see."

Ruby's eyes burned from crying. Her chest hurt—so much—like someone was standing on her heart. Earlier, Rhonda Bailey, one of the critical care nurses, had come out to tell her the doctor didn't want her to visit Peanut for a while. They couldn't tell her he would get better, and they couldn't tell her he wouldn't. Amnesia and head injuries were tricky. Right now, they didn't want him agitated.

She'd been banished.

She took a deep shuddering breath. "I want to go home now."

"I'll take you," Vesta said. "Do you want me to stay with you? I can."

"No. I need to be alone for a while. I need to figure this out. There's something I'm missing here...something God needs me to learn."

"But I don't—"

"I'll be fine," Ruby said. "Twice I should have died and didn't. I have a purpose here, and I'll find it. My heart is broken, but it healed before and it will again. All that matters is that Peanut is alive. I won't be selfish enough to ask for more."

Vesta was crying now. "I'm sorry. I'm so sorry."

Ruby closed her eyes, willing herself not to shed another tear. "Oh God, Vesta, so am I."

Vesta wiped away tears and got up.

"Well then, come on, honey. I'm taking you home."

Vesta drove without trying to strike up a conversation.

Ruby rode with her eyes closed, too wounded to look at Blessings because today had forever changed the way it made her feel. She'd been invaded here in the place where she had felt the safest. Not once, but twice. She needed to see the town in the light of day and hope it was still enough.

"We're here," Vesta said, as she slowed down and pulled up in Ruby's drive. "Here's your house key."

"Thank you for the ride. I'll see you in church Sunday. I need to pick up the donations from the clothing drive and get them to the Conroy family so Charlie and his little sister can enroll in school."

Vesta was speechless. Ruby was already thinking of others. Maybe that would be her salvation. She couldn't fix her world, but she could help others fix their own.

She waited until Ruby was inside the house and the door shut behind her. She continued to wait until she saw Ruby turn on the lights. After that, she drove away, too numb to cry.

Once again, Ruby's home had become a place of great
betrayal, and now she had to come to terms with it
before she could feel safe again.

The last happy place she'd been with Peanut was
in the kitchen, and so she went there, expecting ruined
food to still be on the table and dirty dishes in the sink.
Instead, it was as if the lunch she'd been making had
never happened. She suspected friends again, coming to
mop up the continuing mess of her life.

Ruby glanced at the clock. It was nearing four a.m. It
would be daylight all too soon. Twenty-four hours since
food had touched her lips, almost that long since Peanut
last kissed her, never imagining that it might be their last
kiss. And so being alone was her reality again.

She began going through the house like she did every
night, locking up, pulling shades, tidying up what had
not been put away. She would never have a baby to put
to sleep, but as the years had passed and the pain of that
had lessened, she realized she'd been putting the soul of
her little house to sleep instead.

Satisfied that all was well, and secure in the knowledge that there was no one left in the Dye family to come
after her, she got to her bedroom and stripped, took the
hottest shower she could bear, and then pulled back the
covers and crawled into bed, too exhausted to dry off.

The bed that used to be her sanctuary felt too big—
even empty. She grabbed the extra pillow and hugged it
to herself, then buried her face within the softness.

"Thank You for his life," she said, and closed her
eyes.

When she woke again, it was daylight and someone was knocking at her door. She lay there, listening until they stopped. She heard a car start and felt no guilt as they drove away. She glanced at the clock. It was after ten a.m., time to begin the day. The ache inside her was still there. Might as well get used to it because she didn't know how to turn off the pain of being banned from seeing Peanut.

A few minutes later, she was dressed and in her kitchen making coffee. She'd been all over the house and had yet to look out the kitchen window again. She didn't want to see the backyard. She didn't want to remember, but the horror of what had happened wasn't going to go away until she faced it.

Angry at Gary and Jarrod for bringing their ugliness and evil into her world, she yanked the door open and stepped out. The burned area was like a big, black spill of ink, and the scent of burned grass was still prevalent. She glanced toward the back fence, and for a moment, it was as if the energy of what had happened was still there…like looking at a shadow of the past. In her mind, she still saw Gary pointing a gun from the other side of the fence.

She pointed back.

"You're dead," she said, and went back inside.

Chapter 15

PEANUT KEPT DRIFTING IN AND OUT OF CONSCIOUSNESS. Every time he came to, it was triggered by the reality of pain, and the blessed numbness of pain meds put him out again.

Awake, the only emotion he had was panic. He knew he was in a hospital and that he'd been shot because his doctor had told him, but he had no memory of anything before waking up here. His doctor also told him that would likely pass as he healed, but the fear that it might not was there. Peanut was so focused on remembering himself that he hadn't been awake long enough to wonder if anyone was looking for him.

He was lost—as lost as a grown man could be.

No roots.

No identity.

Nothing to remember.

~~~

Ruby was holed up in her house, licking emotional wounds and preparing herself for the pity she was going to face. It was inevitable and nothing she could control. Yesterday had been a hell like nothing she'd ever known—worse than surviving Jarrod's beatings, far worse than being kidnapped, because people from *her* past had done this, and the guilt was eating her up. She'd begged God to save Peanut, and He had, but the cost of Peanut's life was the loss of his love. As much as it hurt, the relief of knowing he was alive was worth any amount of pain.

She wanted healing for him.

She prayed he'd get his life back.

And if she wasn't part of it, that would have to be okay.

―――

Melissa Dean had gone to sleep last night with the lightest heart she'd had since before Andy died. She'd walked around her house all evening, thinking about what she'd take with her and what she'd sell, because Elmer's house was totally furnished. The Mathis furniture was older, but it was nicer than hers. And she'd taken care of it for him for so long that it was familiar.

She'd thought about which bedroom she would choose as her own, wondering how she would feel about taking Elmer and Cora's master bedroom. But their sleigh bed was gorgeous and one of her favorite pieces in the house. Elmer would be laughing at her, telling her not to be such a goose. That was one of his favorite sayings. Just knowing there would be no more trips to Savannah to visit him made her sad, even though he would be closer when they laid him to rest right here in Blessings beside his sweet Cora.

When she finally gave up and went to sleep, it was deep and dreamless, but then she woke up at her usual time of six a.m. and frowned. Habit was going to be a hard thing to break. She could have rolled over and gotten a little more sleep, but she couldn't wait to go to Elmer's house—her house now. Seeing it as the owner would be far different than going there to clean.

She jumped up, showered, and dressed in record time, and then ate a bowl of cereal while making herself a to-do list for the day. Her phone rang while she was still eating. When she saw it was from Fred at the hardware store, she almost didn't answer, and then her manners overcame her reluctance to talk to him.

"Hello."

"Uh…hello, Melissa, it's me, Fred."

"I know who it is. Caller ID."

"Oh yes, right," he said. "I'm calling to apologize."

"Thank you. Apology accepted."

"Uh, well, I'm also offering you your old job back."

"No, thank you."

"I'm willing to give you a dollar an hour raise," he said.

"No, thank you," she repeated, then heard him sigh.

"Please, Melissa. I'm begging you."

"What happened to Tommy boy?"

"I caught him stealing, just like you said."

"That is not my fault, and your troubles are no longer my own."

"I'll give you a dollar-fifty an hour raise."

Melissa sighed. "Did you talk to your wife yesterday?"

He snorted. "Of course."

"And did she happen to mention seeing me in the dry cleaners?"

"No."

"Ahhh, that explains my confusion about why you think I'd be so desperate as to come back with my tail between my legs just to fix your problems…problems, by the way, that you created."

"What do you mean?" Fred asked.

"Yesterday I attended the reading of Elmer Mathis's will and found out that I am his heir…to everything. I now own a business that I will be running, and I own a house that is paid for, and I am financially set for life."

"You're kidding," Fred said.

Melissa's eyes narrowed angrily. "No, I'm not. You're going to have to hire and train a new employee, and be the one staying late and closing up for a really long time. It's called karma, Fred, and if your nephew wasn't a thief, and if I hadn't inherited Elmer's property, I'd still be out of a job and, pardon my bluntness, you still wouldn't give a shit. Have a nice day."

He was still talking when she disconnected.

She finished her cereal, put the bowl in the sink to soak, and then grabbed her heavy jacket and purse and headed out the door. All of a sudden, she couldn't get to her new home fast enough.

The day was cool and the sky was too cloudy for the intermittent sunshine to make a difference, but she knew it would be chilly in Elmer's house until the central heat warmed everything up, so she went through a drive-through to get a latte to take with her. When she parked at the property, eyeing it from the view of an owner, she could see the woodwork on the house needed painting. Time enough for all of that later, she thought, and grabbed her latte as she got out. The next-door neighbor came out on his porch again.

"Morning, Melissa. Are you going to keep cleaning the property now that Elmer's nieces inherited?"

She grinned. "Actually, as it turns out, they didn't inherit. I did."

A big grin spread across his face. "That is awesome!

I can't tell you how happy that makes me. When are you moving in?"

"Within the week, for sure."

"Well, I'm happy to have you for a neighbor," he said, and went back inside.

"And I'm happy to be here," Melissa said to herself, and headed to the front door.

She let herself in and then turned on the lights. The house was chilly, but it always warmed quickly. She took a quick sip of her coffee as she turned up the thermostat and started going through the rooms, eyeing furniture, trying to decide where she'd put any of her stuff, if she decided to bring it.

So far, the only things she intended to bring were her personal things, like clothes and pictures, and the things from her kitchen. The dishes she had were from her and Andy's wedding shower, and her stainless-steel flatware was a favorite. She would definitely bring that, along with her pots and pans and her big mixer.

She checked the linens, and decided to bring all of hers. Some of these were very worn. Then she made sure there was hot water, that the thermostat was working, and that all of the appliances in the kitchen were in working order.

She moved from the kitchen to the living room and then stopped near the fireplace and turned around, still marveling at her windfall.

"I'll be back," she said, and then left the house.

Next stop, the CPA who did Elmer's books. All she wanted him to know was that she wanted to keep him on the payroll, and she wanted a monthly statement outlining the incoming and outgoing money.

It was a fruitful morning.

It also occurred to her that she hadn't called Niles Holland, her landlord, to let him know she was moving. It had been years since she'd signed the lease, so there would be no problem moving when she was ready.

She sat in the car after leaving the CPA's office and gave Niles a call. As usual, he answered abruptly. He always sounded like he was angry, but she'd learned years ago that was just his way.

"Hello, Niles speaking," he said.

"Hi, Niles. This is Melissa Dean."

Niles was just getting over the mess he'd made with May Temple and wasn't going to fall into ignoring his duties again.

"Melissa! How are you? Is everything okay at the house?"

"Yes, it's fine, but I'm calling to let you know that I'm moving."

"You're leaving Blessings?"

She heard the shock in his voice and was somewhat comforted by the fact that people might actually miss her if she left.

"No, I'm moving into my new house. I inherited the Elmer Mathis estate."

"Well, congratulations! I can't think of anyone more deserving, and you certainly gave years of your life to his care. I will admit I'll miss you as a renter. You were one of the best."

"Thank you, Niles. I'm not taking the furniture, so I'll have to sell it before I can clean out the house."

"You're not taking any of it?"

"No. Elmer's house is furnished and I love the pieces."

"Would you consider leaving it behind? I can get more for a furnished house than I could an empty rental. You tell me what you need to get for it, and I'll write you a check."

"Yes, sure I'd leave it. That would certainly simplify my life. I'll figure up what I think it's worth and let you know. If you don't want it, no hard feelings. I'll just have a one-day sale and sell it from the property."

"Just give me a call," he said.

"I will, and thank you again," she said.

Melissa disconnected, then drove by the Piggly Wiggly to get some empty boxes for packing and headed home.

Chapter 16

RUBY COULDN'T FOCUS. HER HEART WAS BREAKING over what Peanut must be going through. She kept remembering the confusion and then the horror on his face when he said he didn't know his name.

Trying to stay busy, she started cleaning out the cutlery drawer, but needed scissors for the shelf paper, so she went to get the scissors, then saw dust on a bookshelf and began dusting, then decided to take the books out of the shelves and treat the wood. She went to get the lemon oil only to wander off and begin something else. All she knew to do was keep moving, staying one step ahead of losing it.

She turned on the television for noise and then forgot it was on. She kept moving from one room to another and still couldn't find enough to do to keep her occupied.

Hiding wasn't working out.

She was carrying a stack of clean bath towels into her bedroom to put in the master bath, got as far as the desk by the window, glanced out, and saw that damn patch of burned grass and lost it.

The pain in her chest was so sharp she thought her heart had exploded. She turned and threw the towels across the room, then began ripping the pillows from her bed, pulling the pictures from the wall and throwing them into the hall, oblivious to the sound of shattering glass. The rage inside her was choking—a strangling fist at the base of her throat that wouldn't let go.

"Give me a little taste of heaven, and then slap me down with it," she screamed and then started sobbing. "Yank my feet out from under me," she cried. "Give me hope, give me love, dump it all in my lap on Sunday, and blow it up in my face on Friday!"

She tore the covers from her bed and threw them across the room. Then she grabbed a jacket from her closet, her purse and keys from the hall table, and stormed out of the house.

There were things she'd planned to do today, so she was going to do them. People could stare, say anything they wanted, laugh at her, pity her… None of it mattered. Nothing could hurt her worse than she hurt right now. She got in her car and drove straight to the church. There were people in need. She couldn't help herself, but she could help them.

The small door in the back of the church was always unlocked during the day. It was close to the pastor's office, and the one everyone used throughout the week. Ruby strode into the church and down the hall with her head up, knocked once at the office, and opened the door.

Judy Frost, the church secretary, looked up.

"It's me," Ruby said. "I came to see where we are with the clothing donations."

"They're in the adult Sunday School classroom," Judy said.

"Thanks," Ruby said, and closed the door between them.

Minutes later, she was knee-deep in donations, sorting them into three piles…Alice, Charlie, and Patricia.

It was cathartic—folding little shirts, blue jeans, dresses and stockings, sweaters, blouses, pajamas, nightgowns. Ruby stacked the shoes on the floor beneath the pews where she was putting the clothes.

She started on Charlie's clothes next, and again began folding shirts and sweaters, T-shirts and jeans. Tennis shoes stacked. A pair of cowboy boots that she knew he would love. A coat, sock caps, gloves, even backpacks for both of them.

And last, the clothes for Alice. When she was finished, Ruby stepped back, not the least bit surprised by the generosity of the people of Blessings. She knew more clothes might be coming in, but there was no sense waiting to take what was already here.

Determined to stay moving, she started carrying things to her car, an armload at a time. It took her six trips. She stopped back at the office and opened the door.

Again, Judy looked up, and this time Ruby saw the pity in her eyes and it made her angry.

"I'm taking what's already here to the Conroys' house. If more comes in between now and tomorrow, I'll deal with it then. But they need this, and there's no sense making them wait. See you in church."

Then she was gone.

She drove up Main until she got to Carter's Gifts and went in. The owner was behind the counter, ringing up a customer.

"Hello, Erin," Ruby said.

Erin Solomon looked up. "Oh, Ruby, I'll be with you in a minute."

"I know what I want," Ruby said, and headed toward the back of the store where the children's toys were shelved.

Pitty-Pat needed a doll. Every little girl needed a

doll. Ruby looked along the shelf where the dolls were displayed. She picked out a baby doll wearing a pink nightgown and wrapped in a pink and white blanket. Then she picked out a couple of board games and an elaborate Lego set for Charlie to put together, and carried them all to the counter.

Erin eyed Ruby's face, started to make a comment, then caught a glimpse of the fire in her eyes and changed her mind.

"Will this be all?" she asked.

"Yes," Ruby said.

"Do you need them wrapped up for gifts?"

"No, thanks," Ruby said, and popped her debit card into the chip reader and signed her name.

She left the gift shop with her bags, tossed them into the front seat, and then drove to the Piggly Wiggly, knowing her presence would be all the encouragement someone would need to approach her, but the kids needed milk.

She got a shopping cart and went straight to the dairy case, grabbed a gallon of whole milk, swung by the makeup aisle, chose some makeup for Alice, went to the pet aisle and got a big chew bone for Booger. She was on her way to self-checkout when she ran straight into Rachel Goodhope.

Their gazes met, and to Ruby's relief, Rachel said nothing about what had happened. Instead, she pointed to the dog bone and grinned.

"I bet I know where you're going."

The smile on Rachel's face was the lift Ruby needed.

"Booger needs a little pick-me-up too, even though I came to get milk. With two young children, I didn't want Alice to run out."

THE COLOR OF LOVE   221

Rachel pushed her shopping cart aside and wrapped her arms around Ruby. "You have a loving heart, my friend. I want to be you when I grow up."

Ruby swallowed past tears. "No, you don't. I promise."

Rachel shook her head. "Yes. Yes, I do. I admire you more than any one woman I've ever known. You are a survivor, Ruby. You show all of us how to be in the world. Now go give Booger his bone, and let me know if that sad-faced dog can smile."

Ruby was smiling all the way through self-checkout and made it back to her car without losing her composure. She was thinking of little girls and dolls as she drove to their house at the edge of town.

Charlie was carrying a sack of garbage to the Dumpster when Ruby drove up. He saw her and waved, then dumped the garbage and came running back.

"Hello, Miss Ruby!"

"Hello, Charlie. I had some free time and decided to bring the clothes today instead of tomorrow. Would you mind helping me carry them in?"

"Oh no, ma'am, I wouldn't mind at all," he said.

Ruby opened the trunk. "Your clothes and Pitty-Pat's clothes are in here, along with shoes. Your mother's things are in the back seat, so don't mix them up, okay?"

"Okay," Charlie said. He grabbed an armful of clothes for his little sister and headed toward the house.

Ruby got the toys and groceries and walked in behind him.

Alice was smiling as she entered the living room with her daughter. "My goodness, what's happening now?" she said.

"Miss Ruby brought the clothes, Mama. Now we can enroll in school," Charlie said. "All of these here are for Pitty-Pat."

Alice clapped her hands. "This is wonderful. Wonderful!" she said, as Charlie carried the clothes into her bedroom and put them on her bed, then went back for more.

Ruby set her things down on the kitchen table.

"Alice, I worried you might be getting low on milk, so I brought another gallon."

"That is so thoughtful of you," Alice said, and put it straight into the refrigerator.

Ruby grinned at Pitty-Pat. "I also brought the kids a couple of things. Is it okay if I give them to Charlie and Pitty-Pat now?"

"Of course!" Alice said.

When Ruby took the doll out of the sack, the little girl squealed. The joy of seeing her face was something Ruby knew she'd never forget.

"She doesn't have a name, and she didn't have a home. I thought you might like to take care of her," Ruby said.

Pitty-Pat's eyes widened as she fell right into make-believe.

"She can live with me," Pitty-Pat said.

"Wonderful. What are you going to name her?" Ruby asked.

Pitty-Pat looked down at the baby, intently studying her face. "She says her name is Baby Sue."

"That's a good name," Ruby said. "Thank you for giving her a home."

The little girl nodded seriously and wandered off

into the other room, already talking to the baby as if it were real.

"Thank you for that," Alice said.

Ruby shrugged. "Truthfully, coming here today is what I needed. I also brought a few little things for you." She handed the sack of makeup to Alice.

"Oh dear lord, thank you so much," Alice said. "It's strange how a simple tube of lipstick can make a woman feel, isn't it?"

Charlie came into the kitchen. "I'm almost through, Miss Ruby. I still have to get the shoes."

"I brought you something, Charlie. I don't know if it's anything you'll like, but I didn't want to leave you out."

She handed him the sack with the two board games and the Lego set.

"Mama, look! Monopoly! Just like the one that burned. All of us play this game. Miss Ruby, thank you, and this other game looks fun too." Then he saw the Lego set and gasped. "Oh man...I always wanted one of these. Thank you, Miss Ruby, thank you," and for the second time that day, Ruby got a hug.

She was smiling through tears. "You're welcome, honey. Last but not least, this is for Booger."

Charlie grinned, opened the package, and immediately gave the bone to the big hound. Booger woofed then chomped down on it and carried it back to his bed.

"Now, how about I help you carry in the shoes?" Ruby said.

"I'm feeling much better. I'll help too," Alice said.

The last of the donations were carried into the house before Charlie disappeared with his new gifts.

Pitty-Pat was putting Baby Sue to bed on the sofa,

and Alice stood in the doorway, waving goodbye as Ruby drove away.

Ruby didn't want to go home. Instinct sent her to the Curl Up and Dye.

She came in the back door like always, surprising Mabel Jean and the twins, as well as their clients.

"Ruby!" Vera cried.

"You're just in time!" Vesta added.

"What do you need?" Ruby asked.

"Can you fill up the soap dispenser in the bathroom and put out some new toilet paper and a roll of paper towels? We've been so busy today that I haven't had a chance to catch up."

"Consider it done," Ruby said as she put her jacket and purse away, and went to work.

When she was through with that, she grabbed a broom and began sweeping up hair clippings, then got out a new stack of towels for the shampoo station. When the phone rang, she was the one who answered.

"Curl Up and Dye, this is Ruby."

There was a little gasp on the other end of the line, then a slight pause.

"Hello?" Ruby said.

"Oh, I'm sorry. I was just... Oh never mind. Hi, Ruby, this is Precious Peters. I need a new perm. This one has grown out to nothing."

"Just a minute. Let me get out my book, and I'll see what I have." She got her appointment book and flipped to next Tuesday. Her regulars were already penciled in, but there were plenty of gaps. "How about two p.m. on Tuesday?"

"That would be perfect," Precious said. "Thank

you…and Ruby…I'm glad you're feeling well enough to come back to work. We sure have missed you."

"Thank you," Ruby said. "It's good to be back."

She hung up the phone, ignored the ache in the pit of her stomach, and then made herself smile at the next customer who was coming in the door. And so it continued.

By the time the last client had been seen and the girls were cleaning up their stations to leave, Ruby felt like she'd never been gone.

"See you in church?" she asked as Mabel Jean was putting on her coat.

"No, I'm going to Savannah tomorrow. It's my granny's eighty-first birthday. We're all meeting at the nursing home to eat lunch with her."

Ruby smiled. "That's wonderful! Eat a piece of cake for me."

"I will!" Mabel Jean said, and waved as she went out the back door.

Vesta and Vera were putting on their coats as well. "Are you leaving now too?" they asked.

Ruby nodded. "Yes. The front door is locked, and I already made out the night deposit. I'll drop that by the bank on my way home. See you in church?"

"Yes, ma'am," Vesta said. "And let's all go to Granny's afterward."

"Yes, let's," Ruby said. "See you there."

They went out the back door.

Ruby heard their car start, and then they were gone.

She stood for a few moments, savoring the silence as she gazed around at her little shop and what she had created. Without planning it, somehow this place had become a place of shelter. The place where problems were shared and solutions made. A place where things that went wrong were made right.

It had healed Ruby once. She had to have faith it could do it again.

"See you next Tuesday," she said as she turned out the lights, and then she too was gone.

The last scans they'd run on Peanut's head were encouraging. The brain bleed had stopped, and the swelling was beginning to go down as well. The nurses continued to wake him at intervals because of the concussion, and every time they did, they asked him simple questions, like "What do you remember?" and "Do you know who's president?" and "Do you know how old you are?"

Every time, he would ask them his name, and each time they told him, he thought they surely were making a joke.

Paul Quick came in that evening making rounds and woke Peanut up.

"Good evening," Dr. Quick said. "How do you feel?"

Peanut was sick of that question.

"The same," he mumbled. "I hurt and can't remember stuff."

"Well, that's not unusual, considering your injury. I have confidence that will change with time."

"What's my name?" Peanut asked.

Dr. Quick grinned. "Peanut Butterman."

Peanut frowned. "Not funny," he muttered, and closed his eyes.

Dr. Quick chuckled and patted him on the shoulder. "When you remember, you'll realize we're not kidding you, son. Just rest. If you continue to progress, we'll move you out of critical care into a regular room soon."

"Am I married? Do I have a family?" Peanut asked.

The doctor frowned. "No, you aren't married, and you have no family."

Peanut's eyes filled with tears. "I don't matter to anyone?"

The doctor sighed. "That's not entirely true. You have a girlfriend."

Peanut's heart skipped a beat. There was someone who knew him well enough to have real answers. "Then where is she?"

Quick hesitated, then confessed.

"She was here the first time you woke up, and you were so upset I told her not to come back for a while."

Peanut didn't like that."Wanna see her."

"I'm not sure if—"

"Wanna see her, damn it," Peanut muttered.

"Then I'll give her a call," the doctor said. "I'll leave word at the nurses' desk that she will be allowed to visit now."

Peanut sighed again, his eyes already closing.

"Stupid decision," he muttered, and then he was out.

Dr. Quick grinned.

"Your opinion has been noted."

———∾∾———

Ruby stopped at Broyle's Dairy Queen and ordered a burger and fries, then drove home in silence, dreading the moment she had to go inside.

She pulled up into the driveway, and then grabbed

her things and the keys and let herself in. She left the food in the kitchen and went down the hall, wincing at the sight of the broken frames and shattered glass.

She stepped across the threshold into her bedroom, her shoulders drooping in defeat at the sight of what she'd done.

"I owe you an apology," she said. "I'll be back in a little while to fix this."

Then she went back to the cooling food, put her burger and fries on a plate, grabbed a glass of iced tea, and took the food to the living room to watch TV.

She ate without tasting it, trying to fill up the empty feeling in her heart by filling her stomach, but her food choice had not been wise. She nibbled at the burger so she didn't have to open her mouth too wide, and then finally gave up, took it apart and ate the hamburger patty by breaking it up and nibbling on the bite-size pieces, along with eating some of the fries.

Finally, she gave up and threw the rest of it in the garbage, then gathered her cleaning equipment and went to put her little house back in order.

She worked through each task in a slow, methodical manner, beginning with sweeping up the glass and throwing away the frames and pictures. There was nothing personal about any of it, and she didn't want to look at them again.

She had to remake the bed one layer at a time—from the mattress cover to the sheets, then the blankets, all the way to the old bedspread—before she tucked in her pillows and refolded the bath towels. The last thing to do was what she'd come to do earlier—put the bath towels away.

Afterward, she sat down on the side of the bed, trembling from emotional exhaustion and trying to talk herself out of church tomorrow, then remembered she'd already made a date with Vera and Vesta to go to Granny's after church—the same date she'd made with Peanut a week ago today.

She shoved her hands through her hair, then headed for the bathroom, to the mirror above the sink. She eyed the three little stitches in her mouth, got her manicure scissors and tweezers and washed them in alcohol. Then before she could change her mind, she leaned in closer to the mirror, cut the first stitch and removed it with the tweezers. It stung enough to make her eyes water, but she kept going until they were gone.

She laid everything down and looked at herself again, then smiled. The simple removal of those stitches was another step in putting the past behind her.

Her gaze moved from her mouth to her hair and how Peanut had pulled it away from her face. She closed her eyes, remembering...

You are the color of love to me. I don't care what you do with your hair.

She looked at herself again, ran her fingers through her hair, backed away a couple of steps and narrowed her eyes for a different view, then headed for the storage cabinet in the utility room.

She began going through the tints and the dyes, picking one up and then putting it back and looking for another. She was still undecided when her cell phone began to ring. She put down the box she was holding and ran to the living room to answer.

"Hello?"

"Ruby, this is Dr. Quick."

"Oh my God," Ruby moaned and sank to her knees as her legs went out from under her. "What happened?"

"Oh…I'm sorry, nothing, nothing. I didn't mean to scare you. I wanted to give you an update on Peanut's condition. The brain bleed stopped. The swelling in his brain appears to be going down. He still has no memories but is communicating well when we wake him."

"Oh, thank God," Ruby said. "Thank you for letting me know."

"There's a bit more. He has asked if he has family. I told him no, which seemed to make him sad. He asked if there was anyone who cared about him. I told him that he has a girlfriend. He asked why you hadn't visited. I told him that you had been there once when he first awoke, and that he was so upset I asked you not to visit. He was not happy with me, so I told him that I would let you know you could visit now."

Ruby started to cry.

"Oh, thank you, thank you, Dr. Quick. The last two days have been the worst two days of my life…even worse than being kidnapped."

"I'm sorry," Dr. Quick said. "I had no intentions of hurting you. I was so focused on making sure that he didn't cause himself harm by getting upset."

"I understand. So are you saying I can visit any time now?"

"Yes. I told the nurses you were allowed, but not tonight, okay? I want to give him one more night of rest."

"Yes, okay," Ruby said. "Thank you for calling."

"You're welcome. Have a nice night," the doctor said, and hung up.

Ruby pulled herself up and took a deep breath.

"Thank you, Lord," she whispered. She dropped the phone onto the sofa and headed back to the storage cabinet. In a matter of six days, life had yanked her through hell backwards. It was time to turn herself around.

She shoved all of the boxes to one side and grabbed the one in the back corner, took out a pair of latex gloves, her coloring equipment, and a large plastic cape, then headed for her bathroom. This was probably going to set all of the churchgoers on their ears tomorrow, but they'd already seen the ugly part of her past. A new hair color wouldn't be that unusual for her, even if they'd never seen it like this before.

She took everything out and laid it on the bathroom counter, fastened the cape around her neck, and opened the box. The last thing she did right before she started was put on the gloves.

"Here we go again," Ruby said, and reached for her hair.

Chapter 17

PEANUT WOKE WITH A START, HEARD A RHYTHMIC BEEP, FELT the blood pressure cuff beginning to tighten around his arm to take another reading, and thought—*hospital*.

Through the glassed-in front of his room, he could see the circular nurses' station in the center of the unit and the nurses who came and went. He wondered if he knew them from before, or if they were only familiar now because they were the faces he'd seen most recently.

He groaned as he closed his eyes, trying to get past the pounding headache, but when he did, he began to see other faces flashing before his eyes. People sitting in chairs in two rows, one row elevated above the other. Some of the people were motionless. Some were frowning. But they were all staring at him. He didn't know what that meant, and he didn't recognize any of them.

A nurse opened his door and came in to check his vitals and readjust the drip in his IV.

"How do you feel?" she asked.

"Head hurts."

"I'll get you something for that."

"Can I have water?"

"Yes, of course," she said, and poured a little from his water pitcher into a glass and held the straw as he took a couple of sips. "Enough?" she asked, when he stopped.

"Yes. Thanks. What day?" he asked.

She smiled. "It's Sunday…early Sunday morning."

"Church," he muttered. The thought made him anxious, like there was some place he was supposed to be, and then he let it go and fell back into the void.

The nurse left to get his pain meds. He was asleep when she came back. She injected the medication into his IV, and then closed his door on her way out.

Ruby was dressed except for her shoes and taking one last look at herself before leaving the house. As far as she was concerned, her new hair color was a success, and the bruises on her face had faded enough that makeup concealed a good portion of them.

She'd pulled her hair back from her face and fastened it to the top of her head, leaving the rest in a jumble of loose curls. She frowned a bit with regard to the pantsuit she'd chosen to wear, afraid she'd jumped the gun on spring, but then she decided she didn't care. It looked good with her hair and her complexion, and that was what she was going for.

After dinner at Granny's with the twins, she was going to see Peanut, and she wanted to look pretty for him. Even if he didn't remember her, he could still appreciate her appearance.

She straightened the collar on her white turtleneck sweater, picked a piece of lint from the sleeves on the hot-pink jacket, then left to go get her shoes—dressy flats as black as her hair. She grabbed her purse and keys, and headed out the door.

The sun was shining. The air was still as she started

down the steps. A few houses up and on the opposite side of the street, Arlene Purejoy came out of her house, also on her way to church. She saw Ruby about the same time as Ruby saw her.

Ruby smiled and waved.

Arlene lifted her arm to wave and then zeroed in on Ruby's hair and that hot little body in the hot-pink pantsuit and forgot what she was going to do. She was still standing in the yard with her arm in the air when Ruby drove past.

Ruby waved again, then giggled all the way to church.

The reactions as she walked into church were no different. Between the frowns, the double takes, and a few thumbs-up, she made it to the pew where she always sat, slid in beside Vera Conklin, and then poked her.

When Vera turned to say hello, Ruby winked.

Vera's eyes widened, and then she began to grin. She elbowed her sister, Vesta, whose reaction was the same.

Ruby leaned in and lowered her voice. "Dr. Quick called me last night. They think the swelling is going down in Peanut's brain, and I get to go see him now."

"Oh, honey! That's wonderful!" Vesta said. "I wonder what he'll think of the new you."

"He doesn't remember the old me, so I doubt it's going to make a difference one way or the other," Ruby said. "I did this for me."

The woman in the pew behind them leaned up, tapped Ruby on the shoulder, and whispered in her ear," Love your hair."

Ruby turned around and smiled.

Rachel Goodhope was grinning at her from ear to ear. "I also love your spirit," she said, and then settled

back as the organist struck a chord—the signal that services were beginning.

Ruby sang with the others, bowed her head in prayer,
sat at perfect attention as the pastor delivered the sermon,
and when it was all over, didn't remember anything that
had been said. She'd been having her own conversation
with God about giving Peanut back to himself.

Ruby checked on the clothing drive, but there had
been no more donations. Unwilling to entertain anyone
else's curiosity, she made a beeline for the parking lot
and went to meet the twins at Granny's. Her entrance
made heads turn, but she wasn't interested in their opin-
ions as she slid into the booth.

"We already ordered you sweet tea," Vera said.

Ruby gave her a thumbs-up.

"I know Peanut doesn't remember us, but tell him
anyway that Vera and Vesta Conklin send their love and
prayers," Vesta said.

"That is so sweet. I will do that," Ruby said.

"Do you have any updates on the Conroy family?"
Vera asked.

"Yes. I saw them yesterday when I took fresh milk
and the donated clothes. They were so appreciative of
the help. I still can't get over that boy, Charlie. He's
going to do something special with his life. I can feel it."

"We kept that flyer," Vesta said. "I'm thinking about
framing it and hanging it in the kitchen to remind me to
be grateful every day for what we have."

Vera leaned across the table and lowered her voice.

"We've decided we're going to take a cruise this
summer. It'll be one of those five-day ones, so we won't
be gone all that long, but after what happened to you, we

realized how quickly a life can end. We don't want to have regrets."

"That is a wonderful idea," Ruby said. "Where are you going to go?"

"We don't know yet. We're still deciding. Oh, here comes our waitress. Mum's the word," she hissed.

Ruby laughed.

"My favorite hairstylists ever!" Lila said as she swung her tray around and put their drinks on the table, along with a basket of biscuits. "A little something to get you started. Do y'all know what you want?"

"What's the Sunday special?" Vesta asked.

"Turkey and dressing, two sides and dessert."

"We'll have that," Vesta said.

"Me too," Ruby added, and then grabbed her little bread plate and reached for a biscuit as Lila left to turn in the orders.

The food came quickly as the cafe filled up, then spilled over into the extra dining room, which usually happened on Sundays.

Ruby picked at her food, stirring it around some to make it appear that she'd eaten more than she had, grateful for the company. But there was a knot in her stomach that wasn't going to go away anytime soon. The truth was that Peanut was where he was because he'd taken the bullet meant for her.

—⁓—

Ruby's hard-soled shoes made little *clip-clop* sounds on the tile as she entered the hospital, moving at a speed just shy of jogging on her way to the elevator.

When she finally got to critical care, she paused

long enough to take a deep breath, and then entered the double doors and headed straight to the nurses' station.

Rhonda Bailey was on duty again and glanced up, then did a double take.

"Ruby! I love your hair!"

"Thanks," Ruby said. "Okay if I go in?"

"Yes. He's in and out, so don't worry if he falls asleep. He'll wake back up if he hears a voice."

"Okay," Ruby said, and circled the station to get to Peanut's room.

She could see him even before she entered, and said a quick prayer that whatever happened today gave him some measure of peace. Then she pushed the door inward and went inside. Her heart was hammering as she reached his bedside. She put her purse on the chair, eyed the bandage pad on the side of his head, and then touched his arm.

His eyes opened almost instantly. Again, she recognized his confusion, but she wasn't backing down from her role in his life as she leaned over the guard rail and kissed his forehead.

"Hello, you. I'm Ruby," she said, and then took him by the hand.

His fingers tightened instantly. "Are you my girl?" he asked.

She nodded.

"I don't remember," he said.

She cupped his cheek. "It's okay. I remember for the both of us."

He kept looking at her face, at her hair, at the bright pink color she was wearing.

How the hell did I forget someone like this?

"What's my name?" he asked.

She'd prepared for this before she left home. She pulled his business card out of her pocket and handed it to him.

He read it aloud. "P. Nutt Butterman, Esquire? What kind of a name is that?"

"It's the one your parents gave you," she said.

"This isn't a joke?"

"No joke. You go by the name Peanut."

"I thought they were kidding me," he muttered, and then his eyelids closed as he took a deep breath. "That's not even funny. What the hell were they doing, smoking pot when they named me?"

She laughed, and the sound pulled him back.

"That's what you always say," she said.

"Really?"

She nodded, then tapped a finger lightly on his chest. "See, you're still in there. You're just waiting until it feels safe to come out."

He touched her forehead, then very gently beneath her eyes.

"What happened here?"

"Oh…it's all tied to what happened to you and for another day, and we're moving on to a better subject. Dr. Quick said you're getting better."

He looked at the business card again. "Esquire? Am I a lawyer?"

"Yes, the only one in Blessings and very well-loved. And speaking of love, Vera and Vesta Conklin said to tell you to get well and they're sending their love."

"Who are they?"

"Two stylists who work in my hair salon."

His gaze went straight to her hair again. "You make a good advertisement for your salon."

She smiled. "Why, thank you, kind sir."

He was quiet again.

"That felt strange."

"What did?" she asked.

"Like I just flirted with a stranger."

"But I'm not a stranger, and your heart already knows that."

His eyes closed again, and his fingers went limp around her hand.

She let him go and quietly pulled the chair up to his bed. The fact that he didn't know her didn't daunt her one bit. That one comment about his name just confirmed that he was still Peanut.

A few minutes passed and then he opened his eyes, saw her watching his face, and almost smiled.

"You're real. I thought I dreamed you."

She stood. This time he reached for *her* hand.

"Where do I live?"

"In a very pretty house here in Blessings."

"Do we live together?"

"No, but I have spent time at your house when I was first healing from this."

He was silent again as he studied her face. Then he spoke abruptly, as if he'd been holding in the thought too long. "Have we made love?"

She leaned close, whispering near his ear. "Yes. We are quite wonderful together," she said softly, then kissed the side of his cheek.

His eyelids fluttered again, but he was smiling.

"You need to rest now. I love you, Peanut, and I'll come back tomorrow."

He opened his mouth as if to speak, and then couldn't stay awake long enough to say anything.

She backed away from the bed and left his room, more at peace than she had been since this whole awful thing began. On the way home, she stopped off at the Piggly Wiggly, for the first time in two days buying for herself and not someone else.

She started down the fresh produce aisle, looking for inspiration as she shopped, and then she sensed she was being watched and turned around.

Luwanda Peoples was staring at her.

Ruby waved, and went back to looking at lettuce. Moments later, Luwanda had pushed her shopping cart right up beside Ruby's.

"I swan...I almost didn't recognize you," she said. "After your past came back to haunt you and all."

The comment was hurtful, but not surprising. Luwanda considered herself part of the Blessings elite since her second husband was on the city council.

"My past? You surely aren't referring to my ex-husband because you have an ex-husband too. Right? The one who went to Vegas and lost your home in a poker game?"

Luwanda's neck broke out in red splotches that spread to her face. She was mad, but so was Ruby, and she kept on talking.

"I cannot imagine why I am suddenly so unrecognizable. I know it's not because of my hair because I change my hair color at least twice a year, and you know it." Then Ruby took a step closer, lowered her voice, and said, "Remind me next time you come in, and we'll trim up your nose hair again."

Luwanda felt her nose, then moaned beneath her breath and scurried off, pushing her cart toward the checkout at breakneck speed.

Ruby rolled her eyes, muttering to herself as she put a head of lettuce in her cart. "You brought that on yourself, Luwanda Peoples. I do not have the patience for hatefulness."

She added a bunch of green onions, a carton of grape tomatoes, and a yellow squash to her basket, along with a sack of red potatoes, and then she moved to the baking aisle. Tomorrow was Monday, which meant the shop would be closed, but come Tuesday, she was going back to work and wanted some food on hand at home that was already cooked. After adding a brownie mix, she got eggs, a couple of different cuts of meat, and a gallon of milk, then went to check out. She purposefully went to Gladys Farmer's line because she was such a nice person.

"Good to see you out and about, and I just love your hair color," Gladys said. "How's that sweet man of yours?"

"Thank you, and Peanut is doing okay."

"Well, you tell him we're all rooting for him to get better."

Ruby smiled. "I sure will," she said, watching Gladys scan her purchases.

Then she paid and left, anxious to get home before she ran into any more critics.

Melissa Dean had moved everything she wanted to take to her new home, and now she was done. She'd waited until the last trip to bring the food from her pantry and refrigerator and was in the kitchen putting it all away. Once she was finished, she stopped in the middle of the kitchen floor and hugged herself in thanksgiving.

"Oh, Andy, just look at this beautiful old home. I can't believe it's mine," she said, and then moved to the kitchen window to look out at the overgrown garden in the backyard. "It is a mess out there, but nothing that can't be fixed."

She sat down at a chair by the kitchen table and called her old landlord, Niles.

"Hello, this is Niles."

"Hi, this is Melissa. Just wanted you to know I am officially moved. I took my clothes and personal belongings. Everything else I owned is still in the house except my linens, the dishes, flatware, and cookware. I cleaned out the refrigerator and pantry, so you're good to go. I'll get the utilities changed tomorrow when everything opens up, and I left my house keys on the kitchen counter."

"Have you decided what you want for all of your household stuff?"

"I think five thousand is a fair price. If you had to furnish it yourself, the kitchen appliances alone would be more than that."

"Yes, that's fair. I'll put a check in the mail to you tomorrow at Elmer's address."

"Which reminds me," Melissa said. "I also need to stop by the post office and fill out a change of address so my mail will get forwarded."

"Enjoy your new home," Niles said, and disconnected.

Melissa laid down her phone, then picked up the

framed photograph at the end of the table and took it upstairs to her new bedroom.

"This is it, Andy," she said, as she put their wedding picture on a dresser, then gestured toward the elegant old sleigh bed with the royal-purple comforter. "What do you think of this bed? Isn't it amazing? We could have made such wonderful love here."

Then she poked about in the closet, eyeing all of the things of Elmer's she would have to donate. It was going to take a while to move one life out and another life in, but she was grateful Elmer had given her this opportunity.

—∿∿—

Alice Conroy was in the kitchen finishing Sunday dinner. She turned off the fire under the Hamburger Helper version of beef Stroganoff she'd just made, and then gave her sweet tea a final stir to make sure the sugar had all dissolved.

She had opened a can of corn and heated it on the stove to go with it, and dinner was done. The fact that she had food to cook was such a blessing that she had enjoyed the task.

"Dinner is ready! Go wash your hands," she called out, then grinned at the sound of running footsteps as Charlie and Pitty-Pat bolted toward the bathroom at the same time. She knew Charlie would end up making sure Pitty-Pat actually washed.

She took their plates to the stove to fill. She didn't have bowls to dish up the food, and only had these three plates because May at the Blue Ivy Bar had given them to her when they first moved in, along with one paring knife.

Charlie came into the kitchen carrying his little sister piggyback, then plopped her down in her chair.

"Can I help you, Mama?" Charlie asked.

"You can put some ice in the glasses for the sweet tea."

"Yes, ma'am," Charlie said. After he dropped the ice into the glasses, he filled them with tea before carrying them to the table, putting them down beside their old forks and spoons.

Alice put a plate of food at each chair, then sat down with her children.

"Who wants to say the blessing today?" she asked.

Pitty-Pat's arm went up.

Alice nodded, then they all bowed their heads.

The little girl's voice rose on one word and fell with the next, just like the pastor at their old church used to preach.

"Thank you for our dinner, God, 'cause lasterday we didn't have nothin' to eat. Amen."

Alice sighed. "Amen," she echoed.

Booger woofed.

They laughed at the timing. It made it seem as if the dog had echoed his own version of an amen. And then they began to eat, quietly at first because hunger was still a scary thing and the urge to fill up that well was part of self-preservation. But after a bit, the urgency eased.

"Mama, now can we enroll in school tomorrow?" Charlie asked.

"Yes, but we'll have to walk. Once I get you enrolled, they'll be able to bring you home on the bus, and then you two can catch it from here every morning after that."

"I don't mind, Mama. Don't worry. If Pitty-Pat gets tired on the way, she can ride on my shoulders."

Pitty-Pat frowned. She was a first grader and was just

getting used to being in a school when their house had burned down.

"Mama, how will I know which bus to ride?"

Charlie reached over and tickled her ear. "You don't have to worry about that because you have me. I'll find you every day after school, and we'll be on that bus together."

"I can sit with you and everything?" she asked.

"Sure. But I bet you're gonna make new friends so fast that you'll be sitting with them instead of me."

She giggled and took another bite. "Mama, this hamburger stuff is good," she said.

"Yes, Mama, everything is good. Thank you for making it for us," Charlie said.

"You're welcome," Alice said. "We have some kind ladies to thank for this food, don't we?"

"Yes, ma'am," Charlie said.

Pitty-Pat giggled. "I'm thankful for food *and* for Baby Sue."

They smiled, and there were a few moments of silence, and then Pitty-Pat spoke up again. "Mama, I want to wear those new jeans and my new blue sweater tomorrow."

Alice grinned.

"And so it begins. The bane of all women every day of their lives... What am I going to wear?"

Jarrod was still in jail in Atlanta, awaiting transport to a federal prison. A preacher had showed up early this morning and preached a little sermon in the walkway between the cells, then asked if any of them wanted to confess their sins and get right with God.

Jarrod thought about it, but the truth was, if he confessed all of his sins, he might wind up with more charges added to his case, so he sat on the side of his cot staring down at the floor instead.

The morning passed slowly. With absolutely nothing to do, he stretched out on his cot and fell asleep. He woke up a while later with his belly growling and was wondering what passed for Sunday dinner here, when he heard the footsteps of several people. Curious, he sat up, then was surprised when they stopped in front of his cell.

He saw the jailer and a man in a suit who looked suspiciously like a fed.

"Jarrod Dye?" the stranger asked.

"Yeah, that's me," he said.

"Step forward," the jailer ordered.

Jarrod got up and walked all the way to the bars. The man in the suit was staring at him.

"What's going on?" Jarrod asked.

"Did you send a message by your lawyer to call your brother?"

Jarrod's belly roiled. All of a sudden he wasn't hungry anymore.

"I asked him to notify my brother of my situation, that's all. We're close, and I didn't want him thinking I'd gone missing or something," he said.

"What else did you tell him?"

Jarrod shrugged. "I don't think I said anything else. What are you getting at?"

"Your lawyer is in trouble for carrying a message from an inmate to the outside. Partly because it's not allowed, and partly because somehow after that phone call, your brother wound up right back in the town where you kidnapped your ex-wife and tried to kill her. It leads us to assume you asked him to finish her off, because he tried and it got him killed."

Jarrod moaned. Ruby was still alive and Gary was dead? That wasn't supposed to happen.

"Gary's dead?"

"Yes, and you have not been truthful with us, have you?"

Jarrod was crying now. "I don't know what you're talking about."

"Then let me refresh your memory. Of course the police were bothered by the fact that a kidnapper's brother showed up in the same town and tried to finish off the ex-wife who got away. So they began going through Gary's phone for clues. Imagine their surprise when they found a call from your lawyer on his phone. So one thing led to another, and they had a little talk with your lawyer, Mr. Alan Young. Now, imagine his dismay in learning what had happened. To his credit, he was very up-front and helpful. He said he passed on the message you asked him to deliver…about telling your brother where you were and why, and then to tell him Ruby was all right."

Jarrod groaned.

"We thought it a bit strange that you would want to reassure your brother that the ex-wife you kidnapped with malicious intent was okay. Do you have anything to say about that?"

"Uh…well, uh…when we were still married, Gary always thought a lot of Ruby. I just wanted him to know."

"You are asking me to believe that he thought so

much of her that he took a gun and drove from Nashville, Tennessee, all the way to Blessings, Georgia, and tried to kill her? Is that what you're telling me?"

Jarrod swiped the tears off his face and glared. "I'm not telling you anything. I want my lawyer."

"Well, you don't get the one you had. He's in trouble with the Bar Association right now. Another court appointee will be assigned to you, and this information will be added to your file for the judge to review."

"Well, hell's fire!" Jarrod said.

"Very sorry for your loss," the man said, and then nodded to the jailer. "I'm done here."

Jarrod threw himself onto the cot, so mad that he didn't have enough left to grieve. It was all Gary's fault for screwing up.

———

While some lives were in a mess, and others were smoothing out, little Gertie Lafferty's life was winding down. The doctors had done everything they knew how to bring Gertie back to consciousness, but it never happened.

They didn't know that her sweet Bennie had come for her right after she'd fallen against the tree and taken Gertie home. She was already where she had longed to be—with Bennie—and she didn't want to come back. It's just that Gertie's little heart was far stronger than her will to quit, and it was taking it a while to wind down.

The workers from the nursing home were all the friends she had left, and one by one, they were taking turns coming to sit with her. No one could bear the thought of Gertie passing alone.

It was just after three p.m. when the monitor hooked up to her heart began to register an erratic beat. It went from skipping a beat now and then to a flat line.

Nathan Rose, the administrator of the nursing home, two of Gertie's nurses, and the attending doctor were at her bedside when it finally happened. The doctor checked for a pulse, then looked up at the clock and called it.

"Time of death, 3:16 p.m."

"Go with God, Miss Gertie," Nathan said, and then stepped out of the room.

He had the responsibility of calling the funeral home to follow through with Gertie Lafferty's last wishes. They didn't amount to much.

No funeral.

No viewing.

"Put me in my blue church dress and lay me beside my Bennie," she always said, and that's what he intended to make happen.

After Alice Conroy put the kids to bed, she spent the evening washing her hair and picking out nice clothes to wear to enroll her kids in school. It wouldn't take long for people to figure out they were hard up, but she didn't want to leave a bad impression that would fall back on her children's shoulders. People were often unkind, and children were no different. It took life experience to learn true empathy.

After she'd done all she could in preparation, Alice went to bed with both anticipation and anxiety, scooting her daughter from the middle to her own side of the bed so she had room to lie down, then covered them both and cuddled Pitty-Pat close as exhaustion finally claimed her.

Chapter 18

RUBY WOKE UP MONDAY MORNING TO THE NEWS OF GERTIE Lafferty's passing, and shed a few tears in memory of the little woman who had once frequented the Curl Up and Dye. She started to go to the phone to call Peanut, then the ache rolled through her as she remembered. She lowered her head and took a deep breath, trying to move back into her safe place, knowing the ache in her heart would never leave if Peanut didn't recover.

"I hate you, Gary Dye, and God forgive me, but I am not sorry you are dead."

Ruby shoved her fingers through her hair in frustration, then got dressed and started her day.

Since she intended to go back to the salon tomorrow, she fell back into her normal Monday morning routine by cooking for the coming week so that when she got home every evening, she didn't have to cook something to eat.

She started a pot roast in her slow cooker and then stirred up the brownie mix and put it in to bake. All the while she was working, she was thinking of Peanut. She was going to see him today. Would there be another sign his memory was returning? She could only hope.

The alarm went off before daylight.

Alice threw back the covers, slipped on house shoes, and went to turn up the heat before heading to the kitchen.

She'd already made the kids' lunches the night before and put them in the refrigerator. They didn't have lunch boxes, but they did each have a new backpack, so she'd have to put their lunches in those. Someone had been thoughtful enough to put notebooks, pens, and pencils in each backpack, and for that she was truly grateful. The minutiae of details it took to live life were vast when a person was without the means to supply them.

As soon as she had the coffee started, she went to wake up her babies. Even if one of them was already taller than her, he would forever be her baby.

She pushed his door inward and then smiled when she saw his feet sticking out from under the covers and Booger asleep at the foot of his bed. She leaned down and gave the old dog a head rub, then laid a hand on Charlie's shoulder.

"Charlie, wake up, Son. We're going to school today, remember?"

Charlie rolled over, blinking sleepily, then frowned. "What did you say, Mama?"

"We're going to school today. You need to get up."

His eyes widened as a smile spread across his face.

"Oh yeah! I'm up," he said, and threw back the covers as Alice left to go wake up her little girl. Pitty-Pat had slept through the alarm, and Alice suspected getting her daughter up would be more of a challenge than with Charlie.

Alice sat down on the side of the bed and then gave her daughter's leg a gentle pat. "Hey, little girl, it's time to wake up. Today is the day we go to school, remember?"

Pitty-Pat scooted deeper into the covers.

Alice grinned. "You get to wear new clothes to school, remember?"

Alice had said the magic words. *New clothes*.

All of a sudden, Pitty-Pat was crawling out from under the covers and into her mother's lap. Alice hugged her close, marveling at the warmth and energy of such a tiny body.

"Come eat some cereal, and then we'll get ready."

"Carry me," Pitty-Pat said, and Alice picked her up, because she remembered all too well how fast Charlie had grown out of this stage.

Alice gave them their cereal, fed Booger, and then sat down with a cup of coffee and a bowl of cereal too. The kids talked as they ate, excited, but at the same time a little anxious. It was never easy being the new kids at school. When they finished, Alice sent them to get dressed.

Charlie took Booger out in the fenced-in backyard before they left, then brought him back in and settled him on an old rug.

"Gotta go to school now, Booger. We'll be back this afternoon, okay?"

Booger let out a little grumble as Charlie scratched behind his ear.

Charlie laughed. "You cranky old man… You know you like that spot to be scratched. Be good for Mama."

"Come on, Charlie. We need to go," Alice said.

He grabbed his coat and backpack and gave the house a last look before going out the door.

The morning air was chilled but they all had warm coats, and both Charlie and Pitty-Pat had the backpacks for a little added warmth.

Alice felt more like herself than she had in over two years and thought how sad it was that Marty's death

three months ago was what had triggered the change—
that and the good people of Blessings.

They walked past the Quick Stop and were headed
down Main Street when a police cruiser passed them
going the other way.

Charlie saw Chief Pittman behind the wheel and waved.

Lon waved back and then made a U-turn two blocks
up and drove back to catch up. He stopped a few yards
ahead of them, then rolled down the window and waited
for them to catch up.

"Hey, Charlie!" he yelled.

Charlie stopped. "Hello, Chief."

"Where are you guys going?" Lon asked.

"Mama is enrolling us in school this morning," Charlie
said.

"Hop in. I'll take you."

"Thank you!" Charlie said, and got in the back seat
with his little sister, while Alice got into the passenger
seat beside the chief.

"I sure appreciate this," Alice said.

"No problem," Lon said. "Everybody buckled up?"
he asked.

"Yes, sir," Charlie said.

Lon took off up the street, turned off Main a few
blocks down, and then made another turn past the
Baptist church and straight to the school. He pulled up
in the front behind a bus that was unloading.

"Thank you for the ride," Alice said.

"You're welcome, and have a great day, kids."

"Thank you," Charlie said.

The fact that the chief of police had given new kids a
ride to school was something to talk about.

Charlie felt the other children's eyes on him as he walked, but he kept looking forward, then ran ahead to open the door for his mama and sister.

Arlene Winston, the principal, was standing just inside the front door talking to Coach Sharp and welcoming the students as they walked in. When she saw the strangers, she immediately spoke up.

"Good morning," she said. "Welcome to Blessings Elementary. I'm Mrs. Winston, the principal."

"I'm Alice Conroy. These are my children, Charlie and Patricia. I came to get them enrolled."

Mrs. Winston smiled. "Of course. We can get Patricia enrolled here, and then you'll have to go two blocks over for the high school."

"Oh no, ma'am. Charlie's twelve and in the sixth grade."

Coach Sharp grinned as he saw visions of a possible athlete Charlie's size on the sixth-grade teams.

"Charlie, I'm Coach Sharp. Do you play any sports?"

"I played basketball and baseball at my old school."

"Then I'll see you in PE."

Charlie grinned. "Yes, sir."

"I'll see you in class," Coach said, and headed down the hall to his first class.

Arlene gave Charlie a second look. "My goodness, he's sure a tall one for twelve." Then her eyes narrowed as she kept staring at Charlie.

"You look familiar. Have you been in school here before?"

"No, ma'am," Charlie said. "Maybe you saw one of my flyers. I put them in a lot of mailboxes a few days ago."

Arlene gasped. "Yes! You're the boy with the dog that found Gertie Lafferty."

"Yes, ma'am," Charlie said.

"It's a shame she didn't recover, but with her age and everything, I guess it was a blessing."

Charlie was shocked. "She died?"

"This morning, actually," Arlene said. "Follow me. I'll take you to the office. My secretary, Mavis West, will get you both enrolled."

Alice took her daughter's hand and gave her a quick smile, but she was a little irked with the principal for blurting out the news like that to Charlie. It wasn't as if they knew her, but he and Booger had found the elderly woman, and Alice knew this would hurt him.

Alice kept glancing up at Charlie, worried this news would ruin his first day, as they followed the principal. "Are you okay?" she whispered.

He nodded. "I'm okay, Mama. It was just a bit of a shock, but I guess it was her time."

Charlie was super conscious of the curious stares of the kids they were passing, but so far nothing felt challenging. Then they reached the office, and Charlie's greatest wish to get back in school was coming true.

Arlene Winston entered the office talking. "Mavis, this is Alice Conroy. We need to get her children enrolled this morning. They are Charlie and Patricia. Sixth grade and first grade."

"Sixth grade?" Mavis said, as the principal went back out into the hall.

Alice frowned. She could see that look on the secretary's face, thinking about how many grades he'd failed.

"He's twelve," Alice said.

Mavis blinked, then smiled a little sheepishly. "My

goodness. Well, then. Do you have birth certificates and immunizations records with you?"

"No, ma'am. Our house burned three months ago. It's why we moved to Blessings. But their old school has all of that. Can you request the records?"

"Yes, we can. I'm sorry about your home. Write down the name and address of the school for me while I get a couple of enrollment forms."

Alice did as she was asked, and then sat down at a table and filled out the enrollment forms.

"I need to ask about free lunches and getting them on a bus route," she said as she gave the secretary the forms. "We live at the far north end of town."

Mavis checked the bus schedule, then added that info to their enrollment forms so she could enter it all into the computer database.

"They'll be riding Bus Two. The driver is Millard Coffee. Just let him know where to stop when you first get on this afternoon, and he'll tell you what time to meet him in the mornings."

Alice glanced at Charlie. "Got that?"

"Yes, Mama. I won't forget."

"One more thing, Mrs. Conroy. I'll need to see your SNAP card indicating you are receiving family assistance so I can set up free lunches."

"Jewel Easley from DHS just signed us up so I don't have that yet. She said we should get it by the first of the month," Alice said.

Mavis frowned. "The rules are—"

Alice felt the slap even though it never happened, and she damn sure wasn't going to beg. She held up a hand.

"Never mind. We'll manage," she said shortly, then

turned to her children. "You have your lunches today, so don't worry about a thing, okay? Have a wonderful first day, and make lots of friends."

"Yes, Mama," Pitty-Pat said.

"We'll be fine, Mama," Charlie added.

Alice knelt down and hugged Pitty-Pat, then stood up.

"See you both this evening." Then she gave Mavis a cool smile. "I know you're going to take good care of my children."

Mavis had a momentary flashback of facing the anger of Johnny Pine when his little brother had been injured at this school. She didn't want to relive that.

"Yes, ma'am. We take our responsibilities very seriously here."

Alice gave the kids one last encouraging look and was leaving the office as the first bell rang. She couldn't look back or she would cry. She needed to ignore what other people thought of her and not be so touchy. Life had put her on this path, and she was doing her best not to fall off.

The chilly air felt good on her face as she exited the school, and then she headed toward Main Street. Walking back would give her time to shake the chip off her shoulder. She was pleased at how friendly people were as she walked through the neighborhood.

An older woman who was outside picking up a paper waved at Alice. She waved back and walked on as the lady went back inside.

A few houses down, a woman was trying to get her kids in the car. Alice heard the mother fussing and the kids whining. They were going to be late for school, she thought, and kept moving.

She was a block off Main when she met an older man walking his dog and thought of Booger, their gentle giant.

"Morning, miss," the man said.

"Good morning," Alice said. "What a sweet little dog."

"Thank you, ma'am. This is Petey. He's a Yorkie."

Alice grinned. "Hi, Petey," she said, then stepped aside to let them pass.

By the time she got to Main Street and headed north, her heart was lighter. Shopkeepers were outside sweeping in front of their stores. As she approached, they stopped to let her pass, wishing her good morning. She'd been hiding in her house for so long, struggling with the shame of their situation and then her health, that it felt good to be seen.

She passed a travel agency and a pharmacy and was coming up on the newspaper office when a passing car suddenly honked. She looked up and saw one of the ladies who'd brought her groceries waving. She waved back, trying to remember her name.

Oh yes...that was Rachel. Rachel Goodhope.

She noticed the time as she passed a bank. It was moving toward eight thirty. The kids would already be in class.

God, please let this day be a good one.

She saw a store in the next block and smiled at the name. Bloomer's Hardware. She wondered how many times the owner had been teased about that name. But as she got closer, she saw a sign in the window. HELP WANTED. Her heart skipped a beat as she began walking faster.

"It won't hurt to try," Alice muttered, and went inside.

The man behind the counter looked up and smiled.

"Good morning. Welcome to Bloomer's. How can I help you?"

"I'm hoping I can help you," Alice said. "I saw your sign in the window."

Fred Bloomer shifted gears from customer to applicant.

"Have you ever worked in a hardware store?" he asked.

"No, but I've worked in retail and as a checker in a supermarket, and I need a job. I just enrolled my kids in school and was on my way home when I saw the sign. My name is Alice Conroy," she said, and extended her hand across the counter.

Fred's mind was racing. Right now, nearly everyone in town was mad at him for firing Melissa, and this woman was new in town. Chances were he wasn't going to get another applicant for months—until people had time to let bygones be bygones.

"Can you work a register?"

"Yes, but may I look at yours to see if it's very different?"

"Come this way," he said, and she circled the counter for a closer look.

"It's a newer version than the ones I've used, but with a little coaching, I see no problems."

"Do you want to fill out an application?" he asked.

She didn't hesitate. "Yes, sir."

He ran to the office and came back with an application. "Fill this out and bring it back."

"I'll fill it out now, if you don't mind. I don't have a car so it's easier to do it here rather than make two trips."

He frowned. "Why don't you have a car?"

She lifted her head. "My husband is dead. Our car burned up with the house he was in."

Fred blinked. "I'm sorry."

Alice shrugged. "So am I, and I don't need a car to get to work on time."

"Fill out the application," he said.

So she did, and when she was finished, she handed it to him, then waited while he looked it over.

This was the fastest decision about hiring an employee that Fred had ever made, but he was desperate, and from the sounds of her story, so was she. Something inside him felt like this was a test of his conscience, and if he failed again, he was going to be in trouble.

"So, when could you start?" Fred asked.

"Tomorrow, but what does the job pay, and do you pay twice a month or only once a month?" she asked.

Fred became a little cagey and wanted to start her off at minimum wage, but then he remembered her situation.

"Well, I was paying my other clerk ten dollars an hour, although she'd been with me for nineteen years, and I pay twice a month."

"Why did she quit?" Alice asked.

"Oh, it's a long story, and hers to tell," Fred said, not wanting to scare Alice away before she began. "I need a clerk, and I'm willing to pay that much again if you work out."

Alice couldn't believe it. That was sixteen hundred dollars a month before taxes.

"That works for me. One other thing. I don't know what time you close, but because I am a single parent, I can work Monday through Friday, no weekends, and will have to leave by five because of my children coming home from school."

Fred stifled a groan. He'd be on his own on Saturday and have to close every night. But it was his fault he was in this fix, and he needed the help.

"Then eight to five, Monday through Friday, at ten dollars an hour. We'll make this a six-week trial period, and if you work out, then it will be permanent."

"That's fair," Alice said. "I'll take it."

They shook hands again, but this time Alice was grinning. "I appreciate the opportunity and I will not let you down," she said. "See you tomorrow morning at eight."

"Tomorrow at eight," Fred echoed, and shivered as he watched her leave. She'd just said the same thing to him that Melissa Dean had said on the day he hired her: *I will not let you down*. He considered it a sign, and this time, he wasn't going to mess things up.

Alice waited until she reached the sidewalk before she started to grin, and then she couldn't stop. She walked the rest of the way home in a fog before it hit her. This would certainly change what Jewel Easley was setting up for her. As soon as she got home, she'd call Jewel and let her know. If she didn't qualify for assistance anymore, then so be it. Charlie was right. They were figuring things out.

Chapter 19

IT WAS A LITTLE BEFORE ELEVEN A.M. WHEN RUBY ENTERED the hospital. Her heart was racing, and there was a knot in the pit of her stomach. Seeing Peanut was an emotional trip, but she didn't want to convey her anxiety to him. By the time she rode the elevator up to the critical care floor, she felt calmer.

"Good morning," she said, as she passed by the nurses' station.

Rhonda looked up and smiled. "Morning, Ruby. That turquoise looks good on you."

"Thank you, Rhonda," Ruby said, hoping the color would brighten Peanut's day. It was why she'd worn it.

He was asleep again as she entered his room. It had been four days since the shooting, and while the remnants of her kidnapping were fading from her face, the bandage on the side of his head was an ugly reminder of what had happened.

Ruby put her purse on the window ledge and then leaned over and kissed his cheek.

His eyes opened.

"It's just me, Ruby," she said, and caressed his cheek.

He reached for her hand. "You came back," he said.

"I promised I would."

His eyelids dropped again, and then a few seconds later, they opened.

"You're my girl?"

Ruby tried not to let it bother her that he was already uncertain again.

"Yes, sweetheart, I'm your girl."

He looked at her hair, then her face, and then the sweater she was wearing. "So pretty."

She smiled. "That's what you keep telling me."

"I do?" Peanut said.

His confusion was still bothering her, so she changed the subject.

"It's a bit chilly outside today. I'll be ready for warmer weather when it finally comes."

He was watching the way the words came out of her mouth, how her lips shaped as she spoke, and how peaceful the look was in her eyes. Even though he didn't remember her, she felt safe—like he knew he could trust her.

And then a pain shot through his head, moving from one temple to the other so fast and so sharp that it felt like he'd been stabbed.

"What's wrong?" Ruby asked.

"Head. Pain," he mumbled, then light flashed before his eyes, and in a panic, he tightened his fingers around hers. "Help mupple worp!"

Ruby's heart skipped a beat. "Peanut?"

He groaned. "Pluralrolabout," he mumbled, and then his hand suddenly went limp.

Alarms on his monitors began going off, and two nurses were already running toward his room as Ruby cried out, "Help! Help, somebody, help!"

She still had hold of his hand, afraid to let go for fear he'd go too far away to come back.

Rhonda glanced at the readouts as she checked his

pulse, then looked at the other nurse. "His pulse is erratic, and his blood pressure is spiking. Get his doctor in here stat," Rhonda said.

The other nurse ran for a phone.

Rhonda glanced back at Ruby. "What happened?"

"I don't know! He was talking, then said his head hurt. After that, his words quit making any sense."

Ruby heard a page go out all over the hospital as nurses swarmed Peanut's room. She backed into a corner and didn't move for fear they'd make her leave.

It felt like forever, but it was only a couple of minutes before a doctor raced into the room. He saw the readings, flashed a light in both of Peanut's eyes, and then tried to get him to respond, but it was useless.

"I need a CT scan on his head, stat. I'm not sure what's causing this, but my first guess would be that he's thrown a clot. Get them on the phone, and let them know we're coming down," he said.

"Yes, sir," Rhonda said, and headed for the nurses' desk.

"What does that mean?" Ruby cried.

The doctor turned, startled that she was there. "We'll know more after the CT scan," he said.

When they wheeled Peanut out, Ruby started to follow.

"No, Ruby. I'm sorry, but you can't go." Rhonda took her by the arm and led her in the opposite direction. "You need to go to the waiting room. Someone will let you know what's happening as soon as they get a prognosis," she said.

Ruby staggered there on shaky legs, too scared to cry. Thirty minutes turned into an hour and counting before Rhonda came into the waiting room and sat down beside her.

"What's wrong?" Ruby asked.

"There's a blood clot in a part of the brain that controls speech. Doctor thinks it might have something to do with his memory loss as well. They've already taken him into surgery."

"They're going to operate? Oh my God! I thought they tried to dissolve blood clots."

"It's always the doctor's call as to the urgency and need," Rhonda said. "The doctor will come give you an update after surgery. Keep the faith, Ruby."

Ruby felt like she was going to throw up. When one hour moved into the next without a word, she started to cry. She was still crying when her phone began to ring, and when she saw it was Lovey, she answered without thinking.

"Hello."

Lovey Cooper frowned. "Are you crying? What happened?"

"Oh, Lovey, it's Peanut. I came to visit him this morning. While I was here, a blood clot came loose and went to a part of his brain. He's been in surgery for close to two hours."

"Oh lord! Why didn't you call me? I would have come to sit with you."

"Because you can't do anything for me or him except pray. Just pray for him, Lovey."

Lovey hung up, then called their pastor and told him what was happening. The pastor started a prayer chain, and that's how the people in Blessings found out Peanut Butterman's life was still in danger.

Ruby clutched her phone as the room began to spin. She rolled over onto the sofa and closed her eyes, willing the vertigo to stop. She was still there when she heard footsteps. Someone was coming into the waiting room, but she couldn't move. Then she felt a touch on her shoulder.

"It's just me," Lovey said, then scooted onto the sofa beside her.

"Oh, Lovey," Ruby whispered. "This can't be the end."

More than five hours had passed since they took Peanut to surgery. Ruby had paced and prayed, gone through anger and guilt, and for the past hour she'd been standing at the window overlooking the parking lot of the ER, numb to everything around her.

Lovey suddenly called out, "Ruby!"

Ruby turned around as a different doctor in surgical scrubs entered the room. She couldn't tell by the look on his face what he was going to say, and didn't wait for him to speak.

"How is he?" she asked.

"I'm Dr. Rousch, the neurosurgeon who operated on Mr. Butterman. He came through surgery. For the time being, we have him in a medical coma. We'll monitor his progress, and as he heals, we'll slowly bring him out of it."

"Thank God," Ruby said. "Will he come back to critical care?"

"No. He'll be in the ICU during this time with no visitors allowed."

"I understand. Would it be against protocol if I called the ICU to check on him?"

"That would be fine. I'll make sure to note on his orders that you are allowed to receive updates on his progress."

Tears blurred Ruby's vision. "Thank you. Is there anything else you can tell me? Barring problems, what would you say was a normal recovery time?"

Rousch hesitated. "There isn't really a normal when it comes to head injuries. I won't venture a guess."

It wasn't what she wanted to hear, but she understood. "One last thing… Thank you for saving his life."

He smiled. "Go home and get some rest," and then he was gone.

Ruby looked at Lovey, then shook her head in disbelief.

"Come home with me, honey," Lovey said. "I don't want you to spend the night by yourself."

Ruby needed to be alone with this. "Thank you, but no. I have too much to do before work tomorrow."

Lovey didn't bother to hide her surprise. "You're going to work tomorrow?"

Ruby shrugged. "I've been off a week. I can't see Peanut. What good would it do to stay home alone and lose my mind?"

Lovey started crying. "This is breaking my heart."

Ruby put her arms around her best friend's neck and hugged her.

"You are the sister I never had," Ruby said. "Thank you for caring." Then she got her purse.

"I'll walk out with you," Lovey said.

They rode the elevator down in silence, then walked out into the parking lot, got into their respective cars, and drove away.

Ruby went into her house in a daze.

The wonderful aroma of pot roast filled the air, reminding her that the meat she'd put in the slow cooker early this morning was most likely done. She changed her clothes and went to the kitchen.

The roast was indeed done. She turned off the heat in the cooker without realizing she was crying until tears dropped onto the backs of her hands. Her world was crashing, and she had no way to stop it.

She dropped to her knees, rocked back on her heels, and screamed.

But while Ruby's world was coming apart, the chaos of Alice Conroy's was coming to an end. She'd called Jewel Easley at DHS the moment she got home. Jewel was both surprised and delighted that Alice Conroy was making a real effort to support her family.

"I guess you'll have to cancel our assistance," Alice said.

"Not cancel, but adjust it some. You'll still qualify for SNAP because you have children, and we'll see how the rest is affected when I enter the new data. However, huge congratulations on the new job."

"Thank you for coming to our rescue," Alice said.

"You are so welcome," Jewel said. "You'll get a letter with your card and information on what you do qualify for. You'll still be able to qualify for Medicaid as well."

"Oh, that is such a relief," Alice said.

"Call me any time you have concerns," Jewel said, and disconnected.

When the kids came home from school, they were full of excitement. Alice had milk and cookies waiting for them.

Delighted by the luxury of a snack, they began to talk, so Alice listened and rejoiced for them while saving her own news for when they were through sharing their day.

When Pitty-Pat accidentally dropped the last bite of her cookie, Booger bolted toward it and licked it off the floor before anyone could react. Pitty-Pat didn't know whether to cry about losing her last bite or laugh at their dog, and when Charlie gave her his last bite instead, she popped it in her mouth and giggled.

"So, guess what I did today while you two were in school?" Alice said.

They both turned to stare.

She grinned. "I got a job. I start tomorrow."

Charlie shuddered as the weight of the world fell off his shoulders. "Oh wow, Mama! That is amazing. What is the job? Where will you work?"

So she told them, ending up with the assurance that she would be off by five p.m. and home as fast as she could walk and would not be working weekends.

"Who's gonna stay with us till you get home?" Pitty-Pat asked.

Charlie tweaked her nose, making her squeal.

"I will, you silly goof. I'm almost a man. I will take care of you."

Pitty-Pat nodded, satisfied that the burden did not fall on her, and looked back at Alice. "What are we having for supper, Mama? I'm still hungry."

"Beans and wieners. They'll be done by the time you two go wash up."

Charlie grinned. "We ate dessert first today."

Alice laughed. "I guess we did."

They ran out of the room to wash up, and Alice got up and turned the fire off under the pan and got out their three plates.

It had been a good day.

———～～～———

Melissa Dean's first night in the sleigh bed was dreamless. She woke up to sunlight streaming through the curtains and then rolled over. Almost immediately, she remembered the call she'd gotten yesterday from the funeral home in Savannah, where Elmer's body had been taken. They would be bringing his body to the Blessings cemetery this morning at ten a.m. to inter him.

She glanced at the clock. It was just after eight a.m. Time to get moving, because there was no way she would miss this. She got up, made her bed, and then jumped in the shower.

Thirty minutes later, she was on her way downstairs, dressed in dark slacks and a dark-green sweater as she headed for the kitchen.

Making her breakfast in Elmer's kitchen felt like playing house, but it wouldn't take long to put her own stamp on everything.

By the time she was finished and the kitchen cleaned, it was time to leave. She grabbed a coat and her purse as she headed out the door.

She stopped at the flower shop and bought a dozen daisies, then continued to the cemetery. She knew where Cora's grave was located, and as she turned off the road and in through the gates, she could see three people already there. She parked closer, then got out with the flowers and started walking.

When she recognized the nieces from the reading of the will, she was a little uncertain how this would play out. To her surprise, they greeted her first.

"Hello, Melissa. I don't know if you remember our names, but I'm Wilma, and that's Loretta and Betsy. We had a lot to think about on our long drive home and want to thank you for taking care of Uncle Elmer as we should have. After such horrible neglect of our familial duties, coming to see him laid to rest is the last thing we can do for Mama. Come join us," she said.

Melissa smiled. "Thank you. None of you know this, but I had just been fired from a job I'd had for nineteen years. I'm a widow and was scared to death of what was coming next for me when I got the call to show up for the reading. Elmer's gift has been a godsend to me."

The sisters gasped and then all began talking at once and hugging her.

"Mama always said everything happens for a reason," Betsy said. "And this is proof. You needed this. We didn't."

"Thank you," Melissa said, and then pointed toward the hearse coming toward them, followed by another car. "Here he comes. The last time I say goodbye to my old friend."

They stood in silence, watching as men piled out of the car and then pulled the casket from the hearse and carried it to the gravesite.

One of the men stepped out of the group with a Bible, read the Twenty-Third Psalm, then said a prayer before speaking to the ladies present.

"It was Mr. Mathis's request that his funeral be carried out in such a fashion. All he wanted was to lie down beside his Cora again, and now he's with her for eternity. It has been my honor to know him. He was a kind and generous man. My sympathies for your loss," he said.

They watched as the casket was lowered into the earth. Melissa stepped up, grabbed a handful of dirt, and tossed it onto the casket.

"Goodbye, my dear friend. Thank you from the bottom of my heart for how you blessed me. I brought flowers for Cora. Tell her I said hello."

And then she stepped back and put the daisies against the headstone under Cora Mathis's name, as the three sisters each moved to the grave and apologized for failing him, and then it was over.

"Safe travels home," Melissa said, and then left the sisters at the gravesite.

They might have more they wanted to do, and if so, they needed the privacy to do it. As for her, this was the closing of one chapter of her life and the opening of another. She had one more thing to do, but she had to go home to do it.

As soon as Melissa got back, she got the rabbit's foot key chain and removed the extra key.

"Well, Little Bunny Foo Foo, it's time to put you to rest too. I can't look at this without thinking of the rabbit that you were."

She went out the back door, got a little trowel from the tool shed, and then turned to look at the backyard, trying to find the best place to bury the rabbit's foot.

She started walking toward a corner of the yard, then

stopped beside the huge lilac bushes that would be in full bloom come spring and knelt down. She dug a little hole between two bushes, well away from any lawn mowers or planting, and dropped in the rabbit's foot, then covered it back up with the rich, dark earth from the hole.

"There now," she said, firmly tamping down the dirt. "The last bit of Elmer's past has been laid to rest."

About sundown, Ruby sat down in the kitchen to eat, but the food was just a knot in her stomach. It didn't take long for nausea to strike, and she threw up what she'd eaten.

Even her body was rebelling against her. Worn out in both body and spirit, she cleaned up the kitchen and went to bed, after setting her alarm for six a.m. and turning out the lights.

The house was quiet. She could hear the occasional sound of a car driving past, and thought about all the times she'd gone past people's houses without one thought for what was going on inside them. Never once wondering if they were sick, or grieving, or in some kind of despair. It was strange how one person's life could be crumbling around them, while the rest of the world moved on in a normal fashion.

Ruby closed her eyes, but all she saw was the panic on Peanut's face when he was trying to tell her that something was wrong.

Finally, she threw back the covers, then got up and knelt by the side of the bed and bowed her head.

"I don't know how to pray, Lord, because I don't

know what to ask for without sounding selfish, but I want my sweetheart back. Please, God, if You are listening, he means so much to everyone, but to no one more than me. My parents turned their back on me. My husband betrayed me...twice. Peanut was the first person in my whole life who made me feel loved. I am asking for Your grace, Lord. Please give him back to me."

Then she crawled back into bed and cried herself to sleep.

The alarm went off at six a.m.

Ruby slapped at it until it stopped squawking, then swung her legs off the side of the bed and sat up.

"Morning, Lord. Today, please help me curb my tongue, ease the pain in my heart, and take good care of my man."

Then she got up and headed for the shower.

It was time for her to face the life she'd been given.

Ruby came in the back door of the shop, put away her things, and called the hospital to check on Peanut's welfare, but there was no change.

"Thank you for the information," she said, and hung up.

Then she turned on all the lights in the shop, put the change back in the register, and unlocked the front door. She looked out her front windows as she had so many times before, taking a look at the little town she called home, then turned the CLOSED sign to OPEN and went to the back to make coffee. It was time to start the day.

About fifteen minutes later, the twins came in, talking to each other without waiting for an answer, which always made Ruby smile, and today the brief moment of laughter was welcome.

"Do you guys ever hear what the other one is saying?" she asked.

"Well, yes, but we already know the answer, so there's no need to say it," Vera said.

Vesta grinned. "We brought doughnuts."

Ruby glanced at her appointment book. "I have time for one and for the coffee to go with it," she said.

She didn't really want it, but she couldn't go all day on an empty stomach. Surely the doughnut and coffee would stay down, and they did.

Ruby sat in her styling chair, licking sugar off her fingers and listening to the chatter, which increased threefold as soon as Mabel Jean arrived.

"Ooh...doughnuts, yum. I skipped breakfast," she said. "I have three manicures back to back this morning."

"Who are they?" Vera asked.

"The triple threat...Betina, Molly, and Angel."

Ruby rolled her eyes. "Don't let them get started tearing someone's reputation apart today. I'm not in the mood to hear it."

Mabel Jean giggled. "If they get out of hand, they're all yours," she said.

Ruby gave her a thumbs-up.

There was a lull in conversation. Ruby saw them all glancing at her. She knew they wanted to ask, but didn't want to upset her.

"He came through surgery. The doctor put him in a medical coma to heal. He's in the ICU. No visitors, no flowers. I get updates from the nurses in the ICU when I call. Say prayers."

The three of them nodded.

Ruby looked at their faces, these beloved women with whom she'd spent the better part of the last fifteen years.

"And I love you all dearly, but don't make me cry."

"We love you, too, and we won't, we won't," they said.

Then the bell over the front door jingled.

Ruby got up and went to greet her first client of the day.

"Good morning, LilyAnn. Come on back. How's that little guy of yours? I bet he's growing."

Ruby heard something about "three teeth and walking" and then tuned it out as she snapped a cape around LilyAnn's neck and settled her into a chair at the shampoo station.

And so the day began.

When the trouble trio arrived for back-to-back manicures at nine a.m., Ruby was bidding LilyAnn goodbye and sending a hello to her husband, Mike.

"Good morning, ladies," Ruby said. "Mabel Jean is ready. Who's first?"

"I am, because I'm meeting my husband for lunch," Angel said.

"I'm second, because I won the coin toss," Betina said.

Molly rolled her eyes. "And I'm last because I lost."

Ruby patted her on the arm. "Someone has to be. There are doughnuts by the coffee, if you want one. Help yourselves."

The offer of food and drink settled the two who were waiting, as Mabel Jean began to work on Angel.

The day moved slowly for Ruby, and by the time Precious Peters came in at two p.m. for her permanent, Ruby was numb. Everyone asked about Peanut, mentioned her bruises, talked about the little scar on her lip, and then moved on to other news.

"Hello, Precious, ready to get curly?" Ruby asked.

Precious nodded.

"How curly are we going this time?" Ruby asked, as she caped Precious and sat her down at the shampoo station.

"Not as curly as last time. My Rudy hated it, even though it was one of my favorite looks."

Ruby patted her shoulder and smiled. "Who's wearing the hair, you or Rudy?"

Precious blinked. "Uh, well, that would be me."

"How does Rudy wear his hair?" Ruby asked.

Precious frowned. "Well, you know…he looks like an old hippie. That ponytail of his is long, but he's thinning on the sides and top."

"Umm-hmmm," Ruby said, as she squirted soap on Precious's hair and started scrubbing. "How do you like that ponytail?"

Precious rolled her eyes. "Well, I guess I hate it. Long hair in the sink. Long hair in the tub."

"Well, I'll say," Ruby muttered, and began rinsing.

Precious was silent for a few moments, as Ruby began the second soaping.

"You know what?"

"What?" Ruby asked.

"I don't care what that Rudy says. It's my hair. I'll wear it any old way I please."

"Really? Well, good for you, Precious. I like a woman who knows what she wants."

Precious smirked, and then sighed and closed her eyes, unaware that Ruby Dye had already worked her brand of magic by reminding the woman in her chair that she had the right to be who she wanted to be, and look how she wanted to look.

It was just after three-thirty when Precious left. She was beaming when she walked out the door, her curls bouncing as she went.

Vesta came up behind Ruby and hugged her.

Ruby smiled. "What's that for?" she asked.

"For reminding all of us that we are supposed to be sailing our own ships."

Ruby hugged her back.

Vesta grinned. "What was that for?" she asked.

"For reminding me that we're all in this life together."

Then Mabel Jean yelled from the back, "There's one more doughnut! Does anybody want it?"

"You eat it," the others said in unison, and then they all burst out laughing.

Ruby was the last to leave. She locked the front door and turned the OPEN sign to CLOSED, then counted out the money for the night deposit. The last thing she did was call the hospital to check on Peanut. The phone rang twice before the call was picked up.

"ICU, this is Franny."

"Franny, this is Ruby. Just checking on my Peanut before I go home."

"Hi, honey. His vital signs are steady, and there have been no issues."

"Thank you for the info, and thank you for taking care of him."

"You are very welcome. It's what we do," Franny said.

Ruby hung up the phone, then grabbed her things and left, locking the door behind her.

She dropped off the night deposit at the bank drive-through, waited for the receipt, and then went home.

The silence of her little house was exactly what she needed. She changed out of her work clothes, then went to the kitchen, dug out some roast and vegetables from the refrigerator, and this time when she sat down to eat, the food stayed down.

Chapter 20

RUBY'S WEEK HAD TAKEN ON A ROUTINE OF ITS OWN. MOST days, she felt like she was standing outside her own body, watching it go through the motions.

They buried Gertie Lafferty on Wednesday without any ceremony other than the pastor who read the Twenty-Third Psalm as they lowered her casket into the ground in the plot next to where Bennie Lafferty had long ago been laid to rest.

When Ruby heard about it, it made her wonder what she would do if she had to bury Peanut. It was a horrible thing to consider, so she set it aside and went to work, talked and laughed, and fixed hair and shared lunches. Some evenings she went to Granny's and ate supper with Lovey, but it all felt surreal.

It was just after nine a.m. Sunday morning and she was getting ready for church when her phone rang. She turned around to pick it up, and when she saw it was from the hospital, her legs went weak. She was trembling as she sat down to answer.

"Hello?"

"Good morning, Ruby. This is Dr. Rousch, and nothing is wrong."

"Oh, thank God," Ruby said.

"I called to let you know that we have been slowly weaning Peanut off the medicine that kept him in the

coma, and he's showing signs of waking up. I told you I
would let you know."

"Oh my God, oh my God, can I come?"

"That's why I'm calling. Yes, you can come. The
nurses know to expect you. But you have to be mindful
it's the ICU."

"Yes, yes, I'll whisper."

She heard him chuckle. "Have a good day," he said.

"Yes, you too," Ruby said, then hung up.

She jumped to her feet, took off her slip, and ran to
the closet for warmer pants and a sweater because the
hospital was always cold.

Ruby Dye didn't make it to church.

Lovey waited until the preacher started his sermon
before she got out her phone and started texting.

> Where are you? Is everything okay?

Within a minute or two, she got an answer.

> With Peanut in ICU. He's waking up.

Lovey dropped her phone back in her purse and lifted
her eyes above the pulpit to the angel in the stained-
glass window.

"Praise the Lord," she whispered.

There was sound in the darkness.

Sometimes Peanut could hear what people were

saying, and other times it was just a mumble of voices. When he was closest to the voices, he kept listening for her voice, but she wasn't there.

Once he came to just enough to hear someone moaning and someone crying. It made him anxious, and he let go and fell back into the hole. Other times, he woke up trying to climb out. The hole was deep. It had been a sanctuary, but now it felt like a trap.

At times he thought he was talking, and then realized the voices he heard were in his head, but they were all telling him the same thing... *Wake up. Wuke up.* It made him angry. Couldn't they see he was trying?

Then help me! he shouted, but when he talked back to them, they disappeared down in the hole.

He was drifting in and out of sleep when he heard footsteps again, then voices beside his bed.

"Please be mindful of the others nearby," a woman said, and another woman answered, "Yes, I will."

His heart began beating faster. It was her! She'd come back!

He felt a hand on his arm, then a faint aroma of lilac as someone kissed the side of his cheek. He heard the voice again, only softer and right against his ear.

"Hey, you, it's me," she whispered, and put her hand over his fingers.

He inhaled slowly.

—∿∿—

Ruby's heart was pounding. Seeing the bandage around his head, she was afraid of what was to come. The anxiety of not knowing how much more damage there could be had kept her sleepless for most of the past week, and being only minutes from an answer was suddenly scary.

"Can you hear my voice?" Ruby whispered. "Follow it, sweetheart. Follow the sound back to me."

His fingers curled around her hand.

"Oh, honey, you hear me, don't you?"

His grip tightened.

Tears welled from her relief as she leaned over him again, her voice barely above a whisper.

"All you have to do is open your eyes. I know it's hard, but there's so much left for the two of us to share. Just open your eyes."

She saw his eyelids fluttering. There was a muscle jerking at the side of his mouth.

"I'm here. All you have to do is look."

His lips parted.

"Hear," he mumbled.

"Yes, yes, you hear me, don't you, darling?"

His eyelids fluttered again, and then opened just enough that he saw light.

He'd done it! He was almost out of the hole. He tightened his grip on her hand, using her strength to pull himself the rest of the way up.

Light came into his world as he began to blink. It had been so dark, and now there was light.

"I'm here," she whispered.

He turned toward the sound of her voice, and then he saw her face. Yes, she was who he'd been waiting for.

"It's you," he said.

It was all Ruby could do not to cheer.

"Yes, it's me."

He sighed. "My Ruby. Love you so much."

Ruby gasped. "Oh my God," she whispered, and put her hand over his heart, letting the peace of that heartbeat surround her. "You remember. You remember."

He looked confused. "Yes. You're my girl."

"Yes, I'm your girl. You go to sleep now, sweetheart. I'll be back."

"Yes...back," he mumbled, and closed his eyes.

Ruby kissed him goodbye and felt like she was floating all the way back to the nurses' station.

"He woke up," she said softly. "He knows who I am."

"Oh, that's wonderful," the nurse said. "I'll note that on his chart."

"I told him I'd be back," Ruby said.

The nurse smiled. "Yes, you can come back."

"Thank you," Ruby said. "And you will call if there's a change?"

"Absolutely. You are listed as family on his records."

Ruby slipped out of the ward as quietly as she'd come in, but the moment she got in the elevator, she closed her eyes.

"Thank you, Lord, for giving him back to me."

Epilogue

THE DAY HE LEFT THE HOSPITAL, PEANUT WANTED TO GO TO his home, where his things were and where everything was familiar, and Ruby didn't argue. Instead, the women in his life made a schedule between them. Betty and Ruby kept him in food. Ruby stayed with him at night until after the first week had passed, and Laurel came twice a week and kept his house and clothes clean until he was well enough to do it for himself.

At the beginning of the second week, when Ruby arrived after work, he met her at the door, sat her on the sofa, got down on one knee, and pulled a ring from his pocket.

"I got this ring out of the safety deposit box over eight months ago, and it's past time I put it where it was meant to be. Ruby Dye, you know I love you more than life, and I cannot imagine it without you. Will you marry me?"

Ruby's dark eyes welled from the love in his voice.

"Yes, yes, yes, I will marry you."

He slid the single diamond on her ring finger, kissed her hand, and then scooted up beside her on the sofa and kissed her senseless.

When she finally focused on the ring, she was shaken by the size.

"Peanut! What on earth did you do?"

"I mortgaged the house, but I'll get it paid off in—"

Ruby gasped.

He grinned.

Her eyes narrowed. "Are you kidding me?"

"Yes."

"Oh my lord, you nearly gave me a heart attack," she said.

"It was my mother's engagement ring, and now it's yours," he said. "It's been in the Butterman family for a little over two hundred years now."

Ruby was in shock that an emerald-cut, one-carat diamond was on her finger.

"Now I'm afraid to wear it!"

He laid his hand over the ring. "No, ma'am, you are not afraid to wear this ring. You are more than worthy to wear it. It came over from England on an ancestor's finger. It went through the Civil War on another, and if the story is true, the woman wearing it killed the Union soldier who tried to take it from her. Someone pawned it once to save a home and then turned around and stole it back and got away with it. Strong, brave women wore this, and I can't think of a better woman than you to follow in their footsteps."

Ruby threw her arms around his neck.

"Oh, Peanut, that makes me cry. Thank you for loving me."

"I couldn't help myself," he said. "You rock my world."

A couple of weeks later, Peanut had gone back to work part-time. Since it was a Monday, Ruby was home, and he'd gone to her house for lunch to discuss a date for the wedding. After they chose April 8 as the day, the venue was next to discuss, and that's when Ruby gave Peanut an answer he didn't expect.

"I want to invite the whole town and hold it in the park at the gazebo."

Peanut grinned. "The whole town?"

She nodded.

"At the gazebo?"

"Yes," she said. "I can't single out some and leave out others. Not when this whole town and the people in it have become the family I lost."

"I hear you, and I am not against that, but what if it rains?" Peanut asked.

"It's not going to rain on our wedding," she said.

He laughed, as he swept her off her feet and sat her up on the kitchen counter so they were almost eye to eye.

"And how do you know that? What have you done? Made a deal with Mother Nature to do her hair for free?"

Ruby laughed. "No."

"Then okay. So what if it rains? We won't melt," he said.

Ruby just frowned. "It's not going to rain."

Seeing he was not going to make a dent in her certainty, Peanut moved on.

"So we're having it at the park. Exactly how much of this all-town blowout are we paying for?"

"Five hundred cupcakes. They bring their own lawn chairs and birdseed."

"And they throw birdseed instead of rice?"

"Yes."

"You do realize how many people might be throwing birdseed at us at the same time?"

Ruby frowned. "Why am I just now seeing this worry-wart side of your character? What else are you hiding from me?"

"Your wedding ring."

"I want to see!" she cried.

"You won't let me see your wedding gown, and I'm not letting you see the ring."

"What if it doesn't fit?" she said.

"Now who's a worrywart?" Peanut asked.

Ruby laughed out loud.

"Lovey will make our cupcakes... Well, probably Mercy. The preacher will marry us. And we'll set up a few chairs for the elderly who would have problems with transporting their own."

"And what do I need to do?" he asked.

"Pay half the bills and show up."

He grinned. "I can do that," he said.

Ruby shivered. The day couldn't come any too soon.

"Come to bed with me," Peanut said, and he kissed the spot below her ear.

"I have a pie in the oven," Ruby said.

"Then we'll hurry," he said.

She laughed. "Oh dear lord, how I love you. We have twenty minutes."

He set her on her feet, grabbed her by the hand, and pulled her toward her bedroom. What had started out as a lunch break was turning into so much more.

They undressed in haste and fell onto the bed in each other's arms. Laughter lit the fire of joy...and then the kisses deepened, lighting a fire of another kind.

Ruby closed her eyes, focusing on the sensation of building heat as he marauded his way down her body—stealing kisses, cupping her breasts, mapping the shape of her hips, and then moving into dangerous territory—and wanting him in a way for which she had no words.

By the time he moved between her legs and took her, she'd lost focus on everything but how he was making her feel. She wanted it to last forever, but the more it built, the harder it was to bear the ache.

Then his breathing shifted. He was moving faster, going deeper, and she thought she couldn't bear for him to stop, until the feeling grew so intense that she needed that rush of blood to stop it.

It happened in a glorious, mind-numbing, spilling-over-into-another-world climax that left both of them breathless. For one long moment, neither spoke, and then from off in another part of the house, they both heard a ding. The timer on the pie had gone off.

Peanut raised up on one elbow to gaze down at her face—her sweet, beautiful face.

"We get better every time," Ruby said.

He leaned down and kissed her.

"I work best under pressure."

She burst into laughter. "You crazy man. Let me up, or my pie will burn."

He grinned, then rolled over, admiring her bare backside as she grabbed a robe and raced out of the bedroom.

He stretched, then got up. She was still gone when he began to get dressed.

When she came hurrying back, she was clutching the robe together at her waist and laughing so hard she could barely talk.

"What's so funny?" Peanut asked.

"The mailman caught a glimpse of me running through the house with my robe flapping as he came up the steps. He looked back at your car in the driveway and turned red as a beet."

Peanut grinned.

"Well, then it's a good thing I'm making an honest woman of you."

Ruby grinned and then glanced at the clock.

"I love you, mister, but you're going to be late for your next appointment if you don't leave now."

"Yes, ma'am, uh…and I have a question. Are you giving that pie away?"

"No, why?" Ruby asked.

"Well, since I like pie, I thought I might swing by with barbecue this evening and trade you some ribs for some pie à la mode."

Ruby laughed. "I'll be home about five thirty, and barbecue sounds wonderful."

"I'll be here at six with the food. No cooking for either of us tonight."

"And come April 8th, we'll be cooking meals together," Ruby said.

"April 8th can't come soon enough," Peanut said, and then kissed her goodbye. "I'll let myself out."

~~~

Ruby and Peanut's wedding invitation, which came out two weeks before the event, was a full-page ad in the local paper addressed to every resident of Blessings, and anyone else who knew them, stating that everyone was invited to the high-noon wedding, which would be held in the gazebo at the city park on Saturday, April 8.

Bring your own lawn chairs and picnic lunches. Dinner on the ground after the service. Wedding cake provided until it runs out, it read.

The next two weeks were the longest of Ruby's life.

———

Then Saturday, April 8, finally arrived.

Peanut was dreaming about putting up umbrellas all over the park for people to get out of the rain when he woke. After that crazy dream, he jumped up and looked out to check the weather.

When he saw the sun shining and not a cloud in the sky, he laughed out loud. Ruby had gotten her sunshiny day, and he was going to get a wife. He was definitely coming out the winner here. Unwilling to waste a moment, he made his bed, then jumped in the shower.

Afterward, he took extra time with his grooming, trying to find a way to comb his hair so that most, if not all, of the scars on his head were concealed, and then gave it up as a lost cause. He and Ruby were alive and well, and that was all that mattered.

He shaved before putting on a pair of gym shorts and went to make breakfast. It would be the last morning that he would make breakfast alone.

After that, time seemed to fly by. Before he knew it, it was time to get dressed and head for the park.

Peanut's tuxedo and pleated cummerbund were black; his shirt was pristine white—but without the damn ruffles, as he'd told the tailor. He had shiny new dress shoes, and Ruby's ring was in his pocket.

He grabbed his wallet, tossed his suitcase in the trunk of his car, and then locked his house. It would be a few days before they'd be back. He was getting antsy by the time he jumped in the car and drove away.

———∿∿∿———

Ruby's morning was moving along at a similar pace. Her clothes were packed for the honeymoon, and Lovey was taking her to the park so that she could leave her car at home while they were gone.

But when she went into the kitchen to make breakfast, it was a poignant moment, knowing she would never wake up in this house again.

She still hadn't decided what she was going to do with it, but that didn't matter. Today, the only thing that mattered was marrying Peanut.

When it came time to get dressed, she began to fuss. She'd already done her hair and makeup, and now all she had to do was get the wedding dress on without messing it all up. It had been hanging on the outside of her closet door all morning, and she couldn't wait for Peanut to see her in it.

Even though she'd been married before, Ruby had still chosen white, and knowing she was going to be in broad daylight when she wore it, she'd purposefully chosen a dress with lots of sparkle. Since the ceremony was being held outside, she hadn't bothered to look at full-length gowns because she didn't want to drag one through the grass. What she had chosen was in rich white brocade, above-the-knees short, and sleeveless, with a plunging neckline and a fitted bodice. And... there was enough bling on it to light a darkened room.

Ruby managed to get the dress on without messing up her hair but then couldn't zip it. She had to wait for Lovey, who arrived a couple of minutes later in a flurry of anxiety, zipped Ruby into the dress, and then helped her put on the veil.

"Oh, sister, you are so beautiful," Lovey said, and then wiped her eyes and blew her nose. "You and Peanut paid dearly to get to this day, and I couldn't be happier for the both of you. Now where's your luggage?"

Ruby pointed to the bags. "Those two."

"I'll carry them to the car. You gather up what you need from in here. I'll be waiting for you outside."

"Something old. Something new. Something borrowed. Something blue. And a penny in my shoe," Ruby said, then checked to make sure she had them all.

Her something old was the one-carat diamond in the engagement ring Peanut had given her. Something new was her dress. Something borrowed were Lovey's diamond earrings. They'd been given to her by her last husband. And the something blue was the blue garter at mid-thigh on her leg. The penny in her shoe was a 1901 penny she'd received in payment the first year she was in business and had kept for good luck.

She looked around at all of her beloved things, some of which she would take with her to her new home, and some of which would stay here.

"I'll find someone wonderful for you," Ruby said, and then hurried out, locking the door behind her.

The drive to the park felt surreal. She was quiet all the way, thinking of the journey it had taken for her and Peanut to get to this day.

And then they reached the park. Myra Franklin

was waiting on the other side of the street with Ruby's bouquet.

"This is beautiful," Ruby said, eyeing all of the sparkle Myra had incorporated among the white gardenias and the deep green of the waxy magnolia leaves.

Then she looked across the street at the moving mass of people coming in with chairs and blankets and big picnic baskets on their arms, and laughed out loud.

"Just like the Fourth of July," Ruby said.

"But without the fireworks," Myra added.

"Oh, there will be fireworks somewhere before this day is over," Lovey said, and then winked.

Ruby grinned. "Most likely you will be right. So let's get this started."

As Ruby and Lovey started across the street, Lovey made a quick call to the band director from the high school who was waiting for her signal.

"Hey, Justin, we're here. Start the music."

Within seconds, the sounds of the "Wedding March" rang out through the loudspeakers set up around the gazebo.

The last thing Lovey did was pull the veil over Ruby's face. Then she disappeared into the crowd, leaving Ruby alone at the sidewalk.

The moment the music began, people turned toward the street and saw her waiting. There was a group sigh from the crowd as they began moving aside, leaving her a near-perfect aisle to the gazebo.

Ruby's heart was pounding as she started walking across the spring-green grass.

Their wedding flowers were the blooming lilac bushes and the beds of yellow jonquils and bright-red tulips scattered about the park. The birds in the trees were chirping and flying from tree to tree in brief flashes of bluebird blue and robin red.

Sunlight caught and sparkled on every little jewel and sequin as Ruby moved into view, while audible gasps and murmurs of delight followed her every step. She glimmered like starlight, shining only for the man who loved her.

———

Peanut was standing at the bottom step of the gazebo. Their pastor was standing at the top, just beneath the conical roof.

He saw the sparkle, and then he saw her—and for a few moments forgot to breathe. Then the closer she came, the more rapid his heart beat. The music of the "Wedding March" surrounded him and flowed through him as he locked onto her face.

This beautiful woman loves me.

When she was only yards away, he went to meet her. She looked up at him and smiled as he tucked her hand beneath his arm.

"Magnificent," he whispered, and they went the rest of the way together.

———

There were hundreds of people standing as witnesses all over the park, and yet there wasn't a sound to be heard from any of them, not even from the children sitting on their fathers' shoulders. They were convinced that a real fairy had walked into their midst, because what else but a fairy would sparkle like this?

For Ruby, it felt like a dream, but she knew it was real when the music suddenly stopped and the pastor stepped out of the shadow above them and spoke into the microphone.

"Dearly beloved—"

At that moment Ruby shifted to autopilot, answering when questioned. Speaking when spoken to. Never taking her gaze from Peanut's face.

When Peanut pulled a ring from his pocket and slipped it on her finger, she gasped. The white-gold band was encircled with rubies, sparkling as bright as the diamond already on her finger.

Then she heard Peanut's voice ringing out as loud and strong as it did in a courtroom when he was pleading a case.

"I, Peanut, take thee, Ruby…"

Tears threatened, but she blinked them away as she watched his face, lost in the love she saw there.

Then she heard the pastor say, "Ruby, repeat after me," so she did.

"I, Ruby, take thee, Peanut, to be my lawfully wedded husband."

Peanut's grip tightened slightly as she went through the vows as well, and then she heard the pastor saying the words they'd waited so long to hear.

"I now pronounce you husband and wife. Peanut, you may kiss your bride."

Peanut reached toward Ruby, lifted the veil, put a hand on either side of her face, and lowered his head.

And then he kissed her.

When he raised his head, her eyes were still closed, so he leaned down and did it again.

The whole town erupted into laughter as Peanut and Ruby turned and waved.

"Ladies and gentlemen," the pastor said, "it is my pleasure to introduce the newest married couple in town, Mr. and Mrs. Butterman, otherwise known as Peanut and Ruby. And since they're not going anywhere, and we're all about to eat our dinner, now's the time to get that birdseed in the air."

People were on their feet, throwing birdseed toward them, and at each other, and up in the air.

Ruby looked at Peanut and burst into laughter.

All he saw were her eyes, and that smile, and the sparkle. She was shining. He had married an angel. He'd always known she was special, and now it was evident for the world to see.

Then Lovey came running.

"Dinner is ready. Your table is up here in the gazebo. If you ever wondered what it would be like to eat a meal in front of hundreds of people, you're about to find out."

"I don't care where we eat, as long as I'm sharing the meal with my wife," Peanut said.

They walked up the steps and then turned and waved, recognizing friends and customers, townspeople and people from the hills—all who called Blessings their home. She saw Melissa Dean, and then the Conroy family, more people from church, and from the hills beyond the town. All of them were standing. Some were crying, and some were clapping, and some were still throwing birdseed into the air.

When Ruby and Peanut sat down at their table, it was needed for the wedding guests to begin laying Blankets were spread, and families sat.

Food came out and the party began as the air was filled with the sounds of talk and laughter.

Lovey served them chicken and dumplings, the Saturday special from Granny's, and then put on a side table an ornate, three-tiered wedding cake that sparkled just like Ruby.

When Ruby saw it, she beamed. "Oh, Lovey, that is beautiful."

"We have Mercy to thank for this and the five hundred vanilla cupcakes with white icing and silver sparkles."

"Where are they?" Ruby asked.

Lovey pointed to four long tables beneath the trees. "They're putting them out right now."

"Hey, Wife," Peanut said.

Ruby turned, saw the bite he was holding out for her to eat, and opened her mouth, and the meal began.

When they finished, they were guided toward the four long tables set up beneath a swath of shade trees, and to the wedding cake and five hundred cupcakes surrounding it.

Peanut and Ruby cut the cake, fed each other the traditional bite, and then stood talking and laughing with everyone who came to get cake.

Two hours later, Ruby grabbed her bouquet and headed for the steps of the gazebo and reached for the microphone.

"Hey, all you single ladies interested in catching yourself a man…gather around. I caught the bouquet at the last wedding I attended, and look what happened. Now's your chance."

Much giggling ensued as women gathered. Some, like Alice Conroy, weren't ready to join that crowd, but

Melissa's ache was old and familiar—that she was alive and Andy was not.

Ruby climbed up on the steps and gave the bouquet a big toss. Everyone watched as it launched, hit its arc, then started falling, falling, right down into the middle of the crowd, into Mabel Jean Doolittle's hands.

She gasped, then squealed, and everyone laughed.

Then Peanut stepped up and knelt at Ruby's feet, ran his hands up one leg until he felt the blue garter, and slid it down with a gleam in his eye while Ruby laughed and laughed.

Peanut grabbed the microphone. "Got any single men in this crowd?"

A roar of laughter rose as men, both young and old, came through the crowd and gathered around the gazebo.

Peanut winked at Ruby, then pulled back on the garter like a slingshot and sent it flying into the air, right into the outstretched hands of Elvis Kingston, the fry cook at Granny's Country Kitchen.

Elvis turned red and grinned, but he pulled the garter up his forearm, wearing it like a poker dealer in a casino, and walked off through the crowd.

―――※―――

The picnic was still going strong when Peanut and Ruby snuck out through an alley and hopped in the back of Lovey's car so she could drive them to the back parking lot of the Curl Up and Dye.

Vera and Vesta had volunteered to be responsible for the tux and wedding gown and were waiting inside the shop.

After Ruby and Peanut had changed and Ruby had

returned Lovey's diamond earrings, they slipped out the front door to where Peanut had parked his car for the getaway. Lovey was unloading Ruby's bags into the car, and they laughed at what they saw.

JUST MARRIED was written on the back window. There was a big banner tied to the front bumper that also said JUST MARRIED, and red, silver, and black streamers were tied from one end of the back bumper to the other. A big, silver balloon had been tied to each of the front door handles. One said BRIDE. One said GROOM.

Ruby was giddy from the joy.

"Oh, Peanut. This is the most wonderful, most perfect day!"

He looked at her then, saw her cheeks as pink as the dress she was wearing, and leaned down and kissed her.

"Now, it is the most wonderful, most perfect day," he said, and opened the door for her to get in while the balloon bounced above his head in the breeze. "Buckle up. We're about to begin this ride called life."

She slid into the seat as Peanut closed her door, then circled the car and jumped in behind the wheel. Lovey and the twins were waving as Peanut and Ruby drove away. A couple of blocks down, he turned back toward the park.

"Honk so I can wave," Ruby said as she rolled down the window.

Peanut began to honk repeatedly with his window down.

The wedding guests turned just in time to see Peanut and Ruby waving out the windows as they drove by. A huge roar rose from the crowd as everyone began shouting and waving goodbye. Then as they watched, the

Bride and the Groom balloons came loose from where they'd been tied and began floating up, up, up until they finally disappeared from view.

Peanut and Ruby were on their way out of town when they met a big, silver pickup truck pulling a U-Haul trailer.

The driver saw them as he approached, noticed the JUST MARRIED banner tied to the front bumper and the streamers waving in the wind behind them, and honked and waved as he passed.

Peanut glanced up in the rearview mirror and then shook his head. "Well, I'll be. I wonder if he's moving back. I never thought I'd see him again."

"See who?" Ruby asked.

"Aidan Payne. He was a guy I went to high school with. Oh, wow, I'm just now putting two and two together. While I was recovering, didn't Preston Williams pass away?"

"If you mean the old man who lived across the street from Mercy's old landlord, yes, he did."

"Aidan is Preston Williams's grandson."

"So what's the big deal about him coming back?" Ruby asked.

"The whole family moved away during Aidan's last year of high school under a very dark cloud of suspicion. Nothing was ever proven, but everyone thought that Aidan's father burned down his own business for the insurance money. To make matters worse, it burned down the business next to it, and someone died in that fire."

Ruby shivered.

"Poor Aidan, having to grow up with that cloud of suspicion hanging over the family name."

Peanut nodded. "Well, I guess we'll find out if he's staying when we get back. Right now, all I care about is going on a honeymoon with my honey."

"Me too," Ruby said, and leaned back in the seat as they added to the miles taking them away from Blessings.

Still, she couldn't help but wonder what Aidan Payne was like, and if he stayed, would there be trouble for him again?

Ruby sighed. It was always an interesting event when a lost son of Blessings found his way home.

*Keep reading for a sneak peek of the next book in
Sharon Sala's Blessings, Georgia series*

Come Back to Me

Aidan tossed a couple of boxes of cereal into his cart, and moved from the cereal aisle to canned goods, picking out soup and cans of tuna before moving on to condiments and pickles.

He passed shoppers up and down the aisles of the Piggly Wiggly, aware he was being watched. Either it was because he was a stranger in a small town—or because they recognized him from all those years ago. He wasn't in the mood to strike up a conversation with anyone, so he chose not to make eye contact, and apparently no one felt the need to speak to him.

He was halfway down the bread aisle when he saw an older woman coming toward him, pushing a cart filled with bananas and stacks of juice boxes. He recognized her instantly and was surprised at how little she had changed. She glanced at him almost absently, then did a double take and broke into a huge smile.

"Oh my word! Aidan Payne! What a surprise! My stars, you sure take after your grandfather. My sympathies on his passing."

"Thank you, Miss Jane. I see by the juice boxes and fruit that you still have the day care."

Jane Farris rolled her eyes. "The Before and After is still in business, although some days I think I'm getting too old for it. Did you come to wind up Preston's affairs?"

"Yes, ma'am. I'm staying at his house for the time being. I'll likely be putting all of his rental properties up for sale. I live too far away to be an absentee landlord."

"Where do you live now?" Jane asked.

"New Orleans. I own a four-star restaurant called Mimosa. If you're ever in the city, stop in and let me treat you to a meal."

Jane beamed. "That's so sweet of you," she said. "I'll be sure to do that if I ever get up that way. It's wonderful to see you."

Aidan smiled. "Thank you. I'm sure we'll see each other again before I leave."

"Absolutely," Jane said, and gave his arm a pat as she moved on.

Aidan grabbed a loaf of bread and made his way to the checkout stand. He got in the shortest line, and then took the time to recheck his list, making sure he hadn't missed anything. He glanced up just as a tall kid in his late teens walked into the store.

The boy moved toward the registers in a long, lanky stride. When he stopped at register three, Aidan watched him suddenly step behind the checker and put his hands over her eyes.

"Guess who?" he said.

The woman's squeal of delight made Aidan and everyone around them smile. He was still grinning when the woman turned around. At that point, everything faded into the background as he watched an older version of his Phoebe Ritter throw her arms around the boy's neck.

Well hell. That had to be her son.

———— ∿ ————

"Lee, you tease! I didn't know you were coming home!" Phoebe was saying.

"Aw, Mom, you know how it is. I ran out of clean clothes," he said, which made everyone around them laugh.

Everyone except Aidan.

When the woman at his register called out "next" and waved him forward, he began unloading his purchases onto the conveyor belt. He could still hear Phoebe and her son talking, but he couldn't bring himself to look up. Less than two hours back in town, and already his head was spinning. Not only was Phoebe still here, but she was a parent. She'd definitely done a better job moving on than he had. He didn't want to know who she'd married. All he wanted was to get out of the store before she saw him.

He loaded up the sacks of groceries into his cart, paid, and walked out while Phoebe and her son were still talking.

———— ∿ ————

Phoebe cupped Lee's cheek, feeling the burr of a day's growth of whiskers, and thought wistfully that his little boy years were already behind him.

"I have to close tonight, honey. There are leftover ribs in the fridge, and some coleslaw."

"I got this, Mom," Lee said. "I can take care of myself. See you at home, okay?"

"Okay," Phoebe said. "I'm off for the next two days. Perfect timing."

"Great," he said, and gave her a quick kiss on the cheek before he left.

He jogged out of the store and was crossing the parking lot to his car when he noticed a stranger unloading groceries into his vehicle. There weren't many strangers in Blessings, and none of them drove a truck that sharp.

"Nice ride, man," Lee said.

Aidan looked up, startled to find himself face-to-face with Phoebe's boy.

"Uh...yeah, thanks," Aidan said, and shut the door. He walked a couple of cars up to return the shopping cart, then headed back to his truck. The boy was loping across the parking lot, cell phone in hand.

Ignoring a painful twinge of regret, Aidan got in the truck and drove back to his grandfather's house, parked by the U-Haul, and took the groceries in.

Although it had been a long time since he'd been here, he felt at home as he put everything away. It was hard for Aidan to believe his grandfather was gone. He had visited Aidan often in New Orleans, staying active and in fairly good health. Aidan swallowed past the lump in his throat. It seemed like granddad should come striding into the kitchen to greet him.

He was about to go upstairs to unpack when the doorbell rang. He hurried into the foyer and opened the door to a caller he didn't recognize.

The old man smiling at him sported a mane of white hair and was wearing white slacks and a flamboyant blue shirt with puffed sleeves. Aidan's first thought was that all he needed was a Mexican sombrero and a guitar. And then the old man actually bowed.

"Pardon my rude intrusion into your day without calling ahead, but I am Elliot Graham, your neighbor across the street. I came to welcome you to Blessings, and to extend my sympathies for your loss."

Aidan liked him immediately. "Thank you, Mr. Graham. Come in."

"Elliot…please," he said as he stepped over the threshold, then followed Aidan into the living room and sat down. "Preston and I were good friends. I don't mind admitting how much I miss him."

"I'm going to miss him, too," Aidan said. "He came to see me often."

"Oh, I know. He talked about you all the time, so of course I asked why you never came here to visit. When he explained, I apologized, but he assured me none of it was a secret."

"That's true," Aidan said bitterly. "The whole town had a hand in the decision Dad made to leave."

Elliot nodded sagely. "The truth will come out, and soon. You'll see."

Aidan was still struggling with what the old man had just said, when Elliot suddenly stood and headed for the door. "Well, I've intruded too much already on your privacy. I'll be going now, but my door is open to you anytime."

Aidan hastily followed. "Uh, sir…Elliot?"

"Yes?" Elliot said as he stepped out onto the porch.

"What did you mean, the truth would come out soon? It's been nearly twenty years with no suspects for who started that fire."

Elliot waved his hand, as if moving the question out of his space. "Oh…that's just me being me. Sorry. It popped out before I thought."

Aidan frowned. "I don't understand."

Elliot took a neat white square of handkerchief from his pocket, grabbed it by one corner, and popped it open before mopping the sweat from his brow. "I do not appreciate this heat," Elliot said, then smiled. "About what I said…it's nothing, really. Sometimes I just know stuff." He bolted off the porch and down the steps before Aidan could push for more answers.

Aidan watched him as he darted across the street, walking in a little march-step, his snow-white hair gleaming under the late-afternoon sun, past the shade trees lining the sidewalk, and back into his house.

"Odd little fellow," Aidan muttered, closing the door.

—⁓—

Lee pulled into the driveway, parked beneath a shade tree, and sat for a few moments, looking at their little frame, two-bedroom house. He was full of admiration for the way his mother had taken care of them on her own, never complaining, and making what little they had seem special.

He'd known since he was old enough to understand why his grandmother had moved away, why his father was missing. It hadn't made it easier to grow up without a father, but he hadn't held any resentment. He sighed, then picked up his duffel bag from the back seat and went inside.

He took his things to his room, then went across the hall to his mother's bedroom. The worn hardwood floors were clean, her bed was neatly made, and the wall facing the headboard was lined with framed school pictures — from his kindergarten picture to a snapshot of him in his cap and gown at graduation.

Lee had just finished his first year of college and knew his mom would be proud of his grades, but she was going to be surprised that he'd given up his apartment and job to spend the summer in Blessings. His plan was to get a part-time job here and save all the money he made, instead of spending it on rent back in Savannah.

He sat down on the bed and picked up a framed picture from the nightstand. He took out his phone, pulled up the photo he'd just snapped in the parking lot of the Piggly Wiggly, and compared them.

His heart began pounding, his eyes welling with tears. He'd waited nineteen years for this moment, and now that it was facing him, he was scared. What if the story Lee had told himself turned out not to be true? What if Aidan Payne had found out he had a son and didn't want him, after all?

⁓⁓⁓

Phoebe was tired when she clocked out and headed home, but the knowledge that Lee was waiting for her lifted her heart. Seeing the porch light on as she pulled up to the house was just like old times. Lee had done that since he'd been old enough to stay home alone, and she'd missed it. She grabbed her things, ran up the steps, and let herself into the house.

"I'm home," she yelled.

"Me too," he yelled back.

She laughed. Just like old times. She hurried into the kitchen and found Lee at the stove, heating up supper. He gave her a big hug.

"I waited for you," he said. "Go change and get comfy. I'll set the table while you're gone."

"Wonderful!" Phoebe said, and hurried down the hall to her room. She changed out of work clothes into a pair of shorts, an old T-shirt, and sandals, washed up, and hurried back to the kitchen.

"You cooked," she said, eyeing the inviting food.

"I just added some baked beans and fries to the ribs and slaw. Sit, Mom. Let me wait on you tonight."

"I won't argue," Phoebe said, smiling at him as he brought glasses of sweet iced tea to the table. After filling their plates, they talked as they ate.

"My grade point average for the year is 4.0, and I was accepted into an accelerated physics program next semester," Lee said.

Phoebe beamed. "Oh, Lee, congratulations. I'm so proud of you. I know you didn't get that from me."

Lee took a deep breath. "Did I get it from my father?"

Phoebe's smile slipped a little. The sorrow she lived with was once again evident on her face. "Yes. He was very smart."

Lee ate a few more bites, then took his phone from his pocket, pulled up the picture, and pushed it toward her.

Phoebe's smile brightened. "A new girlfriend?"

He shook his head, then waited as she looked down.

Her fork clattered onto the table. She pressed a hand over her mouth, but it didn't muffle the moan.

He grabbed her arm. "Mom? Are you okay?"

"Where did you…oh my God. That's the store parking lot." She looked up. "You took this today."

He nodded. "I saw him by accident. Wasn't sure, so I took a picture, then came home and compared it to yours. He's older, but it's him, isn't it, Mom? That's my father."

She nodded, starting to cry.

"Don't cry, Mom. This is a good thing, right? You stayed in Blessings all this time waiting for him to come back."

"Yes, I did. But he didn't come back for me."

Lee frowned. "How do you know?"

She swiped angrily at the tears on her face. "Twenty years. I waited twenty years for him."

"But he's here now," Lee said.

Phoebe's eyes narrowed angrily. "But he's not *here*, is he?"

Lee was beginning to panic. "Maybe he just doesn't know where you are yet."

Phoebe wasn't having any excuses. "I've been here a long time. All he'd have to do is ask, but I can guess why he's here."

Lee needed answers, even if they would make him sad. "Why, Mom? Why is he here?"

About the Author

New York Times and *USA Today* bestselling author Sharon Sala is a member of RWA, as well as OKRWA. She has more than one hundred books in print, published in five genres—romance, young adult, Western, general fiction, and women's fiction. First published in 1991, she is an eight-time RITA finalist, winner of the Janet Dailey Award, five-time Career Achievement winner from *RT Magazine*, five-time winner of the National Readers' Choice Award, five-time winner of the Colorado Romance Writer's Award of Excellence, winner of the Heart of Excellence Award, as well as winner of the Booksellers Best Award. In 2011, she was named RWA's recipient of the Nora Roberts Lifetime Achievement Award, and in 2017, she received a Centennial Award from RWA for having published her one hundredth novel. Writing changed her life, her world, and her fate. She lives in Oklahoma, the state where she was born.

Also by Sharon Sala